THE POLITICS OF JANE AUSTEN

Also by Edward Neill

TRIAL BY ORDEAL? Hardy and the Critics

The Politics of Jane Austen

Edward Neill

palgrave

Published by
PALGRAVE
Houndmills, Basingstoke, Hampshire RG21 6XS and
175 Fifth Avenue, New York, N. Y. 10010
Companies and representatives throughout the world

PALGRAVE is the new global academic imprint of
St. Martin's Press LLC Scholarly and Reference Division and
Palgrave Publishers Ltd (formerly Macmillan Press Ltd).

ISBN 0–333–74719–4

This book is printed on paper suitable for recycling and made from fully managed and sustained forest sources.

A catalogue record for this book is available from the British Library.

Transferred to digital printing 2001

Printed and bound in Great Britain by
Antony Rowe Ltd, Chippenham, Wiltshire

For Heather, Edmund and Gregory

Contents

Preface

Jane Austen, by common consent a great novelist and literary artist, is equally one of the great formative and founding influences on how we think about 'England' and 'Englishness', as well as class, ideology and gender issues. But the traditional critical convoy for (or cultural custodianship of) 'Jane', as she is appropriatively (but also patronizingly) styled, has aligned her with conservative and traditional views which her texts entertain but by no means finally avow. Attempts to conscript her work for a rather crusty, Tory view of life, (supposedly reassuring but actually inhumanely repressive in its immediate and remote consequences) are, ironically, a way of denying the very artistry which the novels contain, and what, ultimately, she is to be valued for. Thus, although there is a large Austen industry and a fairly settled consensus on what she signifies, it is possible to show (using modern theoretical approaches while remaining reader-friendly and generally accessible) that this is largely illusion, and that much traditional critical effort has been fundamentally misdirected. The book thus seeks to 'liberate' the reading of Jane Austen, to celebrate her achievement and to help its own readers to share in a sense of this, but with a very different critical inflection from those of traditional critical approaches and appropriations.

Briefly, I argue that Jane Austen offers a textual drama in which narrative interest is highly cognate with that of 'the political', while demonstrating that this does not serve to bring Austen's hidden polemic near to that of the tract or the flat ephemeral pamphlet. Yet if works of art may be said to have ideological coefficients, surprising inferences may be made to the effect that Jane Austen's fictional discourse is much more politically destabilized and destabilizing than the critical convoy for Austen's work has been at all eager to acknowledge. (In the process of establishing this, the proceedings are kept as 'light, and bright, and sparkling', in Jane Austen's own phrasing, as the nature of the subject will allow.)

The point is not to assign 'Jane Austen' to an opposing political 'party', but to note the exposure and interrogation of positions she is said to 'hold' and to subvert the (destructive) naivety and even less innocuous snobbism that many forms of Jane Austen criticism uphold and perpetuate.

This critical re-appropriation of Jane Austen acknowledges the paradigm shift in attitudes to Austen enacted in the work of Marilyn Butler, with its magisterial scholarship, its elegant economy of presentation, its clear intellectual sight-lines and wonderful sense of historical context. In quarrelling with her conclusions I have tried to hail other critics as allies or critique what I take to be their misapprehensions without becoming a mere chronicler of previous forms of critical response to 'Jane', not only because I have my own (benign) agenda but because the observations of many critics and theorists with points of general application offer constructive (and deconstructive) suggestions which are potentially as helpful as those of the official critical convoy for Austen.

Indeed, even where this seems to be in pursuit of the ideologically bien-pensant, there is a strongly conservative tradition in literary studies, in approaches to the nineteenth century novel, and perhaps most virulently of all, in relation to Jane Austen, which ensures that even those writings which aspire to march to popular tunes (like those of feminism) offer displacements, substitutions, one might say simulacra, for genuine critique. Even Claudia Johnson, who tried to transpose Butler's historicist acumen into the sense of a slightly subversive Austen, is showing her hand a bit when she describes Wickham, in *Pride and Prejudice*, as a 'propertyless upstart'.

Yet it is hardly inaccurate to the most conventional reading strategies to say that *Northanger Abbey* attacks the 'greedy speculation' which is the character note of modern capitalism, and it is in this context that Henry Tilney's injunction to 'remember that we are English' fails to be reassuring. *Sense and Sensibility* undoes binary oppositions remarked upon as vicious by writers like Derrida and Jameson, and has an Adorno-like awareness of how the falsities of society prevent unironized narrative 'solutions' to the problems it seems to propose. *Pride and Prejudice* enacts a fairy-tale elevation of its protagonist in both Mills & Boon and Freudian Family Romance style, but surrounds the happy event with so much irony that it secretes the opposite meaning to the one that, for its more unwary readers, it appears to 'contain', while *Mansfield Park* is eminently self-deconstructing, patriarchy and the great good place being left in ruins by a textual perspective which seems to anticipate the mischievous wisdom of Freud, Marx and Nietzsche; *Emma* shows how Emma's 'English Ideology' causes her to 'identify against herself', seems ironically to demonstrate a necessary 'subjection' of 'subjectivity', which was Emma's 'problem' as defined by Mr Knightley, and a problem defined by Mr Knightley remains problematic in its solution.

And finally *Persuasion* reverses the Freudian Family romance (the heroine 'opts out' of the gentry, in a scene of writing which refuses to underwrite the text (Debrett's) which snobbish Sir Walter Eliot feels to underwrite his existence, refuses the Burkean perspectives of Lady Russell, while offering a disconcerting homage to 'happy warriors' in an iron time of what David Erdman has called 'war-manacled minds'). Austen's greatness is thus not that of the politically correct, but her exquisite and moving works of art are at all times, and quite correctly, political.

Incidentally, *The Politics of Jane Austen* implies throughout that 'Jane Austen' is a text. Indeed, how could it be otherwise? The 'real' Jane, regrettably for all her necrophiles, lies beneath a dignified slab in Winchester Cathedral. Biographers, accused by Roland Barthes of writing novels that dare not speak their name also dare not, one assumes, claim that their novels rival those of their subject in this case. Note how little, despite their virtues of industrious prudence, biographers' trawls produce, how little one ends by knowing. Even the prima facie absurd claim made of late that Jane may have entered upon a lesbian (and excitingly incestuous) affair with Cassandra herself can hardly be refuted by the nine hundred pages or so of compulsive reading provided by David Nokes and Claire Tomalin. But the culture industry requires an image.

Biography, however accomplished, bypasses much recent sophisticated critical writing which is the authentic cultural convoy for Austen's textualities, Austen as text. Much loved by publishers as they are (and carried, as here, to a high pitch of sophistication, expertise and fascinating incidental insight), the procedures of biography abide many questions. As practised at a lower level, they might even be described as the homage paid by philistinism to culture.

At most one can concede that the real Jane may take three forms among which the reader may choose by elective affinity: she may be imagined as a bag of bones (see under Winchester Cathedral, above). She may also, of course, be imagined as the silhouette summoned by biographers, a product of writing and thus always already a textual absent-presence. The most recent efforts in the genre would also include those by Park Honan, John Halperin,

Elizabeth Jenkins and Lord David Cecil to capture 'Jane', and may indeed be called the efforts of scholarly lepidopterists, as Jane was once famously recalled as 'a husband-hunting butterfly'. But she (as it were) flies by those nets (to filch a holey image from Joyce's Stephen Dedalus). For all our curiosity, all biography is a giving that famishes the craving.

'Jane' is, therefore, infinitely more real in her third manifestation. Unfortunately, this merely consists of orts and scraps, *disjecta membra* – and six overwhelmingly brilliant novels. To put it this way is to be hopelessly 'canonic', no doubt: but the point is, not to proclaim brilliant novels, but to make the criteria which establish this, as Milton puts it, 'not mystical', or at the least, less so. *Hélas* – or should we say, hurrah? Indeed, so far from 'teaching and upholding a canon' in a 'received ideas' way, what this book finally implies is that, as (re-)produced by the wrong critical pharmacy, Jane Austen's novels may indeed secrete 'poison' rather than 'remedy'. *Caveat emptor*!

Edward Neill

Acknowledgements

Parts of my 'Introduction', Chapter 2 on *Northanger Abbey*, and Chapter 6 on *Emma* have appeared in different forms and guises in (respectively) *English, Essays in Criticism* and the *Critical Quarterly.* I am particularly grateful to Stephen Wall and Christopher Ricks of *Essays in Criticism* for their encouragement. The chapter on *Pride and Prejudice* appeared, in a slightly different form, in *Notebooks*, our in-house journal at Middlesex edited by Professor Francis Mulhern. I am most grateful for permission to reprint material.

My reading of *Mansfield Park* takes a somewhat iconoclastic view of things. Reading here may be aporetic, consisting of alternating possibilities of response, each of which is, in some measure, doomed to failure. Here, I have read against the grain, although what might be called a 'with the grain' view is possible, but equally exclusive after its fashion. For those who wish to see what Jane Austen might have called the plain sense of things as *Mansfield Park* develops them, my article on 'Jane Austen and Kierkegaard' in the *Cambridge Quarterly* (due summer 1998) provides some of the clues to the flip side of what might be deemed the flip side taken here. In this case I am also grateful to the editors of that journal, including particularly David Gervais, for his help in making me more readable and reasonable.

To my wonderful family, and glorious colleagues at Middlesex I also offer thanks. I should particularly include Professor Alan Durant, who responded gratifyingly to some of my writings, Mike Walters, a learned companion, and so many others who sustained me. Thanks also to my excellent Commissioning Editors at Macmillan, Charmian Hearne and Julian Honer.

1
Introduction:
The Politics of 'Jane Austen'

Jane Austen has become something of a Tribal Totem, a prime exhibit in a version of Our Heritage more notable for the 'sum of misunderstanding' which its received wisdom represents than the sense of intelligent homage it is meant to suggest. Even among the sophisticated, 'Jane' is understood to serve the Heritage Industry by enacting exquisitely conservative recuperations and ideological containments in her writings – she wrote, we are told, novels for the gentry. If Pascal could say 'we should respect the gentry because ...',[1] then 'Jane Austen' is widely supposed to have spent her time composing a monster footnote to the idea, *authorizing* it, as it were.

In fact 'Jane Austen' is still, one suspects, a name which stands in most imaginations as the 'author' of 'classics of class', high-class treatments of the upper classes, a kind of novelistic 'Debrett's Peerage'. There is also a Burke's Peerage which it is pleasant to confuse with the author of *Reflections on the Recent Revolution in France*, much possessed as he is with thoughts of 'the spirit of a gentleman, and the spirit of religion'.[2] Jane Austen is sometimes felt to offer herself as just such a fictional scribe to the *ancien régime*, entering the political arena as a slashing opponent of progress. Indeed the quality of the novels is often associated (or confused) with the fact of their dealing ('exclusively') with 'the quality' or 'persons of quality'. Yet if Jane's intellectual horizons are composed by Burke's peerage and Paine's persiflage,[3] her 'bantering spirit'[4] makes her, in some respects, more naturally an ally of the latter than of the former.

Indeed, however happily the Austen text is host to 'political' guests, there is a saving modesty in Eugenio Donato's claim that it is impossible to disentangle the literary and philosophical moments[5] of a text, where we might wish to rephrase this as 'literary, philosophical *and* political'.

The recovery of a 'politicized' Jane Austen, of Austen as a swash-buckling Tory whose sword leaped from her scabbard to defend a Burkean view of things was a great leap for Austen studies but brought its own problems. Of course, this seems to imply that there was a time when Jane Austen's novels 'were not thought to have any politics'.[6] She transcended the political; she was 'eternal' precisely because her concerns were. Critics who expressed disappointment, however timidly, at her failure to employ the 'larger canvas' could be pitied, or even relished, for their vulgarity. 'Jane' was by definition an exquisite. If history was a nightmare from which, like Stephen Dedalus, you were trying to awake, one could fly all such feverish contacts with 'Jane', it seemed.

Yet even that form of appreciation of her work which seems paradoxically to annihilate history, happily locked as it is into that 'regression and sterile nostalgia for the past', which Fredric Jameson complains of,[7] also already implies a deeply conservative 'world-picture'. An overtly 'political' Jane Austen, for those who would listen, at least saved us from insipidity and the intellectual stultification of the Janeites.

Ironically, it was Kenneth Clark, the patrician art critic, who saw clearly one feature of the period which 'Jane' grew to maturity: 'Towards the end of the eighteenth century doctrine was found in works which appear to us very harmless.'[8] Yet when he adds that 'from 1780 to 1790 every play and every ballet was "*interpreted in a political sense*"', he seems perilously close to asserting that politics is an imputed figment. Really, art, whose nature it is always to give pleasure, has no political coefficients.

This *seems* to be a mistake, certainly, yet a Macauley-like confidence in what these 'coefficients' are might be an even bigger one. Current wisdom has it that novelists 'formed', like Jane Austen, in the Revolutionary Decade of the 1790s inherited an intensely polarized *genre*, and a quick 'litmus test' by the historically conscious critic would yield very definite results. In the case of 'Miss Austen' these were very definite indeed: 'Jane Austen's novels belong decisively to one class of partisan novels, the conservative.'[9]

It appeared to have been established that the meaning of 'Jane's' novels can be construed by the constricted paradigms of (imagined) authorial intention which can be plotted with reference to a mishmash of sources uncovered by traditional historical enquiry: thus, it's implied, 'Jane' was reared in 'the little ethics of the Rectory parlour' in the heart of the Tory shires at a moment of particular tension when the French Revolution had put the upper classes on their mettle, ergo her work 'means', roughly speaking, shire Tory clichés, the little ethics of the rectory parlour, and a rather hectic legitimation exercise.

This, then is a Jane Austen whose ideological position is naturally on all fours with those who wish to form Tory administrations, reactionaries who write pamphlets, or bad, long-forgotten novels by strident Conservatives saying something rampantly ideological (and unsubtle) which is not part of any subsequent intellectual currency. What she offers, it seems, is a gilded pill of literary suavities and 'light, bright and sparkling' (but finally insidious) entertainment.

Writing as if a sort of secretary to the local Tory agent and as mouthpiece of that eighteenth-century equivalent of the man on the Clapham omnibus (the squire on the Basingstoke barouche, perhaps), her work is nothing if not recuperative, and all her creative energy goes into keeping kings on thrones, bishops in palaces and lesser lights in their places.

(Incidentally, the particular comment adduced by Terry Eagleton in apparent support of Marilyn Butler ['Well, when you get down to it, she's just a straight *Tory.*'[10]] is rather below his usual standard of literary sophistication [indeed he sounds deliberately simplistic to the point of deconstructing rather than encouraging the idea]. Better and more apropos is his point that 'it is not that Jane Austen's fiction presents us merely with ideological delusion; on the contrary, it also offers us a version of contemporary history which is considerably more revealing than much "historiography"'.)[11]

Marilyn Butler notes that Jane Austen is 'an author remarkably sure of her values',[12] but this means that she is very sure of the values 'Jane' is sure of. We all owe her a great debt of gratitude for her charting of the ways in which 'literature' as well as the officially polemic text could be conscripted for ideological frays, the ways in which innocuous novel-writing subtended 'the political' over the whole period of the French Revolution and the wars which followed up to the defeat of Napoleon (although Roger Sales has shown in a lively book that the Regency period was also 'formative').

Her magisterial scholarship in the period, and the disarming clarity of her exposition enacted a 'paradigm shift' in the study of Austen which has subsequently been challenged as well as developed, but has continued to set the terms of debate despite a historicist bias whose perpetuation entails a certain theoretical naivety, a deproblematizing of (inter)textuality and the condition of writing itself. All this leaves considerations of language, representation and subjectivity virtually untouched, and techniques of presentation virtually ignored.

Roger Gard is also right to observe that Butler is possibly the victim of 'a perhaps involuntary exaltation of "research" which issues ... in what seems like a diminished respect and liking for the artist'[13] (which is, precisely, a disrelish for the 'Jane Austen' who is a product of her own processes of critical reproduction).

Perhaps what we need here is a quick reminder of Bakhtin's way of entering the world of the novel by invoking the Dialogic Imagination,[14] or Althusser's refusal to number art among the ideologies,[15] or Barthes' claim that the literary work, is 'always written by a socially disappointed or powerless group',[16] since all such considerations seem irrelevant to this historicized Jane Austen of simple political partisanship on behalf of the socially dominant.

(Even 'the great masters of textuality',[17] Derrida and de Man – both of them *sous rature* in some measure to radical critique because of the murkiness of such political affiliations as they can be discerned to entertain – developed subtle ways of investigating how literary texts came to embarrass their own apparent cases, or causes.) Yet the discovery of 'political Jane' sidelines all such considerations as she doggedly presents, with simple ideological ferocity, what might be styled a *blue*print for no change, like some literary 'Giant with One Idea', to appropriate a phrase by Coleridge.

There is an effect of pretentiousness in adducing such a roll-call of names, to be sure, but I cannot accept Roger Gard's assumption in his well-informed as well as highly cultivated (if 'fogey-ish') book on Austen, that 'theory' is simply irrelevant – or that it necessarily issues in banal critical points as such,[18] especially when so much Austen criticism without obvious benefit of 'theory' is itself so very banal.

We should not, then, feel reassured by the 'warm academic fronts' Roger Gard represents ('against theory' and the like) which ignore intellectually progressive means of analysis and threaten to repress the kind of lively intellectual investigation students (and others) appreciate as a potentially rational route to legitimate literary valuation. To reject all this is to recycle the patrician mysticism of His Master's Voice, dramatized for us in *The Merchant of Venice* as he who irritatingly cries 'I am Sir Oracle/ And when I ope my mouth let no dog bark').

However, I do agree that 'theory' can be a bit worrying when it seems more intent on conveying an interest in its own procedures than 'elucidating' its chosen text. For example, in a lively recent discussion of narrative fiction which presents the restraining of Jane Eyre by the servants, we read that

> Semically, this passage encodes Jane's character as wild ... Pro-airetically, it encodes a sequence of resistance ... Symbolically, it encodes various antitheses ... Hermeneutically, it encodes two enigmas ... As a subject of narration, Jane is ... a site traversed by these four codes.[19]

Unfairly 'filleted' though this is, the reader will recognize that here *Jane Eyre* is helping you 'get' Barthes rather than vice versa. It would seem that, the discussion of novels being in question, this is not quite how to go about it.

On the other hand, Roger Gard as Sir Oracle is an even more problematic presence. His very erudition seems to endow him with a 'trained incapacity' – even if by no means the 'proudly paraded ignorance'[20] of the traditional literary academic as characterized by Nicholas Tredell. Not only does he have the 'Master's Voice' manner which grates, *his* 'Master's' Voice is that of Henry James, which grates even more. Approval from such 'traditional' sources seems unnecessarily tinged by that form of critical patronage which has transparent origins in the 'anxiety of influence'. As a Jamesite he cannot see that James's ponderous recommendation takes more than it gives:

> The key to Jane Austen's fortune with posterity has been in part the extraordinary grace of her facility, in fact of her unconsciousness ... she ... fell a-musing, lapsed too metaphorically ... into wool-gathering, and her dropped stitches ... were afterwards picked up as little touches of human truth ...[21]

The expression 'with friends like these' is well known, and it may lead on to consider whether James or a Jamesian is quite the ideal reader of 'Jane Austen'. We might try to reverse the emphasis. Schoenberg seems to have taken comfort from his enemies,[22] and there is something robust and perceptive about Mark Twain's sustained sniping, as in the following comment in a letter to Howells, for example:

> To me [Poe's] prose is unreadable – like Jane Austin's [*sic*]. No, there is a difference. I could read his prose on salary, but not Jane's. Jane is entirely impossible. It seems a great pity to me that they allowed her to die a natural death.[23]

Ironically, this tone seems to catch the lively iconoclasm of 'Jane' herself. Twain is concerned (legitimately) with the toxic effects of the genteel tradition, as he perceives it, in America, just as we may be concerned with the way Austen's work seems to lend itself to those transpositions into Hollywood kitsch for small and large screen we have been seeing so much of recently (but see Chapter 8 for a more nuanced appraisal of some of these).

Twain's sustained irritation is perhaps with 'the other' who refuses to *be* entirely other. After all, as Kate Fullbrook puts it, if a little too breezily, 'what Jane Austen asks us to laugh at most often is the power structures of her world – wealth, social status, patriarchy ...'.[24] Mark Twain was an early victim of those persistent (and lethal) forms of critical appropriation of 'Jane Austen' which occlude at once the artistic achievement, its radical potential, and the way in which both would seem to be inextricably intertwined. Such misapprehensions make it necessary to liberate Jane Austen from the stultifyingly conservative perspectives which inhibit an appreciation of the rigorous inquisition her work initiates into ideological mystifications.

As I demonstrate in Chapter 2, in *Northanger Abbey*, what looks like a profoundly unworried acceptance of 'things as they are' lies side by side with a profound probing of the darker side of the social landscape. A sardonically 'Blakean' voice deconstructs the Candide-like heroine's Song of Innocence and attacks, if in a more *sotto voce* fashion than Blake, devouring patriarchal iniquity.

As I point out in Chapter 3, *Sense and Sensibility* seems almost Paine-ite in its eagerness to supply something like a rogues' gallery of gentry-folk where the mean-spirited John and Fanny Dashwood set the tone, and what we finally admire about the book is less its clarity in providing a demonstration-model than in its ability to embarrass what initially appeared to be its own case. Setting itself to detect and expel symptoms of Sensibility, it actually becomes more exercised by misapplications of the sense of Sense, and its analysis of the social inferno (once more) has much in common with Blake's.

What fascinates about *Sense and Sensibility* is that at first glance it seems to be quite busy forging mind-manacles here: it actually begins to sound like Iser's definition of the legal text, which 'lay(s) down principles that are binding for the behaviour of human beings'. Yet, when we read it through, we may feel like rhapsodizing in the idiom Fredric Jameson uses to praise Derrida for enabling 'the unmasking or demystification of ... [its own] naturalised binary opposition'.[25]

In Chapter 4 I examine *Pride and Prejudice*. It always looks as if it just might succumb to ideological mystifications, particularly when Darcy appears, but at other points is suddenly alive with a glancing, rampant disrespect and an irony verging on the sardonic. 'Where super-ego is, there shall id be' seems to be the motto of this, at once the most chaste and the most erotic of courtship novels. Volosinov no doubt thought he had abolished 'Freudism' when he observed that 'the unconscious is ideological through and through'[26] but these terms of appraisal are already implicit in, for example, Freud's brilliant essay on the Family Romance, in which the 'self-orphaning' child may seek out a local nobleman to 'claim kin' from a sense of insecurity, and the inadequacy of its own parents. Here Austen arranges – *avant la lettre*, of course – a (sub)liminal doubling of Freud which destroys the unquestioning social basis of the fantasy – the sensible, trade-rich Gardiners challenge Darcy's sense of what, in social terms, 'is fit, and not'; but the matrimonial felicity which ensues offers only a gilded, hegemonic pseudo-inclusivity to celebrants.

Curiously, Darcy and Lady Catherine impinge on Elizabeth as a kind of high-level, fantasy-like 'return' of Mr and Mrs Bennet themselves. Supremely aware of money and property as determinants of gentility, both female 'elders' occlude Elizabeth's unconscious desire (or even project), to make Darcy 'identify against himself' by defining gentility as (mainly) a matter of ethics and education.

As narrative funhouse, *Pride and Prejudice's* march to the scaffold of connubial felicity is sprinkled with annotations, apparently casual but persistent, of those unsuitable marriages whose presentation and representation comes to assume greater *gravitas* than its uniquely favoured and perhaps arbitrarily centralized matrimonial triumph. As it is, the novel ironizes its own conclusion as a site of both marital and 'communal' bonding/bondage. In this respect,

Pride and Prejudice may be felt to undermine the grounding of its own ethical sense, prefigures its own deconstructive reading, and brings together in an 'organic' chemistry some implications of Marx and Freud in a potentially explosive way.

This seemingly favourable but ultimately suspicious approach to Country House culture and happy rural seats is continued in *Mansfield Park*. As Chapter 5 of this volume points out, it seems to embody, and then to deconstruct, myths of Tory patriarchy and the Great Good Place. Its acute diagnosis of the formation of subjects is penetratingly allied to its penumbra of an even more literal slavery. But the Enlightenment it seems to be exorcizing is re-installed by the very processes which seek to expel it. Freud, Marx and Nietzsche, of all people, offering 'convergent procedures of demystification', according to Paul Ricoeur, and thus 'hardly congenial to an English mind' – to pick up one of Charlotte Brontë's many cod-Austenisms – seem all but wandering about the place.

These great demystifying thinkers seem to compose, at an intellectual level, those 'strangers admitted on terms of intimacy' about whom Edmund Bertram frets so histrionically. If, as Marjorie Levinson claims, 'Adorno saw the trouble facing dialectics in an age when the difference between ideology and reality – irony's medium – has disappeared',[27] it may be that the death of irony expunged with Henry and Mary in *Mansfield Park*, is the birth of ideology (in terms of what we have been persuaded to accept about Mansfield Park itself as 'Great Good Place'). Its penumbra of actual slavery is a metonymic enactment of the other forms of slavery with which it coexists, and which operate in the context of patriarchy in the formation of the subject, and in this respect the 'ungovernably' moral Sir Thomas and the ungovernably immoral Henry may be felt to form a strange patriarchal pincer.

In Chapter 6 I explain how Emma's consciousness is a bit of a problem, overdetermining the patriarchality which is, finally, repressing her, and forced to invoke a rescuing nobility as an (ignoble) reaction to her own feminine marginality and insecurity. Yet as an 'imaginist', her refusal, as Knightley said, to 'subject the fancy to the understanding', a process which requires imagining, seems to augur the eventual 'subjection' of Emma to Mr Knightley himself. Curiously, Catherine Belsey, very much *en passant*, mentions *Emma* as an example of a 'classic realist text', with which, implicitly, 'nothing can be done'. But she herself does give the reader the 'purchase' s/he needs when noting, with unconscious irony, that 'classic realism' constitutes an ideological practice in addressing itself to readers as 'subjects', interpellating them in order that they may freely accept their subjectivity and their subjection,[28] rather brilliantly (if inadvertently) articulating the reader's sense of Emma's ambiguous fate and *Emma's* strangely ambiguous politics.

In Chapter 7, I show that *Persuasion* is 'no longer at ease in the old dispensation'; impatient with the false values and false consciousness of snobbism, even if it still plays some 'grace notes' of wistful regret (indignant, one might say, that Mr Darcy has declined into a Sir Walter), it eagerly presses on to new ideological perspectives, 'new thresholds, new anatomies', composing a disconcerting hymn to 'happy warriors', though equally convinced that the pen is scarcely less patriarchal than the sword.

A Jane Austen novel provides so much more than a vicarious (or victorious) *entrée* to the world of the gentry – or the kind of 'Royal Wedding' narrative without the subsequent disappointments brought in their train by flesh-and-blood royalty – which the recent television versions of Austen virtually insinuated themselves to be). Such 'folklore from above' is examined, not too unsympathetically I hope, in Chapter 8.

Hence, Roger Gard's consequent attempt to move Austen out of 'the political' on the grounds that the 'Anglo-Saxon' world has a (healthy) 'disregard of direct political power in everyday life' (p. 16) is strangely complacent about the present-day social realities of English life, about the ideological instabilities of the Austen text, and about sophistications in the act of reading which put him, as literary and cultural critic, decidedly *sous rature* ('Unpolitical, she is *therefore* the realistic novelist of an emerging national democracy' [p. 17]).

From a certain point of view, one of the wisest remarks about Jane Austen seems to have been made en passant by A. Walton Litz when he observes that 'we [can say of her that], like the singing girl in Wallace Stevens' "The Idea of Order at Key West" ... "there never was a world for her/ Except the one she sang, and, singing, made"'.[29] This seems to be an interesting riposte to the apparently commonsensical but actually much stranger idea that 'Highbury [in *Emma*] is a real place',[30] the sort of assumption which seems to govern much of what is written about Jane Austen. But even when such efforts at critical [en]closure (which suggest that 'Jane' offers unproblematic access to her actualities) are overcome, and she is credited with what Stevens would call 'Supreme Fictions', these are held to underpin the 'legal fictions' of landowners and the like.

A genuinely exciting moment in Austen (and literary) studies generally lay in attempts to 'tackle' such issues by 'sons' of Raymond Williams like Roger Sales and David Aers, who seem to situate themselves in a real world independent of textuality in order to complain that 'Jane' is cooking the books for all those 'enclosing' landlords and 'the ordering classes' generally (in D.H. Lawrence's amusing phrase). In this way they reanimate the suspicion most memorably articulated by Étienne Balibar and Pierre Macherey, that 'the literary text' may 'bring about the reproduction, as dominant, of the ideology of the dominant class',[31] something 'Jane' has often been reproved for (if in less sophisticated tones). Sales and Aers are much more interesting, intelligent and *à propos* than the run-of-the-mill Janeite. For this reason they are also a great pleasure to read and certainly raise interesting questions, but they perhaps fail to appreciate fully how 'Jane Austen' engineers an *exposure* of the strategies of dominance which enables their bridling in the first place.

But the startlingly impoverished theoretical and technical aspect of their otherwise 'sympathetic' investigations is surely revealed when, for example, Aers points out that 'what Austen, Fanny, Edmund and now Duckworth [conservative critic] fail to consider' is that the gentry's world is 'actually grounded in the coercive "improvements" and transformation of rural England in the triumph of agrarian capitalism ...'.[32] To lump together a modern critic, the author and two characters with different perspectives from one novel (and to ignore the complex facts of narratorship) is in effect to invite the reader to jump on a critical 'blunder-bus'.

Yet these critics raise interesting questions largely ignored by the strongly 'Fogeyland' traditions of Austen critique, to the effect that 'the novelist isolates individual aberration in a way designed to prevent any critical questions being asked about the total social structure'.[33] What I am arguing here is that Austen's 'greatness' as an artist is involved with the way in which her novels become 'interrogative texts' rather than texts to 'interrogate', and do indeed raise questions about 'the total social structure'.

'Raise questions', yes: we need be in no hurry to attribute party political points. I have some sympathy with Michael Riffaterre's paean to 'indeterminacy' here which has something to say to those who think we do 'Jane' honour by identifying her as a party hack, and reminds us of the violence done in transferring Austen texts into large- and small-screen 'versions':

> undecidability ... makes for the kind of active and strenuous, but disciplined commitment that, more than anything else, characterizes literary response to perceived literariness.[34]

It does look a little, though, as if that 'literary response' of his is, in a key Cowper quotation used in *Emma*, 'itself creating what it sees' when it 'perceives literariness'. Unfortunately 'perceived literariness' is no longer a phrase to conjure with in current critical discourse. We require something more specific by way of academic credentials. As an appreciator of the complexities of 'voice' in Austen, Susan Sniader Lanser notes, for example, the specific unassignability of statements that may proceed from the narrator or the character and may be exhibited for our approval or disapproval – 'doubly oriented discourse'[35] in which the character eclipses the narrator or the narrator the character, and so performs the conjuring trick of the vanishing author.

It is possible to reveal how the author conceals herself, to show how the vanishing act takes place in the linguistic indeterminacies of dramatized viewpoints which have no privileged connection to an 'authorial' press office. In this connection, how much more felicitous would the expert, intelligent and extremely well-informed Tara Ghoshal Wallace's reference to 'Jane Austen's examination of her own narrative authority' be if she had confined herself to referring to 'Jane Austen's examination of ... narrative authority',[36] making of the narrator an 'other' voice. In general, it is a pity that such potentially interesting work as hers enters into such easy intellectual 'intercourse' with traditional Austen critique, perhaps limiting its own theoretical rapports and potential originality and incisiveness. As Susan Lanser puts it in her other book, Austen is 'shifting ... narrative focalisation throughout the text'.[37] Most critics fail to involve themselves with these (sc.) 'nuances' which in fact create much of what we admire in Jane Austen. And although I myself have not embarked on the kind of critical reading which advertises itself formally as a theoretical venture, this book shows some awareness of and interest in other writings which do offer themselves as such – even when they do not specifically speak to the subject of 'Jane Austen'.

Such technical analysis as Lanser offers, as well as those linguistic approaches which seem to offer cumulative critical wisdom, deserve attention. Yet critics, even linguistic ones, it seems, will always have their own little ideological tics. The extent to which works of art themselves might also have these is still a fascinating area of critical speculation. Indeed, Althusser's phrasing in his refusal to number art 'among the ideologies', has a curiously suggestive 'side effect' in that with an author like Jane Austen we are assured that her texts do indeed move 'among the ideologies' without being wholly 'of' them in a way that's sometimes implied. One might postulate, instead, that it is, precisely, inferior/failed works of art (which never emerge from their historical context except to testify to the distinction of their more Mozartian contemporaries) which offer that predictable 'Legoland' of 'ideologemes',[38] with similarly 'cut-out' characters – all those 'Bridgetina Botherims' and 'Harriet Frekes'[39] who offer the bold primary colours of political attitudinizing.

The preoccupation with failed writers of various kinds is partly a by-product of the fact that many books on Jane Austen begin as theses, the thesis being an unhappy genre under pressure to produce arcane and 'strangely' (if justly) neglected figures, so that the general reader has trouble 'staying with' the books that result from such investigations.

Basically, although it helps to put 'Jane Austen' back in her historical context, the ironic justification for doing so in an investigation of 'Jane Austen' is to show *why she emerged from that context* as a massive textual and cultural force, unlike most of the other cultural products, documents and artefacts which may be adduced from the period. Why is it that these texts have acted as continuously circulating cultural energies which have put a girdle round the earth and for many people define 'England', 'Englishness', raise 'gender' and general political issues in a compelling and continuously interesting way, and appear to possess a singular charge and charm for successive generations in very different social and historical conditions?

The chapters which follow are an attempt to answer such questions. The history of Jane Austen's recent reputation seems to be, in David Carroll's phrasing, 'one more of those many attempts to historicize what exceeds and resists historicization'.[40] (As he implies, there should be a concern with history which itself constantly destabilizes concepts of history that would 'absolutize' or 'empiricize' it.)

As it happens, the very opportunity to contemplate a newly 'historicized' Jane Austen led to very different diagnoses of her political and philosophical postures (by Margaret Kirkham and Claudia Johnson, for example). Indeed, there is a sense in which 'Jane Austen' is 'bastilled for life' by an exclusive concentration on the cultural matrix as that is defined by the concerns of the 'Revolutionary Decade'. While it is true that Roland Barthes' claim that we are 'licensed to read the text with an ineluctably modern gaze'[41] should be treated with caution – (doesn't this permit, or even enjoin, pretty licentious reading? Just who is issuing these licences anyway?) – the idea is a useful ally against the simplistic historicism which reduces 'Jane Austen' to a rather pyrotechnic salvo fired off against revolutionism, 'Jacobinism', etc.

Curiously, Roland Barthes himself seems to flinch at the implications of his own insight. His treatment of the concept of 'textuality' is, I would suggest, characterized by its own 'slippage' in its attempt to create a 'roped-off' area for the 'classic text' – 'Jane Austen', might easily be taken to be a *classic* instance of one.

But this is, surely, a residual mystification which should be resisted, and it becomes necessary as it were to chain him to the 'letter' of his own implication when he suggestively observes that

> the classical sign is a sealed unit, whose closure arrests meaning, prevents it from trembling or becoming double, or wandering. The same goes for the classical text; it closes the work, chains it to its letter, rivets it to its signified.[42]

Here he speaks, surely, of something *we* 'do to' these 'classic texts' of his, as opposed to something they might be supposed to 'do to' themselves. As such, it seems to describe exactly what some recent critics have been doing with 'Jane Austen'. They have 'closed the work', 'chained the letter' and 'riveted it to its signified', so that it becomes 'bastilled for life' in the Revolutionary period which also produced the Terror(s) and the ideologically confused (or meaningless) Napoleonic Wars.

Freedom from such 'riveting' will show a Jane Austen with modern rapports who speaks to the conditions described by Marx, Freud and Nietzsche and all that has followed them in the realm of critique. But the point is that 'Jane' gives as well as takes here. If the sovereign image of cultural production and consumption is the famous one from the visit to the underworld in the *Odyssey*, where the 'ghosts' must 'drink the dark blood' of the visitors before they can speak, it is also a curiously reversible one: the artist who fleshes out the abstractions of the theorist is as necessary as the theorist who shows the intellectual and ideological implications of the earlier text.

To enter the world of critique is not to leave the world of Jane Austen, and to enter the world of Jane Austen is not to leave the realm of critique. As D.A. Miller puts it, almost too suggestively, 'her narratives are generated precisely by an underlying instability of desire, language and society'.[43] If, as Edward Said puts it, 'the morality [in Austen] in fact is not separable from its social basis',[44] I have put a rather more favourable construction on the creative upshot of the connectedness than he finds it possible to.

The reader who emerges from contact with my reading of Jane Austen should have, if not an automatic reverence for some canonic texts, at least an informed respect for a creative achievement which still bears on our attempts to think through theoretical issues which have political and social bearings, and thus (and only then) licenses our sense of the pathos of the fate of that 'gifted creature', as Sir Walter Scott movingly put it, who 'died so early'.[45]

2
The Canny 'Becomes' the Uncanny: *Northanger Abbey*

In his memoirs Sir Peter Medawar, describing a meeting with C.S. Lewis, characterizes him (hardly surprisingly, as he studied hard for the part), as 'English in an intolerant, Johnsonian way'.[1] *Northanger Abbey*, too, one feels, sets about being 'English in the intolerant, Johnsonian way', but its very success as a novel depends on its failure to sustain this, like the good, self-deconstructing artefact it turns out to be. It seems to be caught, in the end, with its irony pointing the wrong way, rather like the British guns at Singapore. Nevertheless, as both Claudia Johnson and Raymond Williams would confirm,[2] it fairly bristles with confidence as it sets out to diagnose and mildly defame what Johnson himself would have called Catherine's 'dangerous prevalence of imagination'.[3] Although the importance of this anti-romantic idea to *Northanger Abbey* can hardly be overemphasized, and remains as its essential scaffolding, what the text also discloses is that Catherine's 'dangerous prevalence of imagination' is an indispensable clue to the 'horrid mystery'[4] of an England which is shown to be quite unlike rather than like the reassuring version promoted by the enlightened, patronizing Henry Tilney, as he prattles magisterially by Catherine's side.

Wielding what Olivia Smith has shown to be the (at least potentially) hegemonic discourse of Blair and Johnson[5] – convinced, indeed, that 'reality is sooner doubted than the infallibility' of his own prescriptions[6] – he is entirely 'English in the intolerant, Johnsonian way' *about* England. His trump card, entailing a would-be categorical repression of any claim to insight on Catherine's part, is 'Remember that we are English'. A male chauvinist who patronizes women with apparent authorial indulgence, Henry is also a chauvinist *tout court* who 'produces' a reassuring England as a climax to his genial, placing wisdom. He seems oblivious to the fact that his 'myth of England' – his ideology – is endangered by the language he has used to evoke and articulate it. Henry's political complacency is thoroughly involved with his patronizing attitude to Catherine.[7]

In particular, the rather heavy-handed scene of misunderstanding between Catherine and his sister Eleanor in chapter 14 about whether they are discussing 'fiction' or 'reality', seems to mock Eleanor but is equally ironic about Catherine, and prompts Henry to the reflection that 'Perhaps the abilities of women are neither sound nor acute – neither vigorous nor keen. Perhaps they may want observation, discernment, judgement, fire, genius, and wit' (p. 100).

It is difficult to know whether he is being simply ironic here or more complicatedly ironic about the sort of person – i.e. himself in a less complaisant frame of mind – who makes such remarks. Yet however ironic about his own ironies this ironist may be,[8] what he expresses is in the end an anxiety, perhaps even a somatic anxiety. Henry inhabits his patriarchal uniform, but is haunted by thoughts of an Other, whether in race or gender, nature or culture. 'Jane Austen' is mocking the mockery of her own puppet, and striking a blow for femininity in the very act of celebrating its apparent discomfiture. *Northanger Abbey*, it is confirmed, is the sort of text whose emotional and political direction is on a knife-edge. It seems at once to be almost preternaturally sure of where it's going, yet its reversible ironies at key points momentarily eclipse a sense of intention, of just which reading is 'against the grain'.

Henry proceeds to observe that

> instead of instantly conceiving, as any rational creature would have done, that these words could relate only to a circulating library, she immediately pictured to herself a mob of three thousand men assembling in St. George's Fields; the Bank attacked, the Tower threatened, the streets of London flowing with blood, a detachment of the 12th Light Dragoons (the hopes of the nation), called up from Northampton to quell the insurgents, and the gallant Capt. Frederick Tilney, in the moment of charging at the head of his troop, knocked off his horse by a brickbat from an upper window. (p. 101)

This stirring 'throne and altar in danger' passage from chapter 14 compares very interestingly with Henry's crowning injunction to

Catherine when he realizes that she suspects his father, General Tilney, of having murdered his wife: 'Remember that we are English ...' (p. 172). What this boils down to is the idea, as Auden puts it for another place, that 'nothing serious can happen here',[9] that both social turbulence and violent criminality are essentially alien. His complacency seems to be bolstered by the quoted passage, which purports to describe what hasn't happened and isn't going to.

Unfortunately, however, its tell-tale specificity presents this in terms of what *has* – in this case, the Gordon Riots.[10] These had a limiting context and occasion, but they do in fact evoke the idea of a seething social discontent verging on outright insurrection after the frightening French model, challenging the idea that such depravity is self-evidently alien to the spirit of Englishness. Henry may be playful, but his ludic deflection is itself suggestive of characteristically Tory tactics, assuming a smugly conservative point of view more in accord with the temper of the late 1790s than that of 1817, when the novel was published. This was only shortly before the Peterloo massacre, in which troops violently quelled a demonstration of popular feeling but aroused widespread indignation and protest[11] – brisk military suppression is not invariably what the 'public' wants to see. Although Jane Austen did not live to respond to this event, dying tragically early (as Sir Walter Scott movingly noted in 1826[12]), any creative response to it on her part would have been of extraordinary interest, given her exquisite sense of temporality, which entailed a preternatural alertness to altering ideological inflections.

Imagining Captain Tilney as the victim of violence masks his own potential for inflicting it. (That the scene is presented as being in fact 'imagined' by Henry might make one feel that his prevalence of imagination is more 'dangerous' than Catherine's, and indeed it is he who inflames her thoughts about dark Gothic practices at Northanger.) However, the main point is that he is able to depict the military intervention as part of the order of things, an order of things for which *Northanger Abbey*'s own support might appear to be total.

The early scenes at Bath, despite a briskly satirical tone, put nothing particular into question, especially as, in this hunt for fictional sabotage, not everything is permitted. For example, a very determined 'hermeneutics of suspicion' would perhaps insist that the novel evokes a world of genteel parasitism which an army of 'coolies'[13] is needed to sustain (the favoured method of transport being the Sedan chair), and in which the personal shortcomings of John and Isabella Thorpe et al. lead or feed into some potentially damaging political critique of modes of social organization. This would certainly be insensitive to the initial tone of the book, whose high spirits convey a Regency zestiness its equally coruscating moralism cannot quite repress. At any rate, Catherine's Bath is removed at least as far psychologically as chronologically from the frigid, priggish hauteur of Sir Walter Elliot in the much more rampantly 'ideological' *Persuasion*.

Even so, this 'genteel parasitism' exists; but having no secure tenure, no firm social or semantic anchorage, its warm romantic gestures and professions, developed well beyond the point of mere caricature by Catherine's false friend Isabella, may be a cloak (and a decidedly flimsy one), for flinty, acquisitive attitudes. If it becomes embarrassing, finally, to keep awarding Catherine points for understanding nothing of all this, thus bringing Goodness into dangerously close alliance with Imbecility, her very Errors become instructive. As Joyce's Stephen would put it, as he expatiates on the nature of Genius, they are 'portals of discovery'. The text is itself highly instructive about Henry's urgent need to learn not to teach her. She is a Blakean innocent learning the indignities (and hence the indignations) of Experience, in this (bowdlerized) *Candide* with Henry as a Pangloss of sorts. Finally, though, it's a self-deconstructing little *Bildungsroman* which puts its own didacticism under erasure.

Henry Tilney, then, however amiable (and Catherine's understandable, but uncritical adulation of him is itself mocked), is blinded by both his conservative assumptions and his patronizing 'sexism' to the idea that in Catherine's very 'dangerous prevalence of imagination' she holds what Blake would call 'the end of a golden string'.[14] It's a 'clew' to the social labyrinth – which is, roughly speaking, that 'this England', in its genteel way, *enables* rather than *thwarts* 'villainy'. However, to realize this, the nature of 'villainy' must be redefined, both for us and for Catherine. Catherine correctly intuits that something is rotten in this state of England, correctly associates it with 'ruthless' patriarchy, but wrongly associates this with 'Gothick' acts of spectacular criminality which threaten a fundamentally benign order. In Catherine's construing (or, in her earlier phases, largely misconstruing) of all this, it should be remembered that the meaning of *Northanger Abbey* hangs largely on the 'meaning' assigned to Northanger Abbey itself and what it is seen to 'encode'.

In Catherine's experience of Northanger, everything – from the 'whole parishes' at work in the General's 'hot-houses' to the over-whelming emphasis on a 'devouring' acquisitiveness already sustained by huge estates and properties, a marked emphasis on conspicuous consumption, and a general air of petty intolerance and tetchy authoritarianism – is masked by professions on the General's part completely at odds with his real motivation (and an ironic overinsistence on the part of the unreliable narrator[15] that there is 'nothing special' about Northanger at all). At Northanger Abbey, a 'Urizenic' tyranny actually *uses* an unjust system to advance its own interests, and, while being 'to everything but inter-est blind', as Blake puts it, uses soft, ingratiating language of benevolence and concern for its own ends. Catherine is particularly puzzled by the General because his embarrassing and oppressive 'solicitude' about her derives from a certain misinformation about her own worldly wealth and status put into circulation by the rather pathetic (but also malicious) chump, John Thorpe.

Northanger Abbey, then, for all that it may seem locked into a certain quasi-Johnsonian system-supporting,[16] actually comes close to anticipating Shelley's point about modern forms of 'fraud' which depend upon the 'ghost of gold'.[17] The culminating phrase of *Northanger Abbey*, indeed, is 'greedy speculation', for some the *trahison* of a gentry class for whom 'some deed of noble note' is its 'character note', for others is perfectly consistent with its under-lying *raison d'être*, so that Henry's father, or characteristics we learn to associate with him, stands revealed as 'the cause of misery in society'.[18]

Retrospectively, Tilney senior can be seen to have left an obvious slug-trail across the text, and one of its more piquant ironies is that his rudeness and arrogant insolence are evoked *on Catherine's behalf* – Catherine is, for him, a matter of socio-economic construction, or misconstruction – before the 'peripeteia' turns these hateful quali-ties *against* her, and she is turned out of Northanger as unceremoniously as she was ceremoniously admitted to it. This might be called a moment of truly 'Gothic horror'. In Boswell's *Journey to the Western Isles* (1775), a clergyman, on being rebuked for not offering hospitality to Boswell and Johnson, protested that he considered Johnson might have been a 'little worth person',[19] which is what the General discovers about Catherine, where 'little worth' means 'no money'. In the light of this, it is clear that Henry's celebrated Catherine-quashing address, his exhortation to 'Remember that we are English, that we are Christians', has not found its correct addressee; his deference or passivity in the face of this autocrat of the breakfast-table seems culpable indeed in the light of his own clergymanic fondness for priggish haranguing.

An early sign of the General's patriarchal turpitude follows Catherine's pursuit of the Tilneys after John Thorpe's rudeness in making excuses for her that she did not wish to have made. On this occasion the General 'was quite angry with the servant whose neglect had reduced her to open the door of the apartment herself', and 'it seemed likely that William would lose the favour of his master for ever, if not his place, by her rapidity' (p. 92). Insinuations of snobbery accompany his intimation of disappointment 'in his hope of seeing the Marquis of Longtown and General Courtney' in Bath. Intimations of the grandeur of the Tilney style, with over-tones of somewhat arrogant ostentation attend Catherine's 'admiration' (the word still suggestive of real wonder at this period) of 'the style in which they travelled' to Northanger, with 'fashion-able chaise-and-four – postilions handsomely liveried, rising so regularly in their stirrups, and numerous out-riders properly mounted' (Catherine focalizing this a little too innocuously), while 'General Tilney … seemed always a check upon his children's spirits' (pp. 136–7). As well as being uncomfortably hot-tempered about punctuality, Catherine finds, he is anxiously competitive and complacent by turns about his own property, status and style of life, and a conspicuous consumer ('he did look upon a tolerably large eating-room as one of the necessaries of life', p. 145).

The seriousness of this 'critique' of the General may not be imme-diately clear – perhaps, one imagines, his deficiencies are being listed with playful jocosity in a novel whose intimations of infamy cannot entirely quash a sense of parodic high spirits: on learning that Mr Allen, Catherine's chaperon, has only one small hot-house, for example, he declares 'He is a happy man! … with a look of very happy contempt' (p. 155). Other signs, though, are not so venial. When he reproves his elder son Frederick for coming down late with a severity 'which seemed disproportionate to the offence' (p. 135), we are surely allowed to speculate whether his own domestic tyranny has not partly formed Frederick's unsatisfactory personality, as indicated by the way he seduces the affections of Isabella from Catherine's brother James, then casts her off.

Henry, the professional mentor, condemns Catherine, wrongly, for condemning Frederick. He also condemns Catherine for condemning the General, whom she (wrongly) suspects of having murdered his spouse. Nevertheless, this dangerous prevalence of imagination on her part proves safer than Henry's ironclad rationality; she is, in a general way, correct to intuit the General's turpitude. His villainy transposes into his treatment of *her*, where his false values and his true villainy are *blazoned*. What seems initially to indicate that Catherine is being taught some kind of lesson leaves one instead with the firm impression that she has a nose for these things, the General being truly awful in his fashion and Frederick in his. She is forced to realize that his gentlemanliness proceeds from a false consciousness of her affluence and was subject to an implicit subtextual 'subject to status' clause, like most gentlemanly behaviour, perhaps. Disabused, he hastens to make amends for his misplaced solicitude with as much ill-grace and ruffianliness as he can muster. The General, it seems, would bluffly confirm Luce Irigaray's point that 'woman ... is the object of use and exchange between men'[20] without seeing that there was 'anything wrong' with it.

Catherine's Song of Innocence duly becomes a Song of Experience as she tastes deeply of the malevolence of the Thorpes and General Tilney, and her essential integrity is finally of more import than her lack of sophistication. Perhaps the problem here is one of unmastered irony in a book whose authorial hand is so masterfully corrosive about Catherine and the forces that threaten her, about the genteel style of life and its appearances, yet is still happy to dismiss Catherine to happiness within it. The text's very instability derives from the fact that through Catherine, majestic Johnsonian postures are feminized to produce more ambiguous varieties of experience.

A character here is likely to seem less like a *deus ex machina* than a *machina ex deo* (or rather *dea*), and devices to keep matters under comic control lay themselves disconcertingly bare. How lucky, for example, that Isabella Thorpe should turn out to be her false, affected, and also penurious friend, while Eleanor Tilney proves to be the true, unaffected, and of course rich one. Isabella abuses language, and is guilty of many literary false notes, which puzzle and perplex a Catherine ingenuous to a fault. This should put her in a good light, but reduces her to something of a plot-function, now merely dim and insipid like Harriet Smith in *Emma*,[21] yet also required in due course to sound like Harriet's formidable mentor, Emma herself.[22] One might also be reminded of how completely Isabella Thorpe is a prototype for the vulgar, canting Mrs Elton in that novel – might even be thought of as Mrs Elton in her Bath phase, which lies just beyond the covers of the later novel.

More specifically, Isabella punctures one discourse with another. She has an effusiveness 'lifted' from the novel of sensibility (the 'spontaneous' response with the textual cue) the deflating of which was almost the trademark of the young Jane Austen. 'Had I the command of millions, were I mistress of the whole world, your brother would be my only choice' (p. 107), she tells the somewhat bemused Catherine, too much the *tabula rasa* to require clearing of cant, the text here very much preferring the rhetorical world of Augustan humanism to the equally rhetorical world of incipient Romanticism. Arch and attitudinizing, Isabella is a dubious influence from the start, providing some nicely vulgarized, almost sleazy moments of 'girl talk': 'I have always forgot to ask you what is your favourite complexion in a man. Do you like them best dark or fair?' (p. 39). A spoilt scion of a 'very indulgent mother', Isabella is, with Lydia in *Pride and Prejudice,* a strong contender for the hotly contested title used by Mr De Courcy in Letter 4 of *Lady Susan*: 'the most accomplished coquette in England'.[23]

It seems fair to conjecture, however, that her desperately predatory air owes more to straitened gentility than natural appetite. Apparently convinced, with pretty sententiousness, that 'Where people are really attached, poverty itself is wealth', she is simultaneously possessed by thoughts of 'charming little villas about Richmond' (p. 107). The first phrases were self-deconstructing anyway, and Isabella is, fairly plainly, a prime embodiment of capitalism and schizophrenia rather than simple simpering or lusts of the pampered flesh. Again, however, this threatens to produce in the reader a sympathetic understanding which the text seems not to countenance and she is dismissed (presumably) to unhappiness.

There is something suspicious about the way in which the text sees to it that Catherine becomes positively charged through her very negativity. Too innocuous herself to comprehend others' motives for the misuse of language, apparently, she stands bemused in a crossfire of discourse. She is particularly puzzled, as well she might be, by John Thorpe, who contradicts himself even more egregiously than his sister, and so that she 'knew not how to reconcile … different accounts of the same thing' (p. 60). Thorpe is a rattle, guided by vanity, who speaks for effect on the limited themes of his own prowess in drinking, horsedealing and general rowdiness. Despite his desperate pretensions to sophistication, his pursuit of paradoxical éclat (remotely derived perhaps from some dimly discerned Oxonian paradigm) only issues in lobotomized Wildeanisms, moving gravely towards the unknown region of the boldly meaningless: 'nothing ruins horses so much as rest; nothing knocks them up so soon' (p. 44), or, even more memorably, 'There is not the hundredth part of the wine consumed in this kingdom, that there ought to be. Our foggy climate wants help' (p. 58).

However, Thorpe's *sottises* have their seamy side. Like Isabella, he is on the prowl, and he also proceeds to the opposite assumption – that wine might be helpfully harmful to the childless Mr Allen, since Catherine would be named as heiress and he, Thorpe, will kindly offer to marry her in consequence. Unfortunately, however, he later acquires an unsettling pathos. The dry humour and dry-eyed disenchantment with which Catherine magisterially quashes him goes against the grain of the text, reader responding *cum grano salis* – prompting once more the Northanger Experience of readerly discomfort.

Mrs Allen, too, produces *sottises*, although in a mode of less practised dullness, bringing moral imbecility perilously near imbecile morality. Her triteness might serve the conscientious Kantian concerned to differentiate analytic and synthetic statements: 'She had no doubt in the world of its being a very fine day, if the clouds would only go off, and the sun keep out' but 'If it keeps raining, the streets will be very wet' (p. 74). Anyone would feel licensed to intuit a sardonic young 'Jane' here, less sober Augustan chronicler than fretting female genius ready to scream the place down rather than be pigeonholed with these invincible matrons of mediocrity.

The difficulty in *Northanger Abbey* is not that Jane Austen is not already a past mistress of linguistic registers, but that her very abilities in this quarter seem initially to threaten the serious point of the novel. An air of Pooterish inconsequentiality lightens the tone ('the innumerable capes of [Henry's] great coat looked so becomingly important', p. 137) at some cost. In the very liveliness of its 'Regency' manner it stands ready to be rebuked by the weightier fictions which follow. Although questions of linkage or lineage would see Henry auditioning for Edmund Bertram (genteel clergyman and younger son of the country house complete with domineering patriarch), his ironies, which bespeak class and gender superiority, also have him in training for Mr Bennet. This is particularly in evidence, perhaps, when he (ironically) offers to 'get the Bath paper, and look over the arrivals' (p. 179), in order to find Isabella an even more socially elevated spouse than louche (though lightly etched) brother Fred.[24]

What Fred seems to enjoy is the piquancy of stealing Isabella from Catherine's brother James, yet females bear the burdens of fickleness and flirtatiousness Fred is not expected to be saddled with. Indeed, Catherine's condemnation of his caddishness seems more accurate than Henry's blustering indulgence. Pre-eminently, it seemed, a she who mustn't (or at least needn't) be obeyed, it is suddenly Catherine herself who provides the correct moral perspective rather than her pontificating partner. She repeats, with pained and painful honesty (the voice of honest indignation, said the young Blake, is the voice of God) 'I must say I do not like him at all ... I do not like him at all' (p. 190). A schemer or a conniver would have repressed these responses for fear of alienating Henry. Once more, it seems, Harriet Smith has turned into Emma, and irony at her expense, lavishly provided, is no longer in order, only irony about those who deign to be ironic about her.

Isabella is reprehensible, too, and it is a convincing sign of James Morland's infatuation that he can describe her as 'thoroughly un-affected and amiable' (p. 46); yet her 'tricks' (p. 190) only serve to lose her solid bourgeois fiancé. And compare the conduct of the General, certain traits of Henry, and Eleanor's relative passivity despite her obvious fondness for Catherine, and the Tilneys, all in all, seem almost as disconcerting as the formally cautioned and admonished Thorpes.

Catherine is saved from all this – a brand plucked from the burning – by an exhibition of admirable, if somewhat trite, impec-cability. She is thus allied with power and wealth, one might say, as a reward for not being calculating.

Like Tennyson's 'Northern Farmer', she doesn't marry for money, but goes where the money is.[25] Catherine herself seems to have done this with the best of motives; yet that her 'ethical' and 'worldly' victory converge so smoothly reveals that Jane Austen's famous 'breaking frame' pronouncement about the compression of pages showing a hastening towards felicity is a sign of her embar-rassment at the very patness of its closure. Yeats's image of the box clicking shut was all very well for his kind of poem; but we are more alert to the points that closure is foreclosure, closure is a kind of narratological violence and ideological traduction.[26] As we observed, Dr Johnson wished to see Cordelia 'dismissed to happiness', but when Catherine is simply dismissed one may feel that that would have been an end of the matter, and Henry would have been called to heel with the sort of rhetoric of origins and genealogy with which Lady Catherine de Bourgh afflicts Elizabeth in *Pride and Prejudice*. (Both Blake and Keats were, of course, political progressives, and to see a certain congruence with Austen here is a blow, I trust, to that dominant strain in Austen studies which makes Miss Austen merely a jewel in Edmund Burke's crown.)[27]

If, then, General Tilney is rehearsing for Sir Thomas Bertram and Frederick auditioning for young Tom Bertram of Mansfield Park, Henry the Insufferable is in serious training as a Mr Knightley, ready to cow Catherine as majestically as Knightley does Emma. Yet, rather like Leopold Bloom in *Ulysses*, she emerges intact from much persiflage, much linguistic flak directed at her by the narrator as well as Tilney. As in Joyce's modernist masterwork, indeed, there are at least trace-elements of ironized epic parallel, as attendant mock-heroic turns of phrase suggest, perhaps, what might be called a *Bath*-etic mode, a kind of feminine *Aeneid* (which is not one): 'though by unwearied diligence they gained even the top of the room ... Still they moved on – something better was yet in view ... by a continued exertion ... Miss Morland had a comprehensive view of all the company beneath her, and of all the dangers of her late passage through them' (pp. 43–4).

This rhetoric of muscle-bound heroes is applied to a world of which the text seems to be saying that 'nothing serious can happen here', though this is hardly borne out in practice. We are told to 'despair of nothing that we would obtain' as 'unwearied diligence our point would gain', rather like a modern American text of morale rearmament. (This couplet is conspicuously untraced in the notes: is it merely the cry of its occasion given a prose re-tread some pages later?)

Catherine is momentarily an Aeneas of the Pump Room, it seems, but irony suggests that all that is at issue is the crush and the fact that Catherine's stultifying chaperone, the infinitely insipid Mrs Allen, knows no one. Yet finally Catherine is a heroine in her own way, earning the sort of rhetorical recommendation which Joyce provided for canvasser Bloom, his unheroic epic hero, unique in what Joyce referred to as his positively charged ordinariness.[28] Despite hectoring Henry's blustering put-downs, she achieves ethical centrality as her pleasure trip becomes a distinctly testing *pèlerinage*.

The rift in the novel, the way in which it seems to mingle Johnsonian ethics with a certain cheerful worldly-mindedness (as, indeed, the later Johnson himself did), together with yet another note of totally uncompromising and iconoclastic critique, seems to bear rather heavily on Catherine herself, however. She is seen to transcend Mrs Allen's good-natured imbecility, refuse the sweet social hailings (or halings) of Isabella, sprouts almost alarmingly, indeed, from the originally rather stunted ethical and intellectual ideas we were encouraged to entertain of her.

It's a little difficult, though, to be at once an enchanting *ingénue* who fails to perceive the villainy of others and a character whose ethical basis requires understanding and transcendence of a politely corrupt milieu. Suddenly the text seems to forget its sovereign ironies as Catherine resists the blandishments of the Thorpes and remains, like Milton's Abdiel, 'among innumerable false unmoved'. Cornered by Thorpes when already engaged to Tilneys, Catherine becomes a pilgrim progressing alarmingly well:

> Isabella became only more and more urgent; calling on her in the most affectionate manner; addressing her by the most endearing names. She was sure her dearest, sweetest Catherine would not seriously refuse such a trifling request to a friend who had loved her so dearly. She knew her beloved Catherine to have so feeling a heart, so sweet a temper, to be so easily persuaded by those she loved. But all in vain; Catherine felt herself to be in the right ... '
> (p. 88)

Finally:

> Thorpe would have darted after her, but Morland withheld him.
> "Let her go, let her go, if she will go."
> "She is as obstinate as –"
> Thorpe never finished the simile, for it could hardly have been a proper one. (p. 90)

Catherine's decision and the ways she sticks to it here are impressive, if faintly metamorphic, and she is influenced by the good breeding of the Tilneys, so that a class distinction treads hard on the heels of a moral one.

She seems, then, doomed by plot exigency to grow and shrink in stature like some Alice in Wonderland, threatening the narrator's and Henry's ironies about her by occupying ethical or intellectual high ground, but suddenly diminished, or dim-ish, again just when she seemed to have emerged triumphantly from her rite of passage. When Henry purloins his sister's copy of *Udolpho*, his irony is self-reproachful ('I am proud when I reflect on it, and I think it must establish me in your good opinion'), but Catherine's 'I am very glad to hear it indeed' (p. 96) momentarily lowers her to the John Thorpe level again. She is magisterial once more, though, when she rebukes Thorpe himself; when he claims that he 'does not know anyone like (her)' she replies: 'Oh! dear, there are a great many people like me, I daresay, only a great deal better. Good morning to you' (p. 110), formidable and freezing phrases which recall the worst aspects of English social intercourse. Fortunately, as he 'stands confirmed in full stupidity', in Dryden's sturdy idiom, he may not have got the point.

Yet, curiously, on this occasion, Thorpe speaks in the broken accents of a man – a rather doltish and self-absorbed one, certainly, but also rather a pathetic one – in the grip of strong sexual, even romantic, feeling. A rather less prissy Miss Austen than critics habitually reproduce emerges when he growls that Catherine has 'A monstrous deal of good-nature, and it is not only good nature, but you have so much, so much of every thing; and then you have such –' (p. 110). Good heavens! A truly Freudian incoherence seems to be articulating, or failing to articulate, itself here.

We have already seen how Catherine's 'dangerous prevalence' correctly intuits knavery. It can also be claimed that her Gothic curiosity encodes a pronounced sexual curiosity, or 'sublimated' libido (and it is at least interesting that Henry feels threatened by female sexuality, very transparently so in chapter 10, for example). Something definitely surfaces from Catherine's overwrought state, and here language seems to be structured like an unconscious, when it is observed that 'Her passion for ancient edifices was next in degree to her passion for Henry Tilney – and castles and abbeys made usually the charm of those reveries which his image did not fill. To see and explore either the ramparts and keep of the one, or the cloisters of the other, had been for many weeks a darling wish …' (p. 124). That nice little shuffle, from 'the one' to 'the other', permits the reader to correlate Catherine's desire to explore ramparts and keep with her desire to 'explore' Henry (although the prospect of Henry as a potentially passionate Gothic ally seems remote).

Gothic fantasy, which is mocked and extirpated from 'respectable' consciousness, encodes both the sexuality which is one theme of the novel, and the underlying truth for Catherine on what we come to see as her entry into experience. The narrative is itself a libidinal investment, a rite of passage, in which the sexual and the textual are strangely mingled. In fact Austen is quite close to Blake here (consider the cancelled motto for 'Songs of Innocence and Experience': 'The good are attracted by men's perceptions/And think not for themselves/Till Experience teaches them to catch/ And to cage the fairies and the elves',[29] which might act as a kind of epigraph for the Austen text, although it glides over the likely unpleasantness of the experiences which would lead to this particular form of Enlightenment).

Even if *Northanger Abbey*, without much irony, throws Catherine her bone of consolation in the end – (Henry himself[30]), the narrative is not so much 'about' the happy, if banal, progressing of maiden to marriage chamber as about Catherine's Keatsian exit from her 'Chamber of maiden-thought', which is only Keats's way of broaching the Blakean theme.

One must concede that Catherine is rather too easily seen as a function of the whole process, with the limited autonomy often remarked on in the case of Thomas Hardy's more hapless characters. Her disappointment with (or of) Isabella combines with her revised impressions of General Tilney and Northanger to provide a deeper sense of what might be said to *lie behind the black veil*. The answer, by due process of elimination, points irresistibly to *the body politic*, and those workings of capitalism which ensure that the cuckoo of 'culture' supplants 'nature', bemusing Catherine at one social extreme with the puzzling General Tilney, and, at another, with Isabella, in her financial insecurity, not helped by a shadowy mother, just offstage, who is obviously quite as bad for her as Mrs Bennet was for Lydia.

Northanger Abbey is not only a novel about the novel, but also about fictions as well as fiction, about imaginary relations to real existences. Beyond this temple of English gentility lies a Marxist horizon, with Tilney senior as the archetype of those conventional minds who have the power to resist energy, in Blake's phrasing,[31] the great 'cause of misery in society' for whom everyone is 'in chains' (whole parishes at work in his hothouses, Catherine notes).

In this sensè, the 'transcendental signifier' of *Northanger Abbey* is Northanger Abbey itself, built for a religious community and transferred to an absolute sole lord with an army of serfs.

The irony of its ironies is finally to watch the novel bursting from its Johnsonian carapace (or chrysalis).[32] The 'perfect felicity' towards which its compressed pages hasten bespeaks an embarrassment about a euphoric conclusion so much at odds with the spirit of the author of *Rasselas*, who had seemed to be installed as tutelary deity, and his probable scepticism as to whether wedding bells equal eternal felicity or whether the sound of wedding bells were likely to be bursting on the tympanum in the first place. Henry has perhaps been given too much to answer for here.[33] However, by his postures and turns of phrase he is, like that later pedagogue, Mr Knightley, repressively ironic.

Johnson tried to pin the charge of a 'Turkish contempt of females' on his surly republican alter ego Milton, attacking something that, on earlier occasions, he was not too far away from himself. The reader finally feels that Catherine's last victory is not the self-overcoming which various trials and temptations entail, but rather victory over the very irony with which the novel surrounds her progress.

We can perhaps catch something of the 'tone' of *Northanger Abbey* if we compare Catherine's moment of mortification at Henry's hands with Emma's at those of Knightley in the more ideologically 'policed' *Emma*. Both Henry and Knightley are wielders of a hegemonic moral discourse. This in turn seems to derive from the fact that both are scions of the landed gentry with large country properties including an Abbey – questions about how the family came by it are, on the whole, not in order (although much nearer to being so in *Northanger*).

Emma, one remembers, was crushed into a temporary premarital submission by Knightley for her impropriety, and Catherine was similarly humiliated by Henry for her speculations about his father the General. Yet Emma's is fictionally an open-and-shut case. Emma should not have been rude to Miss Bates, although she was sorely tried, not so much by Batesian prolixity as the deceptions of Frank Churchill and the fact that her situation in life was not quite so advantageous as it looked. Catherine, on the other hand, is finally convicted on a technicality (the General did not murder his wife, as she momentarily supposed), but her 'improper speculation' acquires its own propriety when his 'villainy' (itself the fruit of 'improper speculation') is exercised towards herself.

Catherine, then, supposedly characterized by 'getting things wrong', seems a reassuring sort of female much in need of male correction: the General did not murder his wife, Northanger Abbey wasn't sinister, or not quite in the way she imagined, Isabella was a vain coquette not a choice companion, and Laurentina's skeleton was not to be found *behind the black veil* (see p. 36). However, not only is she not absolutely wrong, she ends by seeming closer to being right than anyone else. It is hard not to feel that getting things wrong isn't rather to her credit. There are so many *black veils* between the imagination and reality, that he who offers to read with confident aplomb fails more profoundly than the stammering schoolboy – or girl. Perhaps Gothic fiction itself is one of them, but, if so, only because it encodes rather than simply states the dark version of reality which so much strives to conceal from Catherine – including Henry.

One way of summarizing this might be to say that *Northanger Abbey* appears to seek to repress the 'uncanny' in the name of the 'canny': 'remember', it seems to say, 'that we are English'; 'the common feelings of common life'; 'nothing serious can happen here'; and many such saws which a Gramsci would see at once to be 'in ideology'. An Enlightenment rationality joins hands with traditional religious scepticism about human motives and potential to celebrate a victory for common sense over the Gothic novel and the adolescent imagination it at once feeds and feeds on. However, this victory fails to occur. The 'canny' secretes (both hides and discloses) the 'uncanny', and Northanger Abbey itself figures this. Northanger Abbey contains the meaning of *Northanger Abbey*, as Catherine, in her way, intuited. Perhaps even the laundry bills she was ashamed to discover had more relevance than she originally suspected. At any rate, as Shlomith Rimmon-Kenan has unsuspectingly put it, in *Northanger Abbey* it is, paradoxically, the canny which becomes 'the uncanniest of all guests'[34] – or hosts.

3
A Sensitive Subject:
Sense and Sensibility

If Pascal could say 'we should respect the gentry because ...',[1] then 'Jane Austen' is widely supposed to have spent her time composing a monster footnote to the idea, *authorizing* it, as it were. But *Sense and Sensibility* is a crucial text to consider here. For one thing, it seems, much of the time, to be *against* rather than *for* the gentry, in a mode of rampant disrespect which might be felt to bring it closer to Paine than to Burke. Although the closure of the novel seems to compose a flourish for what Burke called 'the spirit of a gentleman, and the spirit of religion',[2] as its heroines Elinor and Marianne are married off, respectively to the spirit of religion in the form of Edward Ferrars, and the spirit of a gentleman in the form of Colonel Brandon, this conclusion has often been felt to be somewhat spiritless. And there is something questionable about both of these as wooers, as prospective husbands, and in what they might be said to 'personate'. However, a charitable view would state that both the Colonel and Edward are fairly decent chaps, forced to skulk against their better natures, and to be rather low-spirited as a result of the selfishness and skulduggery (legalized) which surround them. More to the point, critically speaking, is that this *is* what surrounds them.

Marilyn Butler maintains that 'the concept of sensibility is mocked, not argued over', a point made, strangely, in relation to Fanny Dashwood, and not Marianne, its major embodiment. Yet it is also a major mistake to assume that 'mocking sensibility' *is* the central preoccupation of *Sense and Sensibility*.[3] What is certainly mocked here is the claim to sensibility where the effect of such a claim causes suffering to others and becomes its opposite – 'stark insensibility', in Johnsonian idiom. Sensibility, it seems, is not itself. Later in the novel, 'affectionate sensibility' (Marianne's) is not only specifically approved and encouraged: in the social 'dispensation' diagnosed, one is made to feel, such currents of feeling need all the help they can get.

Thus, in *Sense and Sensibility*, not only is sensibility *not* unequivocally mocked, it becomes an indispensable weapon against what the novel defines as really 'evil' – i.e. the acquisitiveness which is 'to everything but interest blind', as Blake puts it. In detecting and analysing this social/unsocial 'element', not only does a rogues' gallery of gentry-folk threaten to appear, the 'element' itself would be firmly pigeonholed as *sense*, or 'sense of a kind' (to adopt a phrase of Elinor's own). We dip our toes in what Marx described as 'the icy waters of egotistical calculation', and are vicariously regaled by the slight tortures inflicted by that 'instrumental reason' attacked by Habermas and Marcuse as 'not rationality as such, but a specific form of unacknowledged domination'.[4]

Sense and Sensibility, then, is a book with compelling claims to attention, but unexpected ones. Or perhaps we might use Joe Fisher's interesting comparison and contrast of what he calls 'the traded text' versus 'the counter-text' in relation to Hardy's novels[5] to illustrate the curious duplicity of this one. On display, certainly, is a braiding of a noble ('Johnsonian') rhetoric of self-command and firmly repressive 'self-government' with dangerous currents descending from the Sorrows of that Young Werther to whom Marianne bears such a startlingly close resemblance. Its central proposition might then seem to suggest that, if the *ancien régime* can be signalled by the mature pronouncements of Samuel Johnson, then there is much to be said for the *ancien régime*.

A more complex assessment of the 'counter-text' might begin with its obvious *tours de force*. Consider, at the outset, the virtuoso display of triumphant mean-spiritedness in which Fanny Dashwood persuades her husband to do virtually nothing for his half-sisters Elinor and Marianne and their 'romantic' mother, despite a promise made at the death-bed of the father. Laced with significant abuse of language ('I'll lay my life he meant nothing more', etc.[6]) this 'hinge' of future events has, among other things, a decidedly 'feminist' inflection deriving from the 'marginalising' and exposure of Mrs Dashwood and her daughters. This was combined with the presentation of what would appear to be a pronounced feature of the period, described by John Barrell as that of the 'pressing importance to [the gentry] to preserve and pass on their wealth from generation to generation, by a ruthlessly prudent management of their estate, by (in England) careful entailment, and by a ruthless parsimony towards all but the heir himself'[7] – a process represented here by John and Fanny Dashwood and their 'poor little [Harry]' (p. 7).

'Better be without sense than misapply it as you do', says Mr Knightley to Emma, and of the misapplications of sense and sensibility we have to reckon with here, it is the former which are incomparably more destructive in their social effects, yet it is more significant to note here that both words are highly ambivalent, and not merely positive and negative vectors respectively. It is a point that William Blake would have appreciated. He, after all, wrote that 'without contraries is no progression' and that 'a contrary is not a negation' – difficult points, but well illustrated by his apparent contrary, 'Jane': conditions called 'sense' and 'sensibility' may actually differ less from each other than conditions with the same name but an opposed significance.[8] Here the initial point seems to be that Elinor is Augustan humanism and Johnsonian control, Marianne incipient Romanticism and emotional open-ness, or display, Elinor 'hide' Marianne 'reveal' – and thus Elinor 'right', Marianne 'wrong'. But this itself seems to be a wee bit wrong, we come to realize, and the text itself becomes a process rather than a demonstration model for those cut-and-dried Johnsonian results.

Sense and Sensibility, then, is rather trickier than it looks. If it evokes, it also refuses the smartly diagrammatic oppositions it appears to ground itself on.

Of course it doesn't always look like this from the outset. Potshots at 'sensibility,' the wanton indulgence of emotion by Marianne, Mrs Dashwood and anyone else who gets in the way of an Augustan narrator are what the text seems to require of itself, in the interest of some downright Johnsonian growling which has tempted many, indeed most, critics to discuss it as if it were called *Sense and Nonsense*. Marianne indulges feeling and wounds the feelings of others. By contrast, Elinor, whose watchword is that 'self-command' for which the Age of Johnson and Adam Smith would have so commended her, possesses a precocious prudence nurtured in the forcing-house of her mother's romantic impracticality – 'her feelings were strong but she knew how to govern them'. Yet things start early to go wrong – wrong for this idea, that is, – but not, ultimately, 'wrong' for a novel with more to do than its 'programme notes' lead one to expect. Norman Sherry points out that Elinor's faintly smug emphasis on 'prudence' and 'address' can make her sound a little like her tormentor, the deviously manipulative and grasping Lucy.[9] In fact Lucy torments Elinor as Mrs Elton torments Emma. Emma's snobbism makes her vulnerable to the one, Elinor's own caution makes her slightly less than honest with the other.

In particular, after Lucy's disclosure of her secret engagement to Edward, Lucy is lightning-quick to detect an element of 'bad faith' in Elinor's response when she asks Elinor to advise her about whether or not to relinquish her secret engagement. Elinor protests that 'it raises my influence much too high; the power of deciding two people so tenderly attached is too much for an indifferent person.' Elinor may be thought of as seeking to relieve her feelings with a peck of irony here, but Lucy pecks back. ''Tis because you are an indifferent person,' said Lucy with some pique, and laying a particular stress on those words, 'that your judgement might justly have weight with me. If you could be supposed to be biassed in any respect by your own feelings, your opinion would not be worth having' (pp. 129–30). *Touché*, as they say – too much so, indeed from someone whose lack of education was supposedly primarily to be deplored, but who is here not so very behindhand in Big Bow-Wow orotundity as she ought to be.

Indeed, at her very worst, Elinor seems to be bent on upholding the ignoble ethos of the 'noble' Lord Chesterfield, counterfeiting a spontaneity of manner that conceals something – basically, a desire to manipulate and to dominate, and his *suaviter in modo, fortiter in re* is still daily played up to, no doubt, by City yuppies and all who play the game of bourgeois self-advancement. It's a most unattractive motto. 'Jesus was all virtue, and acted from impulse, not from rules,' wrote Blake, contrary to Chesterfield and perhaps conscious of him as he wrote.[10]

Elinor, then, attaining 'ends' by 'prudence' and 'address' is to that extent closer to Chesterfield than to Blake's Founder of Christianity. Marianne, although she may trample on the sensibilities of others in displaying her own, not a fault everyone would find venial, certainly, seems a bit nearer to Blake's emphasis on a bit of 'open heart' surgery for the *surgélé* world of Chesterfield and the like. She is also a bit further away from the devouring 'underclass' represented by Nancy and Lucy Steele, who burst on the social scene to 'agree 'em to death and destruction',[11] (to take a suggestive phrase from Melville's *Benito Cereno*), and toady their way to the top.

Resisting authorial attempts to direct the jury as enjoined by Walter Benjamin,[12] and combining the idea with the announcement of the death of the author by Barthes and Foucault, together with a Derridean concept of intention which goes beyond the New Critical enlightenment to see it as less an origin than a product,[13] helps to liberate the play of textuality from unsustainable hermeneutic constrictions. Here, for instance, it's obvious that the 'governing idea' – that Marianne's 'cult of sensibility' is a menace to herself and others – is shadowed by an emerging awareness that what 'the author herself' calls 'a kind of sense' (roughly, flinty acquisitiveness), is altogether more objectionable. In fact, 'Marianne' seems sometimes like a slightly schizophrenic function of the discontented narrative. Unlike her flighty, romantic mother, after whom she is, after all, supposed to 'take', she has a certain formidableness to hand in the form of a Johnsonian downrightness, even truculence, which bespeaks a measure of 'sense' alarming to the insipid propriety (and stupidity) of a Lady Middleton.

The point then seems to be that sense, or true sense, and sensibility, or true sensibility, are, in Wordsworth's voice of the common-man romantic idiom, 'inveterately convolved' with each other. They have large areas of emotional and ethical overlap. And if the avatar of sensibility, Marianne, has lots, or pots, of sense, we are specifically warned not to 'correlate' Elinor's 'sense' with any kind of cold-heartedness. For example, 'her sensibility was potent indeed!', a pronouncement tried out ironically on Marianne at one stage (p. 71), might be used unironically of Elinor at several others, particularly when she sheds 'tears of joy' when the rather dismal Edward, against what appears all narrative odds, comes in quest of her: 'Oft he seems to hide his face/But unexpectedly returns,' chants Milton's barbaric chorus, and Edward, as clergyman and thus *vicariously* goddish, a *Deus* not quite *absconditus*, (although he seems to be threatening to do a bunk throughout), is a relevant concept. And especially so given that Austen, as Robert Polhemus observes, is inclined to substitute *marital* for what in (say) Johnson could only be a religious 'solution'.[14] Pascal, it will be remembered, shed 'tears of joy' in a once-famous passage concerning the mathematician's intensely emotional 'acceptance' of the 'bridegroom', Christ, and perhaps Elinor's winning of Edward, vicar of Christ, could be seen as a 'transposition' of this, especially as eligible men who are not *salauds* are frighteningly hard to come by, apparently.

There is not much need, then, to continue to dwell on the idea that Elinor has feelings. Revealing, though, and the narrative here is certainly one of Revelations, is the trick whereby the mean-spirited Lucy allows the servant Thomas to petrify the Dashwoods by a report of a sighting of a 'Mr and Mrs Ferrars' (meaning Lucy has grabbed the nearest available meal ticket in the form of narcissistic brother Robert). This causes Elinor's deep feelings about Edward to surface in an alarming manner.

This is particularly of interest because it enacts and unites a false sense of narrative 'closure' with a false sense of ideological significance: at last, Elinor's response alerts Mrs D. to a capacity for suffering already severely tested in her self-bridling, self-commanding daughter.

This might well be the final exposure of a more humdrum novelist, but 'Jane' has a few more tricks up her sleeve. For example, even here, at Elinor's nadir, when she might reasonably expect a spotlight or two, Thomas's most unfortunate announcement, which seems to evoke a convincingly 'Edwardian' characteristic – 'he never was a gentleman much for talking' (p. 311) – it is *Marianne* who 'falls back in her chair in hysterics' (p. 310).

We have grown used to the idea, especially as broached and bruited in the immensely powerful work of Derrida, that binaries, or 'binarising', may be a 'vicious' procedure, which creates one image in the antithesis of an other, reducing the necessary autonomy and structural incompleteness of relations which, really, stop nowhere, to transplant James's useful phrasing. Jane Austen may be said to be bringing forward the occasions for the creation of such binarisms and then deconstructing them. Marianne, for example, seems a type, an embodiment, at once an English and a feminine 'Werther', who has carried the new 'heart religions' (in an interesting phrase of Anne K. Mellor[15]) with which Jane Austen herself was at some point to sympathize, into a positive religion of feeling. Although her reading has only taken her as far as Cowper, she sounds more than a little like later figures who offer a rather less decorous and more full-blooded, and rebellious romanticism – that of Shelley, perhaps.[16] By contrast, it seems, Elinor is etched firmly in the Augustan, perhaps even Augustinian, mode of a rather sternly renunciatory Christianized Stoicism. Yet in a sense it is as true of Elinor as of Marianne that, in the famous formula of Byron's Julia, 'man's love is of man's life a thing apart/'Tis woman's whole existence'.[17]

Such statements make feminists, quite understandably, bridle, but they are interesting as statements of how women 'are', not naturally, but culturally – i.e. under pressure, as the Dashwood young ladies themselves are – virtually disinherited, and assiduous, industrious and studious without having any outlet for their employments – except as those may render them more attractive to right-minded suitors. Femininity, in Austen, is definitely under siege.

Although its lively presentation of the contemporary scene and setting entail what can only be called an 'advance' on the Johnsonian model of creative fiction, the novel itself retains the almost smartly diagrammatic contrasts, antitheses, and parallels in achieving 'structures of feeling', demonstration-models for some heavily ethical seminar with a strange, almost paradoxical 'rubric': 'Please, don't be "spontaneous", but I trust you have some spontaneity to restrain.' Marianne and Elinor are walking Blakean contraries who create a kind of sibling dialectic, and it is interesting that *Sense and Sensibility* was being drafted contemporaneously with *The Marriage of Heaven and Hell*, where Blake observes that 'a contrary is not a negation', and here we seem to have to have 'negations' of both sense and sensibility – for example, in the person of spouse-dominating Lady Middleton with her insipid propriety and static calm, apparently embodying but actually parodying sense; and Fanny Dashwood, cold-hearted and selfish, it is said, but capable of formidable fits of hysterics when she feels her own interests threatened. The revelation of impecunious Lucy's engagement to brother Edward sets off one such fit.

Instead of merely expounding a 'nem. con.' idea, then, *Sense and Sensibility* warms to the idea of a war of ideas, and such set-pieces as the 'disputing about tastes' between Marianne and Edward are characteristic of its 'agon-ising', very reminiscent of Schlegel's claim that the novel was the Socratic dialogue of the day. Even if we have been taught by (bullied by?) Derrida into regarding the Socratic dialogue as a scene of intellectual bullying (or even gerrymandering), this too is relevant. Indeed, S and S sets off in this Socratically-bullying fashion, as if to dispatch sensibility was all its care. It still feels 'stratified', showing and hiding this fairly crude 'primal' intention. Title and treatment strongly suggest Mannheim's unfashionable but still perfectly debatable claim that 'Romanticism developed from the Enlightenment as thesis to antithesis'.[18]

What fascinates about *Sense and Sensibility* is that at first glance it seems to be quite busy forging mind-manacles here, so that it actually begins to sound like Iser's definition of the legal text, which 'lay(s) down principles that are binding for the behaviour of human beings'. Yet, when we read it through, we may feel like rhapsodizing in the idiom Fredric Jameson uses to praise Derrida for enabling 'the unmasking or demystification of ... [its own] naturalised binary opposition'.[19]

Marianne's cult of sensibility, then, was to determine against her. Perhaps, in a way, this was 'Jane's' way of 'identifying against herself' as Judith Fetterly puts it.[20] I have in mind specifically 'Jane's' relationship with sister Cassandra, in which the Marianne role looks more likely for her than the Elinor one.

But whatever the biographical tap-root of this may be, it seems to be established, against the grain, that Marianne's stance, in a world of empty or malevolent chatter, is finally attractive, particularly as the society which surrounds her is established as a powerful, destructive engine. On the one hand, what seems a fierce integrity is less easily reducible to neurosis than the postures of Fanny in the 'inferiority-complex'-inducing world of *Mansfield Park;* and on the other, she seems to have little power, and her naivety is easily exploited. Indeed, my only real worry about her is in terms of how many people she is expected to be in this rather exacting text. On the one hand, there is the alienation expressed by slightly truculent adolescent silences; on the other, there are rather sturdy, Blake-like 'interventions', particularly on behalf of all-too-forbearing 'big sister'.

For example, the incident of the screens, on which Tony Tanner has focused nice attention,[21] enacts a challenge to accepted power-relations unusual in a world marked by conspicuous sycophancy towards anything that moves with wealth or power. In vol. 2, chapter 12, Mrs Ferrars (the mother of Edward), arrogant and avaricious, is slighting Elinor's painted screens, symbol of her own tendency to hide feeling. (Marianne, who [in one of her textual 'incarnations' anyway], is determined to live 'without screens', may be said to be 'removing the screens' here by drawing attention to Elinor's, much to the latter's embarrassment.) In attendance are John and Fanny Dashwood, Lady Middleton and Lucy Steele, who all accept, with relish, the necessity for worldly-minded toadying, duplicity and acquisitiveness. What a set! The occasion is well orchestrated and the situation it enfolds is a piquant one: Lucy is holding a depressed Edward to a secret engagement which would actually be held to be less eligible than one with Elinor, while Mrs Ferrars suspects only Elinor and wishes Edward to marry a Miss Morton for money and social position. In this world, people are always being punished for their good qualities, and in fact the way in which the language of natural affection can be conscripted for this kind of power-broking itself shows that some kind of 'radical' 'Jane' is scarcely a figment of the imagination. Indeed, if this is supposed to be a didactic occasion the point of the lesson seems to be less that Marianne should learn not to embarrass Elinor than that Elinor should learn not to be embarrassed.

Here, however, Marianne's sensibility is a bit of an ambiguous gift. It enables the defiance, but self-destructs as 'the rage of her idealism' (to steal a phrase from Adorno) becomes, specifically, a melting sentiment, that is, a sentiment which melts itself:

> Urged by a strong impulse of affectionate sensibility, she moved, after a moment, to her sister's chair, and, putting one arm round her neck and one cheek close to her's, said in a low but eager voice,
> 'Dear, dear Elinor, don't mind them. Don't let them make *you* unhappy.'
> She could say no more; her spirits were quite overcome, and hiding her face on Elinor's shoulder, she burst into tears. (pp. 206–7)

Marianne's challenge to the neglect of Elinor here is, in its effects, gender-specific. Or rather, because what's *engendered* is ineffectiveness, it underscores a point made by Toril Moi in *Sexual/Textual Politics*: 'The significance of gestures changes when used by men or women; no matter what women do, their behaviour may be taken to symbolise inferiority.'[22] Indeed, Mary Wollstonecraft seems to have thought that 'sensibility' was annexed to women in an almost conspiratorial fashion.

This is a bit sweeping. Even if a parochial instance like Mackenzie's *Man of Feeling* need not detain us, an international instance of 'sensibility' is surely Werther in Goethe's novel. And Werther dominates the scene in his novel, whereas in the Austen text we see insistently from the Elinor and generally *ancien régime* point of view.

This is not all bad for the Austen text. We need to know that beneath Elinor's too too chastened exterior, 'the life throbs quick and warm'. But no due process of mimesis enables us to judge of Marianne's feelings, and especially when she is courted by Willoughby. It is tempting then to see Werther's meetings with Lotte as a 'version' of Marianne's relationship, supplying details consonant with the mere hintings of 'Jane's' text:

We went to the window. There was thunder off to one side, the glorious rain was pouring down on the land, and the most refreshing fragrance rose up to us with the fullness of a warm breeze. She stood leaning on her elbows, her eyes gazing out into the country; she looked up into the sky, and at me; I saw her eyes fill with tears; she laid her hand on mine and said 'Klopstock!' I recalled at once the splendid ode she had in mind and sank into the stream of emotions she had poured out over me with this password.[23]

With the substitution of 'Cowper' for 'Klopstock', one feels that Marianne and Willoughby must often have used similar 'passwords'.

Finally, of course, Lotte rejects Werther and 'sensibility', just as Willoughby rejects Marianne for 'prudential' reasons. 'Sense', that's to say, governs his conduct, but his good sense is determined by his previous dissipation, extravagance and profligacy. Marianne suffers as Werther suffers and is even more sinned against, sense persecutes sensibility, yet the text is still 'watermarked' by a purring, or purling, current of irony at her expense. But what it nevertheless lets slip is that Marianne is remedial rather than poisonous, and also a scapegoat.

Re-reading, or re-treading *Sense and Sensibility* with a warmer regard for its second term is probably helped by pointing up how congruent Marianne is with Werther. For example, early on in the Austen text Marianne denounces Elinor's glum, half-hearted wooer Edward for general frigidity of manner and in particular his insipid reading of Cowper: 'To hear those beautiful lines, which have frequently almost driven me wild, pronounced with such impenetrable calmness, such dreadful indifference!' She also bridles at the cautious Elinor's minimal admission that she 'likes' Edward: 'Cold-hearted Elinor! more than cold-hearted! ... use those words again and I will leave the room this moment!' (p. 17).

Interestingly, then, Werther in fact combines the literary and the ethical points made here:

You should see the silly figure I cut when she is mentioned in company! And particularly when I am asked how I *like* her! – *like* her! I hate the word as I hate death. What kind of person must he be who *likes* Lotte, whose every sense and every emotion she does not occupy? *Like*! Someone asked me recently how I *liked Ossian*! (p. 91)

The reference to *Ossian* shows the flip side to sensibility, just as there is a bad sense of 'sense'. Dr Johnson, no less, supplier of maxims to the Elinors of this world, intuited that *Ossian* was an artful forgery pretending to primitive artlessness, roughly what Willoughby proved to be to Marianne (and Lucy Steele to Edward Ferrars).

That Marianne's very high-mindedness makes her an easy dupe of Willoughby itself softens the reader's response to her occasional social atrocities. When Edward, himself being duped by another scheming pretender to sensibility, slyly conjectures that 'Mr. Willoughby hunts' (p. 86), he reminds us that 'hunting', both by tradition and some contextual pressure here, may easily be read as symbolizing predatory *sexuality*.

Predatory Willoughby certainly is, and the 'dissection' of his character is one of the many 'fine tunings' of *Sense and Sensibility*. At first blush he is a dashing fellow who instantly captivates not only the fervid Marianne, but also her 'romantic' mother and even the more 'guarded' Elinor. Full, it seems, of a youthful ardour and exuberance, he appears to compose a specific antithesis to the cold-hearted prudentiality exemplified by the Dashwoods' immediate relations, particularly John Dashwood, the very type of the 'enclosing' landlord defined by John Barrell in *The Dark Side of the Landscape* (1980). But, impelled by a fashionable extravagance which knows no abatement, Willoughby's motivation is, one might say, not *materially* different. In Blakean terms, he too is a 'Devourer'. Thus, another 'binary opposition' collapses, and this is hardly a point of marginal significance, since with it Marianne's chances of happiness disappear, more than temporarily, since many a reader finds it implausible, as the narrative formally asserts, that she finds it elsewhere.

Both Dashwood *and* Willoughby, then, embody Adorno's conception of 'the belly turned mind'. In fact, this also sounds a bit Blake-like, and particularly if we remember that Proverb of Hell which states that 'naturally (man) is only a natural organ subject to sense'.[24] Jane Austen's text lets us see that this use of 'sense' will 'skewer' the prudential ethic which this work is often taken to support (or even advertise). And if, as the Blake proverb has it, 'Prudence is a rich ugly old maid courted by Incapacity', Willoughby courts her as assiduously as Dashwood. Indeed, Dashwood is at least uxorious, distinguished by what Byron calls 'constancy to a bad, ugly woman',[25] Willoughby by inconstancy to a good and beautiful one.

In fact the dissection of Willoughby here might be seen as nothing less than an attempt to nip Byronic Man in the bud, in so far as that might be seen to entail an *apparently* unworldly and 'romantic' posture by someone actually rather acutely concerned with the figure he cuts, sexually predatory, and keenly alert to 'money as social element', very much like the figure of Byron himself. And, like Byron in this also, Willoughby's is a disease of desire as well as acquisitiveness. In fact, Byron's wife, Annabella Millbanke herself diagnosed one feature of his personality which was like a side of Willoughby later explained to Marianne by Elinor, and *also* an aspect of Werther dissected by his 'Lotte' – 'I feel it is only the impossibility of possessing me that makes your desire for me so strong' (p. 229). Willoughby deserts Marianne, we feel, not merely because she is without 'invisible means of support' (i.e. pretty penurious), but because she 'owns without disguise' that she loves him. In her sublimated way, she gives herself to him completely, and it may well be understood that one of the text's silences, gaps, its '*non-dits*', to recall the discussion of the novel by Balibar and Macherey, might entail the full-blown seduction and betrayal which a novel engendered by 'Miss Austen' cannot formally countenance.

The more Willoughby can think of himself as having 'had' Marianne and passed on, the greater the tendency for him to undervalue her. (The text cannot 'imply' this, but we can imply it for it, as it were.) He is a wooer whose desire can only be sustained by an uncertainty principle. Marianne, who will never descend to sleights or tricks, has chosen as her only possible lover an impossible lover (although it is possible that only an impossible lover would possibly do). Elinor, having listened to Willoughby's self-extenuation, is acutely diagnostic:

> [with you] he would have had a wife of whose temper he could make no complaint, but he would have been always necessitous – always poor; and probably would have soon learnt to rank the innumerable comforts of a clear estate and a good income as of far more importance, even to domestic happiness, than the mere temper of a wife. (p. 308)

Marianne has become a slightly different character again, here, to fit this binarism. She was distinguished, the reader would probably confirm, not by 'temper', but by high-spirited poeticality, alienation, beauty, intelligence and a certain unbridled chutzpah not wholly compatible with mere amiability.[26] But Elinor correctly senses – in fact, Willoughby is 'there' for the sake of the diagnosis – that Willoughby as 'Byronic Man' is something of a 'double bind' incarnate, he who wishes to possess what he has chosen not to, while remaining unpossessed by what he possesses.

As we observed, Willoughby's abandonment of Marianne for the heiress is rendered potentially tragic by Marianne's sensitivity. An even darker (and actually more 'plausible') 'scene' of seduction and betrayal is hinted at in Colonel Brandon's rather clumsily inter-polated account of Willoughby's treatment of Eliza Williams. Authorial cunning infolds more realistic destructive behaviour than the decorous text can countenance onstage. No parted curtains will reveal a hypersensitive Marianne in the passionate embraces of a Byronic Willoughby, but the reader may speculate whether Marianne's hysteria might not be the fruit of a sexual awakening, emotionally overwhelming for someone hitherto so 'secluded'. As part of the necessary *non-dit* here we can reasonably assume Willoughby's having taken liberties which for her were incompat-ible with less than an offer of marriage, but which he, having been a bit of a roué, could interpret differently.

Marianne, then, claims to see through the social masquerade but is easily duped. This shows her up a little, as the text might seem to want, but also, destabilizingly, creates sympathy. In fact 'Jane' comes close to black comedy in showing how her intensity in no way inhibits, but rather promotes, the choice of a lover who is louche and shallow. Textual logic here seems to imply that her claims to unsocial (if not downright anti-social) 'authenticity' forges a sense of identity based on what Rousseau calls '*la chaîne des sentiments*',[27] which seems to prove to be a bit of a daisy-chain here.

Willoughby provides a kind of mirror-stage for her sentiments, a firmer 'alterity', and indeed his very hollowness makes him, for a time, an ideal echo-chamber for them. He is in this sense a Shelleyan sort of lover whose 'voice is as the voice of my own soul', in the phrasing of his *Alastor* (1817), largely because when they speak, it is 'the voice of her own soul' that she is hearing. When, therefore, he ruptures the hymen (Derrideans please note) of their 'virtual reality' engagement, or, in the rather chilling formula of Mr Knightley in *Emma*, talks romantically but acts rationally, he destroys Marianne's sense of identity and purpose. Her near-fatal illness is a sort of signifier which states, roughly speaking, in Donne's phrasing but without his coarser overtones, '[I] can die by it, if not live by love', and Willoughby's last appearance becomes a kind of 'death bed' (hers) confession (his).

A *Liebestod* ('love-death') is certainly a plausible fate for Marianne, and even her marriage, finally, to Colonel Brandon may be seen, if sardonically, as a version of one, very much in the spirit of the penitential scene which ushers in the novel's 'last movement', as Marianne administers Johnsonian slaps to herself in impeccably 'Augustan' cadences: 'Do not, my dearest Elinor, let your *kindness defend* what I know your *judgement* must *censure* (p. 336) ... Whenever I looked towards the past, I saw some *duty neglected*, or some *failing indulged* ... a *heart hardened* against their *merits*, and a *temper irritated* by their very *attention*' (p. 337; italics mine).

Marianne's palinode, this supposedly central set-piece of resolute self-censoring, is played off against the fact that she is more sinned against than sinning, that society has moved like a powerful engine to crush her and her sister in their marginalized poverty and femininity – the one very much involved with the other. For example, Marianne may propose rising at six in order to study hard – significantly, she seems to be surrounded by chumps and fops – but what is the point of or what prospects open as a result of this talent and application of hers? Yet Oxford, e.g., to take the most obvious e.g., was merely a last-ditch choice for the 'idle' Edward. For Marianne, it seems, there is 'no end-product to what she does'. There seems to be no outlet for the intellectual activity which alienates Lady Middleton and is all Greek to Sir John except as it may find expression in strictly ancillary style in marriage.

And in this social dispensation the very achievements of femininity increase 'its' vulnerability and exposure. Indeed, Marianne is recuperated by that powerful engine the Jane Austen text, rewarding her, rather against her will, by making her a Colonel's lady. This, though, makes her marriage seem too close to a self-repressing retraction made for her to seem altogether apposite. After such knowledge, the kind of 'closure' (the very word is like a knell) that the novel arranges for Marianne has caused some dismay even among traditionally inflected critics.

Of course it may seem inappropriate to protest. The benign irony of the text swings into action to denounce the callowness of Marianne's teenage opinions about second attachments, older men and the like, in demonstrating that the opposite of what she believed and desired was both true and desirable – that the opposite *was* apposite, not only in romantic theory but in marital practice. Curiously, then, to the extent that one feels that Marianne is being repressed rather than rescued, the narrative process of *Sense and Sensibility* is collusive with a social process and pressure it has contrived to put into question. As Elinor herself concedes, the figure of Willoughby continues to 'haunt' after he has been formally discredited and (as it were) expelled from the text. At the very least what might be called Marianne's idea of Willoughby, if not Willoughby himself, defines what Wallace Stevens called 'an absence in reality'.[28]

The sense of 'an absence in reality' recalls the reader to the nature of Marianne's problem, not at all the same thing, as it seemed initially to be saying, as 'the problem of Marianne'. Actually the problem of Marianne is the problem of or for the impoverished female Dashwoods as such, since Elinor's role as putative 'leader' is to *repress the idea of 'the problematic' itself* – all one can do, so to say, is to arm oneself with nobly generic (but not gender-specific) sort-of-Johnsonish maxims which, as it were by definition, proleptically repress or replace anything vulgarly 'sociological' with the sublimely metaphysical.

In fact Marianne's behaviour – everything she does – is indeed a comment on the Dashwood's social position. And it 'contains' anger, in both the senses one would surely wish to hold in place here. In particular, her nature-cult entails a flight from drawing-rooms where sycophantic, manipulative and even more overtly 'destructive' behaviour is consequent on power-relations, and what Blake calls 'the cunning of weak and tame minds ... which have the power to resist energy'[29] is all-triumphant. Kant remarks in his *Third Critique,* 'nature is here called sublime because it elevates the imagination to a presentation of those cases in which the mind can make felt the proper sublimity of its destination, in comparison with ... – Kant says, 'Nature itself',[30] but substitute [that of] 'drawing rooms', and the contrast will illuminate Marianne.

'Rehabilitating' Marianne seems to be 'against the grain' (in Benjamin's much-used phrase) of the text. Deconstructive and other theoretical readings complicate our sense of what 'against the grain' might mean. Marianne's feelings and postures create a 'loop-hole for the soul' here, against both Augustan/Augustinian pressures. Much greater *Lebensraum* is made for the 'Romantic' than it is possible to glimpse at first through the persistent persiflage to which Marianne is subjected. For example, near the outset, on quitting Norland, Marianne is given some quite perilous rhetoric. Her 'pathos' is fringed with aggression: it is partly a way of figuring the 'spiritual' poverty she had encountered at Norland:

> And you, ye well-known trees! – but you will continue the same … unconscious of the pleasure or the regret you occasion, and insensible of change in those who walk under your shade! – but who will remain to enjoy you? (p. 23)

This is a question which is a bit more sensible and apropos than it seems. Marianne finds her antithesis here in John Dashwood, who cuts down the trees to make way for a greenhouse. Like the Blake character for whom a tree was 'only a green thing that stands in the way' he is a 'Devourer'.

For Dashwood is an 'enclosing' landlord whose propriety of manner conceals a ruthlessly exclusive 'care and dear concern' on behalf of the 'sole heir'. If 'man' is 'everywhere in chains', as Rousseau said, and this is to include what Blake calls 'mind-forg'd manacles', then Dashwood is at once more chained and chaining than Marianne, whatever degree of false consciousness her cult of sentiment may have brought her to.

Dashwood here connotes a general stampede of acquisitiveness, and the overwhelming concern with what the good-hearted vulgarian Mrs Jennings calls 'money and greatness' is the insufferable social tone which 'creates' by reaction not merely the wildly 'romantic' Marianne, who will not live the lie which decorum exacts, but also the devouringly 'umble underclass represented by the fawningly malevolent Lucy Steele and her sister Anne. This weighting towards concealed motives again tilts the balance of sympathetic reading towards Marianne, and her tremulous concern for her natural surroundings seems to have something to do with a feeling for 'that which resists commodification'. It certainly spills over the decorous Cowperism she professes. Her Master's Voice may finally be, not that of Cowper at all, but Hopkins in 'Binsey Poplars', where an intensity of anguish follows on those few 'strokes of havoc' which are said to 'unselve' a 'sweet especial rural scene'.

Marianne was to be 'diagnosed' as a 'case', like the elder Goethe considering Romanticism as sickness. But she ends as a *pharmakon*, seen at first as poison, then, gradually, as both cure and scapegoat. Marianne and Elinor are not, in fact, the terms of a 'binary opposition', though such an intention may have supplied the scaffolding, or the scaffold, for the text. Indeed, it seems that, by the time 'Jane Austen' has finished with her, it is impossible to conceive of Marianne as 'one person' anyway. She is a rather variable function in a metamorphic context. At one moment she creeps away in dissenting silence, or bursts into tears, and yet again has a sharp, unaccommodating defiance William Blake would have applauded her for. Elinor, by contrast, is closer to Johnson. On the other hand 'Blake' and 'Johnson' aren't just forms of mutually assured destruction, and their implied siege of contraries is not hateful.

Indeed on many matters they are not even contraries. Marianne, like Emma at the close of her novel, 'loves everything that is decided and open', which suggests a Blakean distrust of creeping and concealment. She is consequently very decided and open with Edward, who seems a bit of a clam. Edward, she says, is

> the most fearful of giving pain, of wounding expectation, and the most incapable of being selfish, of any body I ever saw. Edward, it is so and I will say it. What! Are you never to hear yourself praised! (p. 213)

Yet for Johnson too, 'where secrecy or mystery (begin), vice and roguery are not far off'.[31] Austen can achieve something of a textual merger of Blake and Johnson here. But her mastery of genre, her 'genius', turns them to subtler ends than they usually encompass. For example, Marianne's wooer Willoughby looks decided and open too, but proves decidedly devious and unreliable. The true heroes, Brandon and Edward, by contrast, are constrained to behave in a somewhat hole-in-corner fashion.

Marianne and Elinor, then, are not 'like' Jane and Elizabeth Bennet in *Pride and Prejudice* – where Jane, for example, is positively sweet, suspends judgement, will not think ill of anyone. Hers is a Song of Innocence, but Elizabeth will have none of it.

Nor will Elinor and Marianne. Both, compared with the somewhat 'polyanna' Jane, exercise relative severity of judgement. For example, Elinor's scepticism earns reproach from her mother, who says that she 'would rather take evil upon credit than good', which makes a sort of contrast, I suppose, with a certain guilelessness or gullibility in Marianne when the story finds it appropriate for her to have this. But on the other hand, or so we are told, Marianne 'had never much toleration for any thing like impertinence, vulgarity, inferiority of parts, or even differences of taste from herself ...'. Sensibility which suffers neither knaves nor fools gladly has obviously been misunderstood.

But it seems also that Elinor is not herself defective in sensibility. How easy, for example, it would be to transfer an earlier, ironic observation upon Marianne's indulgences ('Her sensibility was potent indeed!') to that culminating moment when a free Edward Ferrars, just given up as lost, comes to ask her to marry him – 'She almost ran out of the room, and as soon as the door was closed, burst into tears of joy which at first she thought would never cease.'

If we can, after a fashion, define Marianne as sense and Elinor as sensibility, and if this seems, at first, scarcely sensible, it at least (or at last) detaches them from the abstractions of the title, and causes us to realize, along with what seems a curiously unwilling author, that we are dealing with four separate terms, not two, whose relationship is 'dialectic' and dynamic, as the central characters refuse to be the 'fixities and definites' of rigid 'Johnsonian' projection.

However, this is hardly to say that *Sense and Sensibility* is an 'unproblematic' text, or that Adorno's observation that 'the most eloquent parts of the work are the wounds which the conflict in the theory leaves behind' does not apply to it. Attempting to 'correct' Marianne, it finds Marianne is being punished for her finer qualities rather than her social atrocities.

Indeed, its very reward for Marianne at the close has been seen as a kind of punishment. 'The heroines get what they want,' complains Bernard Paris, 'but we have trouble wanting it for them.'[32] Marianne, however, got what she specifically said she didn't want, a middle-aged man in a red flannel waistcoat.

If Marianne is culpable, then, her faults seem venial when compared with either her sufferings or her positive qualities, actions and aspects. At the same time, Elinor's concessions to a well-bred ethos of insincerity and concealment are perilous indeed, where she has also to 'disguise the act of hiding, and to hide the disguise', in Derrida's phrasing.[33] Although the onus of 'telling lies when politeness required', as she puts it, is shouldered with relish, the non-euphemistic *lies* concedes that social rules may themselves be immoral, and a double bind established which corresponds to Adorno's 'in a false life there is no right way to live'.[34]

Elinor may initially be forced into concealments, but is almost forced to enjoy subterfuge in a social environment where prying and prattling abounds and is potentially destructive even when well enough meant. For example, at the Middletons' Mrs Jennings attributes a 'natural' daughter to Colonel Brandon – a sign that matters of remote and rather nasty conjecture may be 'read' as fact. This gentry milieu is one where people read people rather than books, but they do so with culpable crudity and (in general) without the finesse and moral intelligence which Marianne and Elinor actually share, another blow to the 'binary' conception of them. Like Joyce in *Ulysses*, we find that 'Jewgreek is Greekjew', it seems.

Having learned our lesson, we may move with unseemly haste to such imperfect felicity as *Sense and Sensibility* has to offer. But in such matters the novelist is very much at one with her offending characters. Openness, the friend to closure, is the enemy of the novelist, who is forced to suspend the issue. *Sense and Sensibility* is of course extremely clever about all this. For example, it momentarily transforms Mrs Jennings into a plump, inaccurate Sybil ('Mrs Jennings' prophecies, though rather jumbled together were chiefly fulfilled' [p. 329]), partly in order to draw off, it may be suspected, suspicion from what might easily be felt to be the arbitrariness of its own 'solutions'.

It is interesting to review these: Elinor marries her Edward, but after a rather stagey feint which allows her to suppose – in a brilliant moment of comic horror – that Lucy has finally made off with him (in fact, a much more plausible outcome). As we saw earlier, she has actually eloped with his brother, Robert the Fop. Earlier, Mrs Jennings has conjectured that Colonel Brandon is pursuing Elinor rather than Marianne. This is, again, a dangerously plausible idea, for Elinor, with her admirable 'self-command' seems well-placed to become a colonel's lady.

The Colonel himself is an interestingly implacable wooer who pursues Marianne, rather in the spirit of Thomas Hardy's *Well-Beloved*, because she reminds him of someone. His pursuit of her is, it is asserted, rather touching, but it's surely a far from eccentric reader who finds him more than a little off-putting, with a Humbert-and-Lolita touch underlying the sternly ethical ambience here, while the fact that Marianne feels no spontaneous attraction to this man functions, perhaps against the grain of the text, to provide a strong sense of the limitations of Marianne's possibilities. We may construe this as *marital* prospects and possibilities, although when you think of it it seems a pity that those are construable only in relation to matrimony. The 'blank cheque' of female talents and accomplishments needs conjugal 'cashing', it seems. Indeed, strong undertones here suggest that the Colonel's power as a landowner, with his income and status, may hold sway over 'natural affection'.

Interestingly, too, it might occur to the reader that Marianne should marry *Edward*, a clergyman of character who obviously has strong artistic and ideological 'positions'. Blake thought 'opposition' was 'true friendship', and Marianne's passionate high-mindedness has religious overtones. It would have been a lively match.

It is strongly suggested here, then, that *all* solutions or outcomes might be 'jumbled', and not merely those predicted by Mrs Jennings. The 'technical' difficulties placed in the way of a successful 'resolution' are perhaps a pointer to some sort of ideological hesitation.

The piquancy of *Sense and Sensibility* includes the idea of the novelist as a confirmed satirist of all sleights, 'devices' and concealments who is herself doomed to practise them. In a way, they are her very *raison d'être*. And finally what we admire about the book is less its clarity in providing a demonstration-model than in its ability to embarrass its own case. Setting itself to detect and expel symptoms of Sensibility, it actually becomes more exercised by misapplications of Sense, and its analysis of the social inferno has much in common with Blake's.

So although the novel itself never quite tires of hitting 'sensibility' over the knuckles, Blake's verses point to the real 'villains' of the piece: John and Fanny Dashwood in their 'scrupulous meanness'; the avaricious malevolence of Mrs Ferrars; the insipid propriety and parental gullibility of Lady Middleton; Robert, the foppish, self-regarding brother of Edward; and the spiteful, mean-spirited Lucy. We may look a little sceptically at this apparent nearness of 'Jane' to 'English Blake' in his more iconoclastic phase, but a sense of such intellectual kinship is a useful counter to a current over-emphasis on a 'Jane Austen' locked into a strident defence of Toryism. If, as Fredric Jameson says, 'a ruling-class ideology will explore various strategies of the legitimation of its own power position',[35] it is hard to see much in *Sense and Sensibility* which would abet such an exploration, despite the fact that its author has been neatly pigeonholed as an arch-Conservative, singing a sweet soprano accompaniment to the 'great melody' of Edmund Burke.

4
Pride and Prejudice: or Property and Propriety?

As we have seen, current critical opinion about Jane Austen often makes her a label for a particularly stultifying brand of political conservatism. Yet irony – dangerous, disrespectful irony, is almost by way of being her commodity. But although this irony is, at times, rampant in *Pride and Prejudice*, which has the official, the authorized description of being 'light, bright, and sparkling', irony is seen here in its limitations as well as in its strengths. Finally, irony is well bred, and knows when to turn itself off (or away) here. Pity, you might feel, it couldn't be the non-finite negation Hegel and Kierkegaard said it was: it might, in this context, be all the better for it. Positively, especially in Elizabeth's hands, it is shown to be eminently necessary to avoid the 'ideological mystifications'[1] which entomb a Sir William Lucas or a Mr Collins. In this sense (or *'sens'*) it fights alongside Paine's scorn for the 'puppet-show of state and aristocracy'[2] as we watch these Austen 'puppets' rehearse or adopt postures which Adorno and Horkheimer claimed to be widespread – identifying ('upwards') with a system which, all things considered, is belabouring rather than enabling them.[3]

Irony which takes this intellectual direction, then, is close to the mode in which it is recommended by Schlegel's character Julius. He finds that it 'attaches itself profoundly only to what is just',[4] (i.e. 'just that it should') – that is, in this case, only to what is profoundly unjust. When we watch the insufferable Lady Catherine de Bourgh 'determining what weather they were to have on the morrow'[5] (p. 114) for those 'petrified spars' (p. 212) Sir William and Maria Lucas, while the Reverend Collins dances attendance, we feel that Elizabeth has a right to all the not inconsiderable irony she can muster.

It is indeed interesting to watch Sir William being silenced and young Maria being 'frightened almost out of her wits' by a 'condescension' (p. 144) which is, supposedly, to set people at their ease, but is actually a carefully orchestrated form of social 'terrorism'.[6]

(Wilde had very little to do to turn Lady Catherine into Lady Bracknell.) In Elizabeth's tough, coolly registered 'distance and distaste' (in Milton's idiom), a blow is stuck at the insolence of rank. Surely here we rejoice to see what Johnson called 'the great principle of subordination' yielding to the even greater principle of insubordination. At one point Elizabeth carries this breathtakingly far ('I expected at least that the pigs were got into the garden, and here is nothing but Lady Catherine and her daughter' [pp. 141–21]).

Many might feel this to be disconcertingly sardonic, but Elizabeth, after all, has much to put up with: 'She is the sort of woman,' opines Collins of Lady Catherine, 'whom one cannot regard with too much deference' (p. 141). Clearly Mr Collins is a character whose every sentiment we must rewrite in the negative. However, as patriarchy grants him an entail over the Bennet home, he is, in his way, a man with power over women who obviously likes a bit of compensatory grovelling before that impossible She who has power over him.

Lady Catherine is a large, obvious target, and it is clear that the more one casts a cold eye on her ghastly paradigms the better. Part of the trouble is that it is difficult to believe that Elizabeth is wrong when she 'finds some resemblance' (p. 145) between Lady Catherine and her nephew, the 'overpowering' Mr Darcy, and her attempt to withdraw the idea later leads her into a rather perilous would-be-rhetorical question: 'How could I think her like her nephew?' (p. 313), she asks, and is in danger of receiving the answer 'very easily'. And particularly as it appears that Lady Catherine's barkingly explicit bossiness is of considerably less moment than Darcy's silent, judgemental ponderings. Not exactly a smooth man, he is in his refined way a rough wooer erotically provoked by Elizabeth's social defiance.

In this manoeuvring business between Darcy and Lizzie, we may claim what Leo Bersani says of a Baudelaire 'tableau': 'we never leave the terms of master-slave relationship'[7] (whichever way things happen to tilt). And despite Elizabeth's outward defiance there is an inner crumpling which installs Darcy as an 'interior paramour' in the disconcerting form of super-ego or censor. 'Where super-ego is, there shall id be' seems to be the motto of this, at once the most chaste and the most erotic of courtship novels.

Volosinov no doubt thought he had abolished 'Freudism' when he observed that 'the unconscious is ideological through and through'.[8] But these terms of appraisal are already implicit in

Freud's essay on the family romance, in which the 'self-orphaning' child may seek out a local nobleman to claim kin from a sense of insecurity, and the inadequacy of its own parents.[9] This is suggestive, but as a foray into fiction, like most of his cases, it is crude indeed compared to Austen's brilliant variations on the bewitching themes of hegemony, which lead to all this identifying upwards in the first place.

Indeed, *Pride and Prejudice* does such things with the Freudian account as to make Freud look like a 'precursor text'. Family romance is very much in the air. But we must accept that Elizabeth has much to put up with in actuality, 'feeling impaired' by the family's malign neglect and culpable inadequacy. The Freudian paradigm, more conservative in this than Austen is by implication, says nothing about justifications for this behaviour.

In fact, Elizabeth's sense of exposure is 'overdetermined' by a dim, foolish, meddling mother and an improvident, 'absconding' father (true, he absconds, as it were, *in situ*, but 'retiring to his library' sounds almost like a character note). Filling up the picture are two silly-flirt sisters (Kitty and Lydia) and one owlish pedant (Mary),[10] while even the sweetly affectionate Jane is not entirely helpful in her monad-like determination to hear, see and speak no evil. We also learn that Elizabeth was 'the least dear to her' (mother) of all her daughters.

If Darcy corresponds to Freud's 'local nobleman' hereabouts, the Freudian motif seems to be effaced by Elizabeth's specific *resistance* to Darcy. Almost from the start, however, there is a counter-current. Lizzie's 'first impression' (the title which first impressed 'Jane') is based on a misconstruction, it seems. Like Dr Johnson in Goldsmith's exoneration, Darcy too has 'nothing of the bear but his skin'. But Elizabeth's melting moment is that of her fateful visit to Pemberley on Darcy's imagined absence. Almost too Kantian by half, it seems, Darcy's presence was a kind of absence. Subject to congenial forms of representation, his absence becomes a kind of presence.

As a proto-Romantic type who prefers hiking to hitching, Elizabeth is known as a connoisseur of the picturesque who could ask, with imperilled Augustan rhetoric, 'what are men to rocks and mountains?' Cut off from the Lakes by the importunities of Mr Gardiner's business, she arrives well equipped, an as yet unwitting social mountaineer, with those transparently more adequate, understanding and appreciative parent-substitutes, the *Gardiners*.

'When Adam dug and Eve span,/Who was then the gentle man?' Whisper it not in Pemberley, but these toiling Gardiners are figures who will 'raise a blush' only if their social claims, not their personal qualities, are considered.

Thus, if Darcy has the requisite 'landowner magnetism', Elizabeth need not approach him with that abject deference which the Freudian paradigm seems to require. Indeed, a counter-current is set flowing in which Elizabeth only 'thaws' as a result of a reappraisal of Darcy combined with his persistent importunity; and if Darcy has power over women disconcertingly congruent with his social consequence, Elizabeth obviously has power over him.[11] Her crushing rejection of him (pp. 169–77) is combined with a denial that he possesses a sufficiently 'gentleman-like' manner – 'gentleman' being here, even more than in *Emma*, an ideological battleground. Even at the close, when Darcy has 'won' Elizabeth, her spirited, challenging manner alarms his bashful younger sister.

But Elizabeth's repeated 'blushing and blushing' (p. 89), her 'agony of shame' (pp. 89–90) for the family shortcomings, project her own vulnerability, and Darcy is something of a recording angel, writing the Bennet failings large in a letter of insufferable orotundity.[12] For Elizabeth, Darcy obviously has considerable power of what could be called 'subliminal penetration'.[13] As we shall see in the *Emma* chapter, the celebrated 'penetration' of the Knightley brothers in Emma hardly stops short of the epiphanic: no wonder Emma chooses God's chosen Englishman, despite the fact that he 'could not praise her marriage-choices'.

It is, to be sure, in a tone of savage satirical farcicality that, for Collins, the Church of England priest, the ruling class equals, roughly speaking, God. But, as Ivor Morris, himself a clergyman, seems to be saying in his curious book on Collins, attitudes and concerns which his faintly robotic garrulity endlessly rehearses are not perhaps so very different from those which actuate other characters who seem to claim our esteem.[14] (Mr Darcy and Mr Collins both feel their 'worldly position' entitles them to the hand of Elizabeth, and both suffer from angry pride when rejected; Darcy is also vaguely congruent with Sir William Lucas, exquisitely sensitive to matters of rank and unaware that, to Darcy, his implicit principle of exclusivity should exclude himself.)

Indeed, one of the main sources of unease in the book is that 'virtue' seems largely to consist in not avowing feelings which are not in fact different from those of people who are culpable enough to give them expression. This surfaces brilliantly in a sentence one feels should have been writing in red ink, when Elizabeth is dismayed by Lydia's 'illiberal' sentiments about a girl Wickham has been pursuing for money:

> 'But I hope there is no strong attachment on either side,' said Jane. 'I am sure there is not on *his*. I will answer for it he never cared three straws about her. Who *could* for such a nasty freckled thing?' [Lydia speaking]
> Elizabeth was shocked to think that, however incapable of such coarseness of expression herself, the coarseness of the *sentiment* was little other than her own breast had formerly harboured, and fancied liberal! (p. 195)

That Elizabeth, whose character note would be something like 'disembarrassed', should 'blush' for her family under the 'stony British stare'[15] of the redoubtable Darcy signifies the incorporation of the erotic in the ideological.

From the outset he treads on Elizabeth, in the first instance, ironically, by refusing to foot a measure with her. There is a persisting sense of his impulse to cow or crush, of Darcy as the figurehead of some male ruling-class juggernaut which resists the effort to reinscribe him as an acceptable wooer. And even at the happy close there is an obvious need for Elizabeth to provide a check to his influence on the perilously repressed and bashful Georgiana (p. 395). The triumphant aesthetic 'resolution' is shaded with ideological ambiguity. Clearly, even Elizabeth's irony has come up against limits. These are perhaps suggested by the consequences of its own deployment.

Paul de Man has reminded us (in *Blindness and Insight*) of Schlegel's quite pejorative definition of irony as 'permanent parabasis', although he might have been so good as to inform his readers that 'parabasis' is, in ancient Greek comedy, 'a part sung by the chorus, addressed to the audience ... and unconnected with the action of the drama' (*OED*). Perhaps, however, it might be said to be connected by being unconnected, at least in *Pride and Prejudice*, since the 'motor' of its 'subject' seems to be the 'permanent parabasis' of Mr Bennet's irony, as Elizabeth discerns.

We might even call irony his hermitage, particularly as his garden contains one (p. 313). However, as it is presumably not a real one, we might reasonably proceed to call it a folly. The aporia of irony here is that its watchword appears to be 'sick of this folly'; however, although the contemplation of folly has led him to the hermitage of irony, irony itself may be a form of folly. 'Sick of this folly' is actually Elizabeth's phrase for the rejoicing which follows the patched-up business of Lydia's foolish elopement with Wickham (p. 271). However, she is also sick of Mr Bennet's folly in allowing Lydia to be foolish, and in public. To be foolish in public is to be exposed to what Terence Hawkes, citing Ronald Blythe, has called 'that old England which would do for you if it could'.[16] But it might never have happened if Elizabeth had not given up trying to make Mr Bennet give up irony.

There is a particularly strong sense here of what Henry Tilney in *Northanger Abbey* calls 'a neighbourhood of voluntary spies' which would be well pleased to rejoice in the prospect of the Bennet family's disgrace. For example, at the prospect of Lydia's wedding

> The good news quickly spread through the house; and with proportionate speed through the neighbourhood. It was borne in the latter with decent philosophy. To be sure, it would have been more to the advantage of conversation, had Miss Lydia Bennet come upon the town; or, as the happiest alternative, been secluded from the world, in some distant farmhouse. But there was much to be talked of, in marrying her, and the good-natured wishes for her well-doing, which had proceeded before, from all the spiteful old ladies in Meryton, lost but little of their spirit in this change of circumstances, because with such an husband, her misery was considered certain. (p. 273)

There is a sufficiently strong sense of an encircling malevolence here to justify D.W. Harding's famous, salutary emphasis on Jane Austen as a proponent of 'regulated hatred' for a vicious, stunting milieu.[17] What Lydia in particular has failed to realise is that although the economic dispensation stimulates, one might say *entails* savage manhunting, at base this predation is social, not natural. The pursuit, which might be said to entail a scene of *marble* men and maidens *overwrought*, not quite in the Keatsian sense of figures on an urn, is implicitly understood as, in the first instance, a pursuit of *property*. Lydia thus conducts her affairs without *propriety*.[18] What Shakespeare would call her 'strong imagination' sees her tenderly flirting with 'at least six officers at once' (p. 259).[19]

It is of course entirely possible to sympathize with Lydia's attempts to fly by those nets of ideological malformation which produce a Mr Collins, the clerical toady whose kingdom is of this world, who looks up to the rich and never down to the poor,[20] or Sir William Lucas ('Lucres'?), the knighted tradesman and nonentity with a crippling King Charles's Head about royalty. These bow and scrape their way through life aware of power relations, of money as social element mediated by rank. Yet what is wrong here is less their recognition of this than what might be called the behavioural inferences they cull from it. Lydia's revolt against an ethos in the name of 'love' produces only disgrace and exposure. But it is at least interesting that her lack of 'virtue' is made to correlate so highly with her lack of economic concern (see p. 268).

Although Elizabeth says of both Lydia and Wickham that 'their passions were stronger than their virtue' (p. 325), she herself goes far to recognize that 'virtue' here is a shaded, if not a shady, term. Thus, Elizabeth's intelligent friend Charlotte is virtuous. In her case this seems to entail 'marrying without affection' (p. 332) for a prudent settlement. The propriety of finding the joys of marriage entirely transposed into property ('... her home and her house-keeping, her parish and her poultry, and all their dependent concerns, had not yet lost their *charms*' [p. 192]) disconcerts. Charlotte is to count herself lucky, yet she is married to a man about whom and to whom she must hide her feelings as he goes through his social paces with all the agility of a seal in irons. And Collins, according to Elizabeth (p. 159), must count himself lucky although he is married to a woman who despises him. This is indeed morality with a vengeance.

It removes some of the discomfort to realize that Lydia and Charlotte are mainly there for the sake of Elizabeth – 'differences without positive terms'. This novel is already, for all its classical objectivity and brilliant balance of subjective and objective presentation, half way to *Jane Eyre*. But *Jane Eyre* pays dearly for making the subordinate characters and relationships into tableaux representing possible results of Jane's self-determinings, readings on a spiritual thermostat showing, in Lowell's phrasing, her 'lowest depths of possibility'.[21] Thus, for us, Charlotte and Lydia may be assumed to correspond to Georgiana and Eliza in *Jane Eyre*, for whom the implied order to the respective heroines is to be neither.

A sardonic reader might see in *Pride and Prejudice* a blindingly conservative moralism,[22] and its prime-time, back-to-basics marriage is located 'within the City-Crown matrix' in a 'fake model of festive inclusivity' (see Chapter 8 of the present volume). With Darcy in his Pemberley heaven-haven and all right with the world, it is possible to see Elizabeth's almost fairytale 'elevation' with Darcy as, rather, tell-tale, a recognition of the 'impossible possible' (Wallace Stevens) nature of the 'solution' to the 'problem' of 'social security' for brilliant, uncorrupted, genteel young women.

We may rejoice over such 'thoughts of more deep seclusion'[23] as Elizabeth will be able to entertain in the 'real estate' wilderness of Derbyshire – a real estate which is pretty much a royal estate. (See, incidentally, Chapter 8 on recent Austen adaptations for Austen's oneiric geographies: they seem to indicate that nothing 'Ukanian', to use Tom Nairn's alienated coinage for forged Britishness, remains free of hegemonic 'recuperation'.) But, in the end, we will recognize that Elizabeth was 'rescued' by what a famous Frankfurt School anecdote would call a 'source of misery in society'.[24]

To appreciate this it is necessary, in the first instance, to read Darcy as simply a variation on, a mere allotrope of, Lady Catherine, and to correlate the low esteem in which he holds the Hertfordshire crowd with their own tendency to backbiting and general ill-will. This idea is, we have seen, lightly pencilled in but unmistakably 'there', and itself an unmistakable sign of uncertain self-esteem. Bernstein, summarizing Lukacs, seems to drop a point fairly close to what I imply here, in saying that 'he appears to claim that whatever allows an author to displace [her] subjective desire into novelistic form is an achievement of irony'.[25]

In particular, Elizabeth's frequently expressed 'astonishment' at each new turn of events is in danger of seeming quite rational, as Darcy struggles to master his desire but succumbs to his desire to master her. She questions the very narrative in which she appears. Indeed, the novel might almost be said to allude to the implausibility of its own conclusion, at once a cause and an effect of irony.

Here we might consider how we are actually reading this text. When David Lodge points out (of a Hemingway short story) that 'we infer its meaning indexically from its non-narrative components rather then hermeneutically or teleologically from its action',[26] he evokes Seymour Chatman's distinction between the 'resolved' plot and the 'revealed' plot, using *Pride and Prejudice* as an example of the former (traditional novel) and *Mrs Dalloway* as an example of the latter (modernist novel).

But one of the great shifts in evaluation which have 'decentred' modernist texts is the realization that there is no 'clean break' between their ways of working on the reader and those of 'classic' novels (suspending for a moment the claims for Austen's sheer technical uniqueness as advanced by Roy Pascal, for example[27]).

In other words, the 'meaning' of *Pride and Prejudice* is not contained by its plot resolution any more than that of *Mrs Dalloway* is. This absolute 'binarizing' of Chatman's is interesting (but perhaps 'vicious' in the classic Derridean sense). Irony destabilizes all that *Pride and Prejudice* is assumed to 'encode'.

Perhaps the source of Mr Bennet's own irony is that he himself has stooped to folly which an age of prudence can never retract: he has married Mrs Bennet. Her charms have fled, and he has retired to his library. A generation or two later we would have seen him deep in Schopenhauer. By characteristics and empathy he is close to Elizabeth, and his ironic intelligence, ambiguous gift, is kind of patrimony. This spiritual patrimony is once more underscored by *difference*, as a younger sister, Mary, imitating his bookishness, has achieved only an owlish pedantry whose want of sensibility is want of sense. (But one feels sorry for Mary: rejected by their father, Kitty and Lydia have their mother; Mr Bennet loves Jane and 'Lizzy'; Mary, craving paternal recognition, is odd 'man' out here.)

It is certainly interesting that Mr Bennet's guiding principle and Greek gift of irony was pinpointed by none less than Lukács as the 'regulative concept' of the novel. It is certainly in a rather special way the motor of this one. Bernstein, following Lukacs here, sees irony as an '... expression of the split subject'.[28] These are, to be sure, hard words from Kantian Heights, and Mr Bennet's split subjectivity is dramatized in quite down-to-earth ways, ineffective Transcendence in the library being followed by an equally ineffective sortie in order, as Mrs Bennet picturesquely puts it, to 'fight Wickham and make him marry her' (Lydia: p. 263).

Put Mr with Mrs Bennet and it is easy to appreciate why Elizabeth arrives in the grounds of the formidable Darcy suitably equipped with substitute parents more able to cope with things as they are. Yet it is impossible not to feel that Mr Bennet with his 'split subjectivity' ironies has 'reproduced' Elizabeth in a rather special sense. Indeed, apart from Jane (whom we never actually see conversing with him), he may be said to have refused to 'affiliate' with the others, and there is something 'split-level' about Elizabeth too, as she hesitates between deference and defiance, the impulse to comply and the impulse to resist. The split itself reproduces and is reproduced by the structure of the novel.

In Elizabeth's case, the 'fissure' in authority and possible reactions to it are dramatized by the difference, initially quite suggestively hard to pinpoint, between Darcy and his Aunt; Elizabeth bridles at both, then has her responses polarized. It is interesting here that (to 're-employ' the strategy of Freud's family romance) Darcy and Lady Catherine are themselves very like a kind of *Aufhebung*, meaning a return in an at once 'transcendent' and 'incorporative' form, of Elizabeth's own parents and their attitudes to her.

Briefly, there is a resemblance between the bossy interventionist insensitivity of Lady Catherine and Mrs Bennet, and both suggestively undervalue Elizabeth. Lady Catherine wishes to depress her virtually to servant status ('she is very welcome, as I have often told her, to come to Rosings every day and play on the piano forte in Mrs Jenkinson's room. She would be in nobody's way, you know, in that part of the house' [p. 154]); for Mrs Bennet, we hear, Elizabeth is 'the least dear to her of all her children' (p. 93) and for her she is obviously a dish fit for a Collins.

On the other hand, the lowering, withdrawn Darcy, eager to broach the need for 'extensive reading' (p. 34), is a bit like a 'high-level' return of Mr Bennet. Volosinov's point, apparently Freud-killing, that the 'unconscious' is 'ideological' is elegantly made by Freud himself, but not in as subtly 'layered' a way as it is by *Pride and Prejudice*.

Jane Austen has been more persistently associated with Marx than with Freud, perhaps most famously in Auden's glib point that she shows 'the economic basis of society'.[29] This attribution of a radical perspective seems to establish nothing much, although as it postulates a disenchanted, Enlightenment emphasis it might imply a resistance to Burkean mysticisms. What Jane Austen does uncover is an economic platform of *subjectivity*.

Indeed, Austen's novel might be said to be bringing together elements of Marx and Freud in a potentially explosive way, and even its aesthetic resolution and recuperation cannot efface the traces of this. Beneath its light, bright and sparkling surface, it investigates the social heart of darkness. As Lennard Davis remarks, for Marx the villain is capitalism and the insidious character of its ideological mystifications. For Freud, it is the superego, with the severity of its commands and prohibitions,[30] although questions about the origins of that severity might find one once more on Marxian terrain.

Both the severity and the insidious mystifications (suggestively related by Paine to the mystifications of monarchy[31]) are 'mediated' in various ways. This is indeed most obvious in relation to Lady Catherine and Darcy, and the imagination that projects them – in one sense the novelist, in another, Elizabeth – plays subtle games of differencing and 'assimilation'.

It does seem to be intimated that these two 'opposites' are deeply associated. It is not, for example, surprising that Lady Catherine should find the prospect of an Elizabeth at Pemberley a kind of 'pollution' (p. 317), as Darcy has to do a good deal of 'self-over-coming' in order to exorcize the idea himself ('In vain have I struggled', 'It will not do' [p. 168]).

While it is true, as we have seen, that Lady Catherine is straight-forwardly insufferable, Darcy is also seen to be in need of a 'retreading' before he can pass muster. In Jane's own time, one of the domineering Mitfords let it be known as if by decree that Elizabeth in all her sauciness was not a mate meet for a Mr Darcy. Our qualms are more likely to take an opposite turn, as we continue to wonder a little about representations of Mr D. This is to some extent veiled or muffled by making the drama appear to lie in Elizabeth's supposedly inaccurate perception of him, but his 'master-fulcrum' status makes any investigation of such ideas come close to the idea of an investigation of 'social (in)justice' in general.

In Jane Austen's work generally, the emphasis is generally supposed to be on individual relationships based on natural affinities, accidentally complicated, thwarted or stimulated by matters relating to caste. In fact the bulk of Jane Austen criticism has worked to exaggerate this idea.[32] But this novel obtrudes matters of social relations as actual *Bestimmungen* – conditioning or deter-mining elements for the emotions themselves.

This argument also correlates with (as opposed to running counter to) the fact that despite the 'refinement' that caused Charlotte Brontë to bridle, Jane Austen's novels are almost in-decently erotic. But they are overwhelmingly concerned with the social mediation of desire, and even the moral emphasis may be said to be ancillary to it. Richardson (perhaps Jane Austen's central forebear) liked as a good bourgeois to get a vice-like ethical grip on the upper-class characters, but in order to release rather than inhibit the love interest. Austen does a brilliant redistribution of all this. With pride to direct him, Darcy has got a rein on his lower passions which, for his friend's sister Caroline Bingley, is clearly excessive.

This is because of his 'proper pride', which (initially) alienates Elizabeth. Noting Elizabeth's own, he succumbs to a kind of female double. (We sometimes think that the point of the title is that 'pride' is annexed to Darcy, 'prejudice' to Elizabeth. But each has a strain of both.) It is often assumed that Darcy becomes less proud. In fact he is finally allowed to keep his pride because it is the right kind. But even that undergoes a kind of proleptic humbling as a result of his sexual enthralment.

We see this partly through his tendency to perpetrate what would appear to be doubles-entendres or what would be *doubles-entendres* did not his own rigorous propriety almost prevent our attributing them. 'I would by no means suspend any pleasure of yours,' he replies, 'coldly', we are told (p. 84). 'Too hot, too hot!' we might reply, with Leontes in *The Winter's Tale*,[33] as this coldness hardly prevents the word 'pleasure' from receiving wantonly irrelevant connotations like those in *Fanny Hill, The Memoirs of a Woman of Pleasure*.

He explains later that Elizabeth has shown him how unable he was 'to please a woman worthy of being pleased' (p. 378). Anger such as Dr Johnson visited on those who guffawed at the idea of a 'bottom of good sense' ('I say the woman is *fundamentally* sensible!') confirms the 'Freudian' sense it seeks to expel. Perhaps one is primed to see connotations in the scene where Darcy's sexual distress, when he proposes to Elizabeth, is so well dramatized as his fear of *lowering* himself, which it is hard to disentangle from the feeling that desire itself is *low*.

Darcy, who is, par excellence, the 'governor' type, cannot govern his desire for Elizabeth, and this is particularly distressing because he has been able to 'govern' his friend's desire for Elizabeth's sister for reasons which prove insufficient to govern his own. 'That the gentleman was overflowing with admiration was evident enough' (p. 230), confirm the sensible Gardiners, contrasting themselves here as elsewhere with Elizabeth's 'real' parents, who are amusingly, when the time comes, 'so very free from any penetration or suspicion', to steal a phrase from *Emma*. 'Overflowing with admiration' is almost an imperilled phrase here too.

Elizabeth and Darcy see one another as relatively cool and disembarrassed, but each can cast the other into a state of considerable inner turmoil. As we have seen, Romantic emotions are imprinted with ideological 'directions'. In fact Austen seeks to overdetermine these in Elizabeth's case: 'She liked him too little to care for his approbation' (p. 44) yet she blushes a Nietzschean blush for her family's exposure to his scrutiny.[34] It is hard to believe that this blush is the opposite of the romantic attachment which is to replace it; its potential is 'already there' in the aroused sense of social vulnerability and exposure.

Elizabeth is a 'positive term' created by the differential 'neither Charlotte nor Lydia'. In relation to the men she also falls between stools, resisting but rather more tempted by gigolo Wickham than by solid sycophantic Collins. Of both it may be said that their *charms* are their *property*, Wickham because he has no property and thus uses his charm(s) to gain power over women.

This is particularly lacking in propriety because it suggests what, in this milieu at any rate, women are supposed to do to men. (The most outspoken exponent of this game is perhaps John Dashwood in *Sense and Sensibility*: 'those little attentions and encouragements which ladies can so easily give, will fix him, in spite of himself' [p. 195].) Elizabeth appears to fall between these stools, but is finally featherbedded by Pemberley. It is interesting, however, that Wickham is pronounced objectionable as a suitor by the sensible Mrs Gardiner because he offers a 'connection imprudent as to fortune' (see pp. 127–9) *before* his moral turpitude becomes generally known.[35]

Yet, although finely disillusioned, Judith Lowder Newton surely overpresses when insisting that 'Elizabeth Bennet … *must* marry; she must marry with an eye to money; and the reason she must marry is that the family inheritance has been settled on a male.'[36] Elizabeth's spirited scorn for prudential attachments, a Blake-like theme, give her a lively interest in the blandishments of Wickham, a shadowy character made out of differences from Mr Darcy without positive terms – money/no money; ethics/no ethics; charm-less/charming (in the 'flatters to deceive' idiom), and so on.[37]

Elizabeth, however, also rejects the initial 'image' of Darcy. As has often been remarked, there is a 'cruel' version of this, in which, as the objection is to Darcy's 'improper' pride, she sees his property, becomes convinced of his propriety, and finally assures Mr Bennet that he has 'no improper pride' (p. 335), perhaps because his pride is merely coextensive with his property, and is thus well grounded ('at that moment she felt, that to be mistress of Pemberley might be something!' [p. 215]). The exclamation mark is hard at work here in making Darcy's grounds insufficient.

If *Pride and Prejudice* shows Elizabeth 'in the act of finding/what will suffice',[38] in Wallace Stevens's words, how insufficient was

Darcy to begin with? It depends how you read, of course, and this might be 'against the grain', Benjamin's way of reading against history which associates itself easily with his way of reading texts like *Elective Affinities* against the sense the author/narrator wishes to impute.[39] Perhaps the 'early' Darcy's truculence is too Johnsonian. Johnson's defiant downrightness registers differently in issuing from a 'slow-rises-worth-by-poverty-depressed' figure[40]: when great landowners start to bellow feisty opinions, alienation may ensue.

Sardonically earnest, Darcy seems a member of that class of persons who thinks that the approach of anyone else is a kind of insult. 'Every savage can dance', he barks at the grindingly winsome Sir William, who has the temerity to suggest that dancing might be an agreeable pastime. Darcy is obviously a practised hand at knowing whom 'to trash for over-topping',[41] as the Shakespeare character puts it, well on his way to being a prototype for the cruder Rochester.[42] If he has the winning ability to bully potential bullies, he may indeed become one in the process. As such, he is dangerous to the defenceless creatures who invoke his power.

Rochester, and much else in *Jane Eyre*, incidentally, seems completely parasitic on the Jane Austen officially patronized by Brontë.[43] In Austen's subtler art,[44] and unlike the ambiguous figures of Darcy and Knightley, Rochester seems practically to be wearing, not merely the phallus, but the jackboots. But I think that through him we learn something further about Darcy (or even understand the 'point' of Rochester as something of a critique of Darcy).

Certainly Darcy himself is understood to be in need of reconstruction at this stage, and has to be shown delivering a few ruling-class kicks to reassure the reader that Elizabeth's *perestroika* (of him) is really necessary. The danger is, of course, that the reader will have been shown the need for a much more thoroughgoing restructuring than a great man's admiring wife will see fit to administer. Georgiana, his younger sister, is alarmed by the degree of her defiance, akin to that of contemporary Romantic poets like Blake, Shelley and Byron: 'Souls that dare look the omnipotent tyrant in/ His everlasting face, and tell him that/His evil is not good!'[45]

Darcy may not be deity exactly, except to Collins and Co., although the Gardiners pronounce him 'infinitely superior' and his friend Bingley describes him as an 'awful object' on a 'Sunday evening' (p. 95); and of course, on a more mundane level, he owns large tracts of Derbyshire and is known to have 'extensive patronage'.

Wickham has a seductive charm which finally fails to seduce. Darcy scorns to charm or to seduce. This is in danger of being a seductive quality from the outset. He is a Nietzschean nobleman, pleased with his own volitions,[46] and he thinks Elizabeth has the same admirable stand-offishness: 'We neither of us perform to strangers' (p. 156). Her voice is as the voice of my own soul, he thinks. Yet Darcy is in danger of attracting by virtue of what the novel seems to say are his faults.

For example, he is to his amiable but weak-minded friend as the spirited Elizabeth is to her charming but insipid sister Jane. Darcy, it is plain, will indeed be able, to use the famous formula applied negatively to Miss Bates, to frighten those who might hate him into outward respect. In fact not even outward respect is necessarily going to save you from Mr Darcy's lash, as Sir William finds to his cost. What Darcy is astonished to 'learn' from Elizabeth is that she must 'civilize' him somewhat – the last lesson he expected to have to learn. From a Nietzschean perspective here 'civilize' would mean 'weaken'.

Jane Austen is not supposed to be Nietzschean, but Darcy is clearly from the outset to be reckoned more highly because very much to be reckoned with – for example, if we compare his 'nature' with that of the 'good-natured' Bingley who is unable to brace himself sufficiently to tell even the unprincipled Wickham to be off. The Austen scholar R.W. Chapman said of Darcy that 'it has even been doubted that he exists'. This is critically naïve but a propos, in the sense that, if Darcy exists for Elizabeth rather than vice versa – and Elizabeth of course *is* the ironic femininity which is the text's deepest register – then the theme of the book is presumably to be Elizabeth's attainment of a True Hermitage, which Darcy's grounds, consequence and formidable manner will confirm.

The formal scheme of the book insists on an innocuous tale of Elizabeth's finally buckling resistance to Darcy's importunities when accompanied by enlightenment as to his true character. But what is supposed to give offence about him actually recommends him, and the book works so hard to reform him it almost shows its hand in doing so. There is a threefold re-presentation of him when Elizabeth visits Pemberley. 'Imago, Imago, Imago'[47] is strange line in Wallace Stevens which underscores how even the most brutally practical activities, in this case the prosecution of war, are subject to the airy nothings of imagination. Here it may well stand as a formula for the three sources of Elizabeth's formal transposition of

Darcy into an object of desire: the admiring housekeeper, the family portraits suggesting ancestral dignity and distinction, and the grounds which, like those of Knightley submitted 'neither to fashion nor extravagance', bespeak a 'natural[ized] gentility'.

We might say that they give Elizabeth's Gilpinesque romanticism about the wild scenery of the Lake District a 'proper direction', in Darcy's idiom.[48] That Elizabeth's anticipatory admiration is couched in ironic, Johnsonian terms makes it particularly susceptible to recuperation for an idea of *natural gentility* which makes Darcy's estate an objectivizing of his *qualities* – or, shall we say, his *property* bespeaks his *properties*?

The properties of the landscape begin to bespeak Darcy in an incipiently erotic way, and combine quasi-ontologically with the housekeeper's account and the unshowy elegance of the pictures and furnishings. Just as Milton's Eden infuses and is infused with the erotic qualities of its human inhabitants ('Enormous bliss'),[49] the landscape, for Elizabeth, orchestrates a modulation of feeling:

> The hill, crowned with wood, from which they had descended, receiving increased abruptness from the distance, was a beautiful object. Every disposition of the ground was good; and she looked on the whole scene, the river, the trees scattered on its banks, and the winding of the valley, as far as she could trace it, with delight. (p. 216)

Eros is abroad,[50] but there are positively religious overtones to the contemplation of the portraits: 'She beheld a striking resemblance to Mr Darcy, with such a smile over the face as she remembered to have sometimes seen when he looked at her. She stood several minutes before the picture in *earnest contemplation*' (p. 220). Is Mr Darcy in some danger of becoming an icon here? It is just at this moment when the reader is supposedly to rejoice at Elizabeth's *éclaircissement* that, by 'negative dialectic' if you will, s/he might rather experience dismay that a book which bid fair to be a brilliantly disenchanted and diagnostic document should make haste to entomb itself in the very mystifications it seems in its other dramatic projections to make such short shrift of, and to unite itself with 'that extensive class of literature which makes Gods of Baronets or Dukes'.[51]

Given an aura by his worshipping housekeeper, frozen eternally as an icon of gentility whose house and grounds speak for themselves, even Darcy's absence has a certain resonance here. 'Absence is the highest form of presence', goes a Joycean joke, a serious one, which has, ultimately, a religious basis. Of course in *Pride and Prejudice* there is a special dramatic impact in Darcy's sudden unanticipated reappearance: 'Oft he seems to hide his face/but unexpectedly returns.'[52]

All this is a severe test for Elizabeth, but the reader too may wonder just who or what is on trial or what is at issue. The aporia may be indicated by pointing out that Elizabeth is at once armed and vulnerable when accompanied by the suggestively named Gardiners. On the one hand, since they are sensible and polite by comparison with the eccentricities of her 'real' parents, she has every reason to feel relatively buffered.

On the other hand, they are, as Emma's phrasing has it, 'in a low way, in trade, and only moderately genteel'. In particular, as they live in the unfashionable part of town 'within sight of their own warehouses', they exhibit that 'visible relation to the economy' which the fashionable world of Bingley and Darcy goes to considerable lengths to suppress.[53] *Sense and Sensibility* presents this London scene in close focus, and Christopher Gillie has acutely noted the characteristically down-to-earth decision about where to live in London taken by no-nonsensical John Knightley.[54]

Thus, when Elizabeth looks to see how Darcy 'bears' (p. 224) the social provenance of the Gardiners, the idea grants power to Darcy's judgements, but he will also be judged by his response. Darcy's family pride, it is felt, might find the very virtues of the bourgeoisie to be something of an insult. Thus the reader's own response is split to the extent that, on the one hand it will be abominable if Darcy cannot accept the excellent Gardiners, while it is obvious that the inadvertently prepared pill to the effect that 'the rank is but the guinea's stamp,/The man's the gowd [gold] for 'a that'[55] is a particularly hard one for Darcy to swallow. Darcy might well claim that he was merely being 'pleasant', and irrationally so, on account of his infatuation for Elizabeth.

Surely it is clear that for Darcy trade in England does *not* make a gentleman, as Defoe averred? Or is it indeed 'clear' what *Darcy* is 'thinking'? Focalized through Elizabeth, what we are mainly aware of is Elizabeth's hypothesizing accounts of Darcy's reactions. We know the text is 'handling snobbism', but whose? Darcy's, or Elizabeth's? Is her discomfort over what he may feel on being introduced to people she knows are perfectly sensible, amiable and

congenial excessive? In wondering how he will 'bear' the introduction, is she a little too sure (in her unsureness) that there will
indeed be anything at all to 'bear'? How strange that a light, bright
and sparkling work with a saucily insouciant heroine should leave
one with such a sense of wincing exposure.

Wondering whether one is genteel enough is very much
compounded by worrying just what gentility consists of. Finally it's
a floating signifier, it seems, prone to more than a little semantic
wobbling over Wickham's 'gentleman's education' (p. 178) – is that
an education which helps fashion a gentleman, or an extra for the
already 'fully-fashioned' gentleman? If the latter seems more likely,
it seems odd to attribute the kind of importance to it that Darcy
appears to. As P.N. Furbank has reminded us, 'the social status of
"gentleman" gains its suggestive force and its enormous potential
for rhetorical and ideological exploitation, from its vagueness and
lack of semantic anchorage.'[56]

Clearly Darcy himself senses that, and although Elizabeth's insecurity makes her more vulnerable to him than he is to her, she
neatly pinpoints his Achilles heel in accusing him of lacking,
perhaps only momentarily, a 'gentleman-like manner' (p. 171). On
the one hand, Darcy knows that he has a gentleman-like manner
because he 'is' a gentleman, with a country estate, a distinguished
family, ancestral portraits – in short, all the signifying agents and
practices, all the evidence anyone could require. Ergo, anything he
says or does or indicates is necessarily 'gentleman-like', since he
himself spontaneously defines what this is.

However, as part of a profound historical 'slippage', the hold on
'gentleman-like' is weakening (partly because more, or at least
different things are being demanded of gentlefolk before they can
be defined as such), Elizabeth is able to 'wound' Darcy in a way that
a Darcy of a generation or two earlier would have found inexplica-
ble:

> 'Your reproof, so well applied, I shall never forget: "had you
> behaved in a more gentleman-like manner". Those were your
> words. You know not, you can scarcely conceive, how they have
> tortured me; …' (p. 326)

Freud would, I am sure, have been quick to note that it was Mrs
Bennet, the Inadequate Mother, who most stridently defined gentility – and thus eligibility – in terms of *money* and *property*. This is, of

course, insufferable and must be denounced loudly as erroneous, and all the more loudly if it should happen to be true. Elizabeth, by contrast, and no doubt by reaction, correctly intuits that Darcy wishes to 'spiritualize' gentility by redefining it largely in terms of *ethics* and *education*. In this sense she might be said to 'know' him, with a 'spiritual' knowledge which leads on to carnal[57] – not to mention the money and property which Mother so despicably 'fore-grounded'.[58] Elizabeth did in fact tease Jane with the idea that she fell in love with Darcy when she saw his beautiful house and grounds at Pemberley. But that, of course, was only a joke.[59]

5
'Capital Gratifications' and the Spirit of Mansfield

Mansfield Park seems to be determined to have everything to do with principles and nothing to do with principles of indeterminacy. It appears that anything like spirited critique or 'hermeneutics of suspicion' is as it were 'devolved' to (or on to) Mary Crawford. And her discomfiture seems to be a 'project' of the book's narrative strategies. This disconcerts, particularly as Mary seems at first blush a little like a return of the apparently unrepressed and approved-of Elizabeth Bennet of *Pride and Prejudice*. And, as Lionel Trilling rightly points out, we are inclined to visit our suspicions on her severe critic and rival, the severely repressed Fanny. Trilling's reading is itself a return of the repressive, as he proceeds to vindicate the 'sternness',[1] the austerities and censoriousness of the Cinderella-like, perhaps Cordelia-like, figure of Fanny.[2] Yet, finally, a displacement of Trilling's reading is not quite the same as defiance of *Mansfield Park*'s 'intentions'.

But if critical theory would deconstruct the patriarchal perspectives that *Mansfield Park* seems to announce, Fanny in particular to ratify, and Edward Said naively to assume,[3] it initially seems it would be helped to do so by reading 'against the grain' of 'Jane Austen' herself – at least in her 'light, and bright, and sparkling' role, suggestive of subversive irony and challenging impertinence (or pertinence). As Alison Sulloway reminds us, Shaftesbury's prototypically feminist "Tis the persecuting spirit has raised the bantering one' (1790) also seems to announce a Jane Austen 'programme' while insisting, not without justice, that 'there was much to be "revenged" by the bantering spirit'.[4]

Curiously, however, it is finally Fanny herself, fan and supporter of patriarchy, much possessed by the need to iron out any ironies about it, suspicious of hermeneutics of suspicion, scandalized by thoughts of scandal in high places who contributes most to the 'decentring' of that patriarchy which *Mansfield Park* seemed poised to celebrate, rather than 'bantering spirit' Mary (who has seen enough of *Rears* and *Vices*, as she startlingly puts it [p. 54], to regard conventional assessments of social value with contempt).

As Nina Auerbach puts it, Fanny 'rises from being the prisoner of Mansfield to the status of its principal jailer'.[5] If Elizabeth Bennet is, as one critic puts it, 'a fantasy of power',[6] Fanny seems equally a 'fantasy of powerlessness'.

Modern critical theory is fed by the spirited critiques of Marx, Freud and Nietzsche. Paul Ricoeur has called these 'three convergent procedures of demystification'.[7] And if *Mansfield Park* is indeed 'visibly ideological', its effect is to make such 'procedures' seem 'hardly congenial to an English mind',[8] to steal a phrase from a novel which offers less guarded forms of priggishness than *Mansfield Park* displays – Jane Eyre, as the 'creeping creature' of Thornfield is clearly modelled on Fanny. Yet Mansfield Park itself as 'signifier' of Tory patriarchy, is glimpsed as an *ideal* only by the 'wonders' (p. 188) of Fanny's memory, as déclassé in Portsmouth, she stands in tears amid the alien who constitute her nearest, but not dearest, kin:

> … she could think of nothing but Mansfield, its beloved inmates, its happy ways. Every thing where she now was was in full contrast to it. The elegance, propriety, regularity, harmony – and perhaps, above all, the peace and tranquillity of Mansfield, were brought to her remembrance every hour of the day, by the prevalence of every thing opposite to them *here*. (p. 357)

Not exactly what we were 'shown' about life at Mansfield! By this point, we have learned enough about Mansfield to detach ourselves from Fanny, and, in acknowledging the novel as 'a bitter parody of conservative fiction'[9] and a 'horrifying picture of family life'[10] to detach ourselves from Mansfield also. Indeed, Arnold Kettle's correct but unfocused concern about the 'parasitism' of Jane Austen's world,[11] invoked in relation to *Emma*, has much more powerful resonance for the ethos of Mansfield, where, under the eye of Sir Thomas, it is much too commendable to be, as dull Mr Rushworth puts it, 'sitting comfortably here among ourselves, and doing nothing' (p. 167).

Fanny's feelings in exile at Portsmouth ask to be described as 'perfectly natural', yet what they tellingly reveal instead is how ideological 'formation' can govern natural affection. It seems a disastrous mistake, unless Fanny as focalizing consciousness is relevant here, to close the chapter (p. 357) by applying the tired Johnson adage about marriage and celibacy to Mansfield and Portsmouth, the former with 'some pains', the latter with 'no pleasures'.[12] It evokes the fatuity of Kingsley Amis's 'nice things are nicer than nasty ones' to enact a complacent acceptance of class divisions (and it isn't clear that Mansfield *is* 'nice' in this sense). The effect is to expose the noble musings of Fanny as somewhat ignoble, but perhaps in this way she really does confirm that she belongs at Mansfield Park, very much a place of pettiness, bickering and jealousy rather than a Great Good Place which rises above such unworthy feelings.

In fact David Lodge[13] shows how defective Mansfield actually is when its candidature for Great Good Place is considered. Avrom Fleishman shows how defensive and neurotic are Fanny and her memory, as she tells her psychic rosary.[14] Portsmouth, after all, provides a curiously reversible image. We are told, roughly speaking, that Fanny's family hold her at arm's length, but it's not so clear that what we are shown doesn't consist largely of Fanny holding them at arm's length. Trilling, whose well-known essay is surprisingly full of critical wrong notes, thinks the Portsmouth episode 'most engaging' (p. 225). Surely it isn't? For example, Fanny has an acute sense of the defects of her home, yet these defects largely arise from a want of *propriety* arising directly from a want of *property*: 'She was taken into a parlour, so small that her first conviction was of its being only a passage-room to something better ...' (p. 343).

Watching Fanny reading the signs of her estrangement here, in her sojourn in the social 'Hell' of Portsmouth (a fate measured for her with solemn unctuousness by 'Heavenly Father' Sir Thomas), where the slaves have no decent sense of servility, makes Fanny herself a little more legible. She has a highly censorious emphasis on what might be called house-keeping (her horrified avoidance of various forms of dirt perhaps projects a Freudian fear of becoming a *dirty girl*). Portsmouth, it appears, is full of reminders of the physical basis of life in a way that Mansfield mysteriously is not. Moreover, her determination to see the conditions of life in the wretched naval dwelling as mere signs of disgusting incompetence and incontinence – rather than a social wrong to those forced to undergo it – is also disturbing for a firm sense of Fanny's simple rectitude or the moral basis of her morality. (Sailor families, after all, are the 'saviours' of English freedom who keep the sea clear for Sir Thomas and his [slave] trade.)

Portsmouth, it seems, is a place where things fall apart, the centre cannot hold, no fiscally powerful patriarch sits at the centre of the web. God made the country but man made a town like Portsmouth, a place where no one, not even servants, knows their place.[15] Yet, at the point where Maria elopes with Henry Crawford, Mr Price becomes as ungovernably *moral* as anyone could desire, indeed revealingly so, for his unfortunate 'coarseness' perhaps shows more about the 'genealogy' of morals than the fastidious Fanny cares to contemplate – when he observes, on reading of Maria Rushworth's elopement with Mary's brother Henry, that ' ... by G--, if she belonged to me, I'd give her the rope's end as long as I could stand over her' (p. 401).

This happy vision of the punitive knout comes close to invoking that very 'aggressive' sexuality which has been the character note of Henry Crawford himself. Yet although this is indeed a little too coarse for the delicate and fastidious Fanny, one might ask if his imagining of the condignly punitive is any crueller than the punishment devised by the authority of Sir Thomas Bertram. He, after all, 'would not have [his daughter] Maria received at home' (p. 434) after her elopement. We are surely a long way here from Mr Bennet's amusement over Mr Collins' notion of Christian forgiveness in response to Lydia's improprieties in *Pride and Prejudice*: 'You ought certainly to forgive them as Christians, but never to admit them in your sight, or allow their names to be mentioned.'

So if Mansfield Park rises in Fanny's consciousness as something of 'another Eden, demi-paradise', this ironically exemplifies Fanny's own remarks earlier in the novel on the 'wonders' of memory. These are used to underpin romantically conservative views on the continuity of selfhood, but perhaps from the outset somewhat aporetic because forced to note the capriciousness of memory (p. 188). Fanny in fact identifies so desperately with Mansfield because her removal *from* it is a literal statement of her own 'overdetermined' marginality.

If Mansfield Park reassuringly excludes the alien, the alien might be found, not at all reassuringly, to include oneself. (It is commonly assumed, for example, that the question of the propriety or otherwise of the theatrical 'experiment' at Mansfield depends entirely on matters relating to the moral status of impersonation, though what Edmund really frets over is the *proposed admission of a stranger on terms of intimacy* and similar threats to what might be called the mystique of Mansfield (p. 138).

Indignation here has a 'sliding signifier', as questions of morality seem very intimately related to matters of *propriety* – *principle* is uncomfortably close to *interest*, to use terms which recall Marx's famous discussion of Toryism. Fanny herself also identifies so desperately with the ethos of Mansfield because her initial removal *to* it confirms her sense of her own threatened, insecure marginality. This has been engineered by the solemn injunctions of Sir Thomas himself, but is overdetermined by the arrogance and neglectful treatment of her by his daughters and the barkingly explicit repressiveness of the censorious Mrs Norris, who, as Mary Poovey has remarked, is anxious to 'project on to her little niece the worthlessness, inferiority and indebtedness she is anxious to deny in herself'.[16] Thus, although in terms of class and status she has been consigned to a kind of limbo, she desperately identifies upwards, i.e. with a system which is, itself, in some measure, 'giving her the rope's end'. It also, as the Portsmouth episode recognizes, 'purloins her from herself',[17] in Paine's phrasing.

Thus, in Fanny's case, we are shown not only what and how she thinks, but what governs and controls her thought-process. Although it is true that *Mansfield* may in some sense be radically blind to the light it emits, it is clear that its final effect is not one of ideological 'recuperation' for Tory causes. Similarly, Mansfield Park might be held to destroy an apparently intransigent moralism in the very act of seeming to enunciate it. Paradoxical though it may seem, it is the English *Genealogy of Morals*, and its high-toned hests are shown to have what Auden calls, 'a vague and dirty root'.[18] We see that not only in base Antigua but in superstructural Mansfield it is 'difficult to leave the terms of the master–slave relationship'.

Although of course *Mansfield Park* does not exclude foreign bodies of thought in the same way that Mansfield Park closes ranks against the socially unacceptable, it might be said to militate against all that is 'scandalous' in the 'demystifying' work of Freud or Marx or Nietzsche. Yet, precisely because the text (or the Park) seems to be doing the work of a moral and intellectual Censor, all such demystifications seem to stage a 'return of the repressed' in the face of its return of the repressive.

Freud seems the least difficult to countenance here, as Jane Austen is, in an innocuous and literal sense the most *libidinous* of novelists, her invariable theme that of the social mediation of desire, love and the thwartings and enablements of caste.

Clive Bloom is one critic who, bravely and perhaps rather

controversially, has scrutinized the 'libidinal economy' at work in the name and the nature of Fanny Price, finding in her a paradoxically non-erogenous zone which offers appeasements for the sexual excesses of her mother.[19] Marginal to the point of invisibility, that particular Fanny Price has her hands full with the results of her inconsiderate incontinence.

This is certainly a critical *trouvaille*, especially as Fanny herself is so severely repressed; yet entertaining such ideas threatens to turn the reader into a thoroughgoing 'Crawfordian' – not something she or he would wholeheartedly enter upon, however priggish or prudish the face of 'goodness' in this novel might appear to be.

Nevertheless, when Mary Crawford observes that Maria, after her prudent marriage to the stupid Rushworth, has certainly got her 'pennyworth for her penny' (p. 359), she may certainly lack scruple, but she can scarcely be said to lack perspicacity. 'Now do not be suspecting me of a pun' says Mary, in a famous passage (p. 54) in which she mischievously reinforces the reprehensible association she pretends to repress. This tactic, however, might also be seen as characteristic of what might be called the textual 'Jane Austen', who in (as it were) asking the reader to avert her or his eyes from sources of disillusionment or scepticism, discloses by the attempt to hide, or the apparent attempt to hide. For example, in the context referred to, Mary claimed that the higher officers in the navy were characterized by 'bickerings and jealousies' (p. 54). Edmund's response to this is a tone of grave rebuke. As a trainee ('rehearsing') clergymen he certainly makes clear that the claim that clergyman must not 'set the ton[e] in dress' (p. 83) has nothing to do with not setting the tone. Yet, protective of interest rather than principle, Edmund's high tone or occupation of the moral high ground, is impotent to muzzle the sense of corruption, pettiness and self-seeking which Mary has evoked.

It is at least interesting that Fanny's own brother William is (corruptly) 'made' as an officer through his Mansfield connection. 'Everybody gets made but me,' he grumbles, ignobly (p. 226). For females there is no possibility of 'getting made' without awakening a sexual connotation of 'made', which shows how much more sheerly sexual pressure there is on femininity, even at the most 'privileged' social levels.

This might seem a consideration to mitigate the ferocity of the judgement which is actually brought to bear upon the errant young women of Mansfield.

Another small incident which hints strongly at the 'aporetic' nature of the mores of Mansfield concerns William's candidature for promotion. The point appears to be that, as Robert Burns puts it, 'the rank is but the guinea's stamp', but is actually the reverse. William complains that 'the Portsmouth girls turn up their noses at anybody who has not a commission' and Fanny replies that 'when you are a Lieutenant, how little you will care for any nonsense of this kind' (p. 225). Fairly plainly, William has in fact to *get made* in order to *make* this 'nonsense', so that this nonsense is seen to make pretty good sense.

Nietzsche is equally germane here, as Fanny, flanked by Mrs Norris, is a classic case of *ressentiment*, the inverted 'revolt of the weak and slaves', in Fredric Jameson's paraphrase, with its 'production' of the secretly castrating ideals of resignation and abnegation.[20] Fanny, then, triumphs by being ungovernably compliant, 'not in movement, but in abstention from movement'. In this she is specifically differentiated on a gender basis from her brother William, distinguished by his noisy and strenuous careerism. William in fact knows his place well enough to want to quit it as soon as possible. Henry Crawford enters with great piquancy here, as he abets William's desire to be 'made' in order to 'make' Fanny, both in the vulgarly erotic but also in something of a 'promotional' sense, as marriage for a young woman in her situation *is* a kind of promotion.

One might say that he hopes by making a woman of her to make a lady of her, so that his achievement will be a characteristic combination of pleasure and high-mindedness. It will be, to use his own phrase, a 'capital gratification' (p. 309).

As we have seen, Mansfield Park in its intellectual orbit comes fairly close to the tone of Marx's famous analysis of Toryism in its treatment of the archetypal patriarch Sir Thomas Bertram. Just as he is in a measure a study of how principle is perhaps finally a function of interest in the way Marx suggests, he also furnishes materials for the study of what Nietzsche discerns as the non-moral *Bestimmungen* of morality, and particularly perhaps in his role in moulding Fanny's character. While it is not entirely clear that 'the good' *itself* is quite so easily 'reducible' as Jameson's summary of Nietzsche here appears to suggest, the description and claims of the analysis are particularly suggestive for the effects and the procedures of *Sir Thomas*: Nietzsche, he says, 'demonstrates [sic] ... that what is really meant by the "good" is simply my position as an unassailable power centre, in terms of which the position of the other, of the weak, is repudiated and marginalized in practices which are themselves ultimately formalized in the concept of evil' (p. 117). Sir Thomas is obviously vulnerable here, as his serene occupation of the moral high ground and his unctuous tone sit uneasily with his (putative) slave-owning and his destructively unimaginative authoritarianism. This reduction of moralism is rather like Marx's reduction of Tory landowner's principle to Tory landowner's interest, which he finally identifies with their rents.[21]

Mary Crawford is the only character with enough bad taste here to make the connection between moral 'weight' and economic status or dispensation, most strikingly when she mentions the stage-struck intruder Yates in a letter to Fanny, and comments on his poor prospects as a wooer of the younger Bertram daughter, Julia: 'if his *rents* were but equal to his *rants*!' (p. 359). It is at least interesting that such playing on words seems itself to constitute a kind of 'diabolism' in *Paradise Lost*, where the devils invent punning ('scoffing in ambiguous terms', as Milton puts it), in conjunction with gunpowder, in the War in Heaven episode (Bk. VI), where it accompanies their malicious euphoria. Some of the 'Hebraism' (Arnold's term), the moral fierceness and even phasing of Milton's poem seems to have effected an entry to Mansfield Park.

Rents, then, might be said to correspond (basely) with super-structural *rants* (indeed, the whole base/superstructure metaphor might be said to turn on this wordplay), as, in Yates's case, his rents *are* equal, are *merely* equal to his rants – since 'ranting' suggests moral invective without real power to intimidate or impress. For slave owner Sir Thomas, on the other hand, whose rents are equal to his rants, and in a much graver and weightier mode, 'none dare call them rants'. Yet there *is* actually something 'exsufflicate and blown' about the way he delivers himself of his pronouncements. For example, there is one which embodies something like 'a Turkish contempt for females',[22] in his statement that independent-spiritedness in them is '*offensive* and disgusting beyond all common *offence*'. Sir Thomas obviously has good ranting potential; on the other hand, he must be taken seriously. There is, however, some-thing quite 'histrionic' about him, and never more so than when we see him casting a cold eye on the 'theatrical nonsense' which has disfigured Mansfield. His sudden arrival from Antigua, where he might be well imagined as having quelled something like 'an insurrection of the negroes' to find something uncomfortably like a revolt against his hests and ordinances at home is a splendid *coup de théâtre*.

Mary Crawford, then, though she may be cast off at the close (in a narrative closure of some severity), has points that stick or stain. The moral high ground of Mansfield – at least as occupied by Fanny's imagination – is found to be more than a little muddy underfoot. Infecting Fanny with 'the anxiety which later becomes conscience', or, in Nietzschean terms, the 'sense of compulsion' which 'becomes' morality,[23] this ambiguous 'good' comes out of 'evil' (even where, at the least, this is only construable as want of sympathetic imagination).

Sir Thomas as a pompous, coercive patriarch has considerable symbolic resonance. At one level he might seem to impersonate that famous Althusserian invention, His Majesty the Economy, Lear-like with his 'revolted daughters' and particularly as, we are told, 'he had never seemed a friend to their pleasures' (p. 28), he is also suggestive of that 'Majesty' to whom, in Lacan this time, all too much honour is given – the Ego. Shoshana Felman, paraphrasing Lacan, observes that 'the ego ... is not even master of its own house, but must content itself with scanty information of [*sic*] what is going on unconsciously ...' (and, in fact, the etymology of *economy* itself suggests a concern with the running of the *house*).

The phrasing is cumbrous, but specifically suggestive here of the return of Sir Thomas, like some *deus ex machina* from his Antiguan estate, to find his 'house' in such disarray that 'house' might almost bear the theatrical connotation ('the house lights were dimmed', etc). Having quelled, as one might feel some licence to imagine, the '[latest] insurrection of the negroes in the West Indies'[24] to find revolt at home establishes, subtextually, an uncomfortable connection between base Antigua and superstructural Mansfield here: in line, perhaps, with what the text itself does not appear to concede, but what it nevertheless prefigures, Julia, Maria and Tom behave rather like 'revolting' slaves. Perhaps the point is that they are enslaved by their own desires. In addition, though, Engels' statement that 'the product enslaves first the producer and then the appropriator', seems curiously suggestive.

Edward Said is eloquent about the sugar plantations of Sir Thomas's Antigua.[25] If we combine this with the narrator's point that as a father at home who is 'no friend to their pleasures' and 'not outwardly affectionate' (p. 16), the connecting theme of

Antigua/Mansfield is what Yeats, meditating on country house tradition, calls 'the sweetness that all longed for night and day'.[26] Julia and Maria in particular are embittered and disaffected (the rivalry of Julia and Maria has more emotional thrust than their affection for Henry Crawford), more substance in their enmities, as Yeats would put it,[27] than in their love. They see not the Sir Thomas 'little Fanny' (p. 160) sees, but rather a distant, alienating figure strutting and fretting on an uncongenial stage. He sees intimate family connections as the foundation of all things, they experience only 'distance and distaste', in Milton's idiom.

What is noteworthy here, then, is the pejorative account of Sir Thomas, ratified even by traditional critics like D. Devlin, who legitimates the conclusion that *Mansfield Park* 'appears to let conservative ideologues have their way' – only to 'let them discredit themselves with their own voices'.[28] In Sir Thomas's case, although there is nothing deliberately malevolent about him, his worldly minded, inflexible posture seems to give a good many people the idea that they have nothing to lose but their chains.

Here, however, one must be cautious. If Henry Crawford is at hand to provide new mind-forged manacles for Sir Thomas's daughters, and their subsequent miseries are to some extent laid at his door, the text never abandons itself to a wholeheartedly unsympathetic treatment of Sir Thomas himself. The assumption of a continuing interest in his 'welfare' combined with a sustained peroration designed to exorcize the wraiths of the banished Crawfords, of Maria and Julia and Mrs Norris, counters the incipiently disruptive effects of his exposure.

Yet 'visibly ideological'[29] as it is in this complicated way, it is still not so easy to make *Mansfield Park* into a flagship of Burke-like conservatism as Marilyn Butler and the too-easily credited Alastair Duckworth of *The Improvement of the Estate* contrive to suggest. Why, for example, make its prime patriarch an Antiguan slave-owner? Why endow him with such a potentially destructive lack of imagination? Considered as a principle of stability in family and society, Sir Thomas clearly has considerable destabilizing force or potential.

Fanny herself is, in a key phrase of the later *Persuasion*, something of a 'new creation' of Sir Thomas himself, and Nina Auerbach is surely right to describe her as a kind of Frankenstein monster wound up to march to his tune so that she (the copy or 'simulacrum', as a Baudrillardian might say) comes to 'replace' the original. Marilyn Butler feels the novel is finally some kind of failure in terms of the low empathy count the reader would have in relation to low-spirited Fanny. But that hardly prevents her from starring in her own way in some brilliantly ironized and 'theatrical' moments which are as relishable as the overt fencing of *Pride and Prejudice*, particularly perhaps in the wonderful set-piece in which Sir Thomas comes in quest of her to make her accept Henry Crawford. He asks her with highminded obtuseness if she has any reason to 'think ill of' his 'temper': 'She longed to add, but of his principles I have' (p. 287) is her unuttered reply, one principally learned from Sir Thomas's own emphasis on principles.

Elizabeth Bennet may speak her mind at all costs, but inferiors generally think of wondrous answers and bite their lips. Yet finally, symbolically, if not 'master' of Mansfield, she, the former slave, is finally its 'mistress'. Ironically, the staunchness of Fanny's opposition to Henry Crawford, in his 'false homage' to Fanny as 'a thing enskied and sainted'[30] is derived from a Sir-Thomas-like sense of propriety which actually outdoes his own, as Sir Thomas himself is angry to find her unenthusiastic about the prospect of union with one so ostensibly eligible. Although the matter is complicated by the fact that her heart is already secretly pledged to the obtuse and unsuspecting Edmund, the secret of the attachment itself lies partly in the attachment of Edmund to the postures and proprieties of Sir Thomas (for which the other children have no regard).

Yet the issue is also complicated by the fact that Fanny resents Crawford's pretension to honour women in sexual terms as a refusal to consider them as 'rational creatures'. According to Margaret Kirkham, this constitutes Jane Austen's refusal of Romanticism in *Mansfield Park*, as a movement tainted with ('Rousseau-ish') 'sexism'.[31] This could be confusing. Fanny has her own kind of Romanticism to hand, a Sir Walter Scott-like attachment to a 'feudal' past which gives honour to rank and royalty, and a specific cult of nature, Cowper and memory, for example, using a quotation in which Burke himself might have found an 'emotional synthesis' of what he was trying to say.[32] Romantics, as Marilyn Butler reminds us in the most scholarly way, may be 'rebels' or 'reactionaries'. (Fanny's musings on the name Edmund also remind us strongly of the musings of *Edmund* Burke, polemic sustainer of the *Ancien Régime*: 'It is a name of heroism and renown – of kings, princes and knights; and seems to breathe the spirit of chivalry and warm affections'(p. 190). We may take it, then, that Fanny's defence of 'Edmund' is one of 'Jane's' little jokes.)

Fanny's nature-philosophy – 'one cannot fix one's eyes on the commonest natural production without finding food for the wandering fancy' (p. 189) has a cool, taxonomic quality, rather as Elizabeth's nature rhapsody' in *Pride and Prejudice*, by being couched in Johnsonian terms, negates or at least strongly qualifies itself. But it is also prissy and priggish, almost neurotically fastidious in a way that bespeaks incipient aggression towards and disapproval of Mary here, whom she's addressing. Her linguistically 'overdetermined' gentility combines with her unavowable jealousy.

Yet, whatever the ambiguities involved in presenting Fanny, we must concede that in Henry she meets a 'type' of Don Juan – in any case, one who would certainly say, with Molière's Don Juan:

> La belle chose de vouloir se piquer d'un faux honneur d'être fidèle, de s'ensevelir pour toujours dans une passion. – La constance n'est bonne que pour les ridicules. Pour moi la beauté me râvit partout où je la trouve. On goutte une douceur extrême a reduire, par cent hommages, le coeur d'une jeune beauté[33]

and indeed this brushes past some of Henry's very phrasings.

Yet, although he is, fairly plainly, a version of Byronic man, Henry inhabits a text which would not permit, as it were on-stage, the overt coarseness of conduct which issues in the full-blown affairs and seductions of reckless gallantry. Such are dwindled to damaging flirtations and intimations of sexual power-play which 'joys in another's loss of ease',[34] and set one woman against another. For the same reason, Henry could obviously not be allowed a coarse maxim like Byron's 'cant is so much stronger than c-nt nowadays'[35] (the latter term is glossed by Isobel Armstrong as 'aggressive sexuality'), but he acts in accordance with it, in the sense that his function is to exploit the gap between high moral tones and real motivation or intention.

Here then, he might be said to expose the world of difference between 'marriage vows' and 'lover's vows', the title of the Inchbald version of the Kotzebue play enacted at Mansfield, where the former, as proffered by Maria to the 'booby' Rushworth shows marriage and giving in marriage transposing physical and other charms into charms of property (in Maria's case for the sake of a sizeable estate and a house in town), rather in the spirit of Bulwer Lytton's later remark that 'in England the heart is remarkably prudent, and seldom falls in love without a sufficient settlement.'[36]

Marrying and giving in marriage thus form part of a 'social contract', which actually effaces the traces of the passionate feeling it appears to express and fulfil.

Yet Henry himself is hardly an apostle of spontaneity, and after his elopement with Maria after her marriage, the famous D.H. Lawrence formula, 'it is so, let it be so, with a generous heart', could be applied to Maria, but hardly to Crawford himself, whose attitude might be described as ludic. His concern, with 'the narratable moment',[37] as D.A. Miller puts it, in a suggestive phrase, brings him dangerously close to the spirit of the novelist, with her plots and stratagems, her suspensions of closure. In short, he has designs rather than desires, and his wooing of Fanny has the air of a project:

> No, I will not do her any harm, dear little soul! I only want her to look kindly on me, to give me smiles as well as blushes, to keep a chair for me by herself wherever we are, and be all animation when I take it and talk to her; to think as I think, be interested in all my possessions and pleasures, try to keep me longer at Mansfield, and feel when I go away she shall never be happy again. I want nothing more. (p. 208)

There is something genuinely odious in all this, of course, certainly enough to call in question Trilling's claim that Mary is conspicuously more degenerate than Henry. ('Moderation itself!', she exclaims here). It also shows how what could be called the nature of his interest in the subject brings him well into line with Nietzsche when he asks.

> Is it really his 'carnal nature' that makes him sin again and again? And not rather, as he himself suspected later, behind it the law itself, which must constantly prove itself unfufillable, and which led him into transgression with irresistible charm?[38]

And, as Nietzsche again says:

> In the end this transformation of Eros into a devil wound up as a comedy: gradually the 'devil' Eros became more interesting to him than all the angels and saints, thanks to the whispering and secret-mongering of the church in all erotic matters.[39]

Thus, the observation already made, that in *Mansfield Park* it is difficult to leave the terms of the master–slave relationship, attracts the further idea that Sir Thomas has slaves, while Henry has 'sex slaves' in the sense of emotional dependents whose desires he has aroused: see Mary on the extent of his conquests on p. 329 – 'Were I to attempt to tell you of all the women whom I have known to be in love with him, I should never have done'. These conquests include the Bertram daughters, who are between as it were the upper and the nether millstone of 'sexist' Sir Thomas and equally 'sexist' Henry, respectively no 'friend of their pleasures' and false 'friend of their pleasures'. If, then, Sir Thomas's daughters are 'bastilled for life', it is apparently by the idea of the 'prudential marriage' but, in terms of the more complex trap sprung by Crawford, of their own desires.

It may be difficult to see in Henry a creature of clerical cut. He is shown toying with the possibility of the role, although his main function here seems to be to play wrong notes which emphasize the correctness of Edmund (speaking of sermons as 'capital gratifications' [p. 309]), but saying that making them 'would not do for a constancy' and so on [p. 310]). No doubt Henry's main preoccupation here is impersonation, and he 'is what for a moment he thinks he is'. However, it is possible to argue that Henry is never more than (precisely) a clergyman manqué, or rather what might be styled the 'verso' of a clergyman. Listen, for example, to Dr Fordyce – who was, as it happens, a particular *bête noire* of Jane Austen, and whose sexism causes a modern critic like Margaret Kirkham to see her making common feminist cause with Mary Wollstonecraft:

> Let their confidence in you never be abused. But is it possible that any of you can be such barbarians, so supremely wicked, as to abuse it? Can you find it in your hearts to despoil the gentle trusting creatures of their treasure, or do anything to strip them of their native robe of virtue?[40]

In fact these rhetorical questions are somewhat perilous and actually foreground the Nietzschean point: the answer 'yes' would produce a Crawford – i.e. a 'subject' 'produced' by ecclesiastical rhetoric, fascinated by the idea of transgression and actually oscillating between the 'good' and 'evil' responses to such rhetoric. Such talk, however well-meaning, is rightly arraigned as an instance of what Mary Wollstonecraft calls 'a false system of education, gathered from the books on the subject written by men, who, considering women as females rather than as human creatures, have been more anxious to make them alluring mistresses than affectionate wives and rational mothers'.[41] That Wollstonecraft and Austen can make common cause is a large part of the point of Margaret Kirkham's book, and again inhibits any desire to present 'Jane Austen' as simply a Tory ideologue.

A similar inability or refusal to be ideologically cut and dried attends the presentation of Fanny. After the manner of such 'structuralist' X-rays, which never quite fit in any case, Fanny is customarily seen as a Cinderella-Cordelia confronting (or rather failing to confront) Julia and Maria as Ugly Sisters or Goneril and Regan – suggesting, that is, black and white oppositions. A finely shaded account would perhaps suggest a more ambivalent Fanny than this suggests (an ambivalence Geoffrey Hartman has already been prepared to see in Cordelia), and a feminist theme stirring (and disrupting hermeneutic complacency) when the reader contemplates Maria's and Julia's fates.

'Slavery' is the thematic link for all the females specified here and in the text generally, and it is women in particular, who are seen to be 'everywhere in chains'. Fanny, a critic like Devlin keeps telling us, is 'free',[42] but, not to speak of her officially sanctioned 'repression' with its attendant personality traits, her eroticized Christian slavery is 'sealed' with a cross and chain suggestively (and extraordinarily) said to be 'so full of William and Edmund', brother and adoptive brother respectively. It is perhaps implied that 'natural affection' crosses sibling feelings with sexual ones.

Surprisingly, at least for us, when St. John Rivers says in *Jane Eyre* that 'natural affections only' have power over him, he means his relationship with his sisters, not his 'rearing' affections for Rosamund Oliver. Fanny's thoughts of a menage are with brother William (p. 341), although her heart is said to be Edmund's and Edmund is by way of being a brother-protector at Mansfield, yet she feels critical of Mary because she 'loves only her brother' (p. 386). 'Brother and sister – no indeed!' says Mr Knightley, in humorous indignation with Emma for supposing that their dancing together might be seen as improper, although their marriage has suggested to many the even more excitingly incestuous tie of father and daughter. Sir Thomas finds that 'Fanny was indeed the daughter he wanted' (p. 431), and particularly so as his response to Fanny is so pronouncedly erotic that the stolid

Edmund, the only one of Sir Thomas's children to have adopted his attitudes, seems to arrive at the idea that Fanny may have romantic charms via Sir Thomas's 'warmth'. This is first in evidence on his return from Antigua and strongly confirmed thereafter. Is it that she is the only one to conform to the truly slavish pattern which excites him?

> As she entered, her own name caught her ear. Sir Thomas was at that moment looking round him, and saying 'But where is Fanny?' Why do I not see my little Fanny?' and on perceiving her, came forward with a kindness which astonished and penetrated her, calling her his dear Fanny, kissing her affectionately, and observing with decided pleasure how much she was grown! Fanny knew not how to feel, or where to look. She was quite oppressed. He had never been so kind, so *very* kind to her in his life. His manner seemed changed. His voice was quick from the agitation of joy, and all that had been awful in his dignity was lost in tenderness. (p. 160)

Such a passage has all the more impact from the fact that the official disclosures of love by legitimate wooers are in Jane Austen's texts characteristically elided – for example, there is nothing to compare with this in the courtship of Edmund and Fanny, in which we are held at ironic arm's length.

A.S. Neill, the educationist (or anti-educationist) has remarked that many parents seem, paradoxically (and unhappily) to succeed in the parental role with children other than their own.[43] This is potentially tragic rather than matter of course, and it actually seems to be a prominent theme in *Mansfield Park* without *Mansfield Park*'s quite intending for it to be.

This is, of course, because we are supposed only to have a sense of deep 'solicitude' for certain people whose righteousness is as it were guaranteed and underwritten. Yet as it moves to expel or eliminate those who 'cannot have a proper way of thinking', to use Elizabeth Bennet's suggestive phrase in *Pride and Prejudice*, the phrase is itself problematized or put in question. Sir Thomas himself, for example, is led to mildly agonized reappraisal and a vague sense of the need to be less world-minded, yet his agony is over his own false values rather than a genuine feeling for the daughters whom he has helped to destroy. In his very insight he seems to have found a way to continue his blindness. Conversely, one might say that, although Maria is more emphatically shown not to have 'a right way of thinking', yet, being high-spirited, passionate and intelligent, Crawford is surely right when he muses that 'she [Maria] is much too good for him [Rushworth]' (p. 202).

Even the compulsively *bien-pensant* Edmund acknowledges that it is 'mortifying' (p. 385) to have to think of Rushworth as a 'brother' during the short times they are forced to be together. The inference might then be that it is much greater mortification for Maria to be on terms of much greater intimacy with Rushworth than Edmund has to endure. She has achieved wealth and social cachet at a high cost, and when she decides that the price is too high for herself, this is dangerously close, surely, to seeming an understandable (if not a good) decision. It is hard not to feel that she is 'very much out of luck' in that her foolish wisdom in marrying Rushworth does not find its converse in the 'wise folly' of an elopement where her passionate feelings would actually be reciprocated, since, true to his ego, Henry has only courted her out of pique. Although Laurence Lerner cannot understand why Maria ran off with Crawford, we were told that she 'loved' (p. 427) him, and that her resentful reception of him reawakened his Don Juanesque desire to '*reduire par cent hommages*' so that finally, 'he was entangled by his own vanity' (p. 427).

It is Edmund's falling in love with Fanny which would take a little longer to explain, especially as Crawford's desire for her elicits, not his jealousy (as Harriet's desire for Mr Knightley in *Emma* awakened Emma's), but his earnest efforts to make Fanny accept him (!)[44]

It is also interesting here that Rushworth is so emphatically presented as a 'ruling-class' Booby with a huge estate – and, as it were, a tiny brain. (A strange point of emphasis in abjectly 'Tory' fiction, surely?) As if in compensation for the all-too-dramatic Mr Yates, it may be said that his 'rents' are *more than equal* to his 'rants', since he is incapable of learning his part in *Lovers' Vows*, obviously in a more complex sense than he could easily be made to understand. About this, Henry has, retrospectively, the dangerously funny comment: 'Poor Rushworth and his two-and-forty speeches! Nobody can ever forget them' (p. 202), that is, except he, for he could never remember them. (Compare Sir Thomas's anxiety to 'forget how much he had been forgotten himself' – *Mansfield Park*, in its narratorly phrasing, is often as mischievous as the 'lighter-toned' novels by Austen.)

As we saw, it is probably hopeless to expect dull, egocentric Rushworth to utter the famous Lawrentian formula 'it is so, let it be so, with a generous heart' on Maria's elopement: but the reader perhaps comes to feel that some such utterance might be appropriate from what Wordsworth calls 'thinking hearts', given the nature of her relationship with Rushworth. Marriage was, for the well-educated Maria, the only available 'career'. In the more morally considerate *Pride and Prejudice* Mr Bennet openly considers the possibility that even for the 'good' Elizabeth her 'lively talents' would place her in the 'greatest danger' were her marriage one of convenience only. There is enough to suggest that, as dominant critical opinion has it, *Mansfield Park* proposes an austere 'Hebraism' (characterized, for Matthew Arnold, by 'strictness of conscience'), it does so rather against the grain of its own creative development.

The subject of *Mansfield Park* is indeed, as Jane Austen says, or seems to say, 'ordination',[45] and in a weirdly 'pure' sense, leaning on the etymology of the word, which is from the Latin *'ordo, ordinis'*, 'rank': the novel is, then, about how people are to be ranked, with surprises in store, perhaps, for those who either naively or not so innocently assume that this will indeed follow the simple fault-lines of conventional social arrangements: 'everybody has their level', as Mr Elton points out in *Emma*, but even a conservative account of *Mansfield Park* cannot fail to notice that persons of consequence are not always the most worthy. The effect is destabilizing, and undermines, for example, the clarity apparently obtained by referring to that other set phrase, 'persons of quality'. Compare here Fanny's key phrase, 'the effects of education', meaning upbringing, as opposed to mere factual instruction, which means to upbraid Mary but also applies to Edmund's sisters, who have earlier mocked Fanny for her want of 'education'.

Perhaps we might add, then, that the book is indeed a study in 'ordination', but with special reference to what Fanny calls 'the effects of education'. Fanny's reference here is to Mary Crawford, and the phrase is (for Edmund's benefit), both critique and extenuation. Her phrase about education also refers more pointedly to Edmund's sisters, who, partly through their earlier scorn for what they see as the effects of Fanny's education (pp. 11; 15–16), actually define the defects of their own education and their defective definition of the word 'education'[46] itself, which for them is radically divorced from *formation* or development, consisting, apparently, mainly of what Donne called 'unconcerning things, matters of fact'.[47] They knew, as the narrator mischievously suggests, 'the Roman Emperors as low as *Severus*' (p. 16), connoisseurs of Imperialism (as Edward Said might have noted but didn't), and perhaps capable, like Jane Eyre, of 'drawing parallels in silence' (between imperial domineering and paternal *severity*).

Ironically, although Fanny herself speaks of nature in terms which suggest Wordsworthian soul-formation, the formative role in her own life has been that of Sir Thomas, whose patriarchal moralism is as it were the horizon of her understanding, and whose strictness of conscience makes her 'rule'.

Yet as source or origin Sir Thomas is decentred, with almost comic effects, although the situation itself is painful, when he confronts her over Crawford's suit and finds nothing amiss with it. Suddenly he is no longer the fixed source or origin for her sense of 'what is fit, and not'. Interestingly, the 'hinge' of this discovery, previously mocked by Austen in *Sense and Sensibility*, is 'romantic delicacy', and seen, in the presence of the massively unromantic Sir Thomas, as no bad thing: 'He who had married a daughter to Mr Rushworth. Romantic delicacy was certainly not to be expected from him' (p. 300). Along the same lines of thought, a hint of 'degrading personal compulsion', attendant upon his laborious misconstruction here, reminds us of the point, inverting Nietzsche, that we tend to label that good which is only powerful: 'Sir Thomas came towards the table where she sat in trembling wretchedness, and, with a good deal of cold sternness, said: "It is of no use, I perceive, to talk to you ..."' (p. 287).

Reprehensibly uncomprehending and harsh, the more Sir Thomas attempts exclusive occupancy of the moral high ground the more vulnerable he becomes, and the text itself speaks volumes as it 'economizes on truth' as if to shield (and yet in effect to expose) him further. For example, in a brief report on a conversation with Sir Thomas, Edmund commends Fanny for daring to ask him a question about the slave trade (p. 178). This is of course (and innocuously) a character note. Fanny is interested in his concerns, as Edmund's brother Tom and his sisters are not. Yet it is also interesting that Edmund implies that with a clear conscience he would have explained measures and procedures he would have felt no need to justify. He would adopt a high moral tone, and no doubt he would never have behaved like the absentee, but not perhaps sufficiently absentee, lords of Gramsci's Sardinia, who enjoyed playing Pozzo to the native Luckies.[48]

Yet the text here is still interesting in that the issue seems to be at once concealed and revealed. If there is no need to assume that the text's comparative taciturnity about this implies a tacit approval, its taciturnity is still more significant than its approval. Antigua for Mansfield Park (and in *Mansfield Park*) is in fact so marginal as to be optionally invisible/visible as the reader chooses, or so it appears. It too is a horizon of meaning which speaks of the master-slave relationships which Mansfield so curiously replicates, and Sir Thomas is the mediator of, as well as in, both worlds.

Sir Thomas is also revealing in what he implicitly conceals when he speaks rather unctuously about Edmund's proposed clerical duties to suggest that 'a parish has wants and claims which can be known only by a clergyman constantly resident', in stern correction of Crawford's notion that a clergyman need only drop in occasionally on his flock: 'If he does not live among his parishioners and prove himself by constant attention their well-wisher and friend, he does very little either for their good or his own' (p. 224).

Implicit here is the idea that 'clerical duties' are ideologically innocuous in ways that might not in fact compel universal assent or approval, just as the comfort a conservative critic like Duckworth is able to draw from the idea of a traditional proximity of the great house and the parsonage of the neighbourhood would not necessarily be shared by everyone. However, this might of itself seem hypercritical, particularly as Edmund here furnishes a kind of paradigm for the serious-minded young man; yet, Sir Thomas also implies, we are to infer that *his own* activities are on all fours with Edmund's professional philanthropy or professions of philanthropy.

In *Mansfield Park*, then, the shadow follows the light to the end, and its moral victory is something of a pyrrhic victory. Sir Thomas, to be sure, stands corrected: 'He felt that he ought not to have allowed the marriage – had sacrificed the right to the expedient – [had] been governed by motives of selfishness and worldly wisdom' etc. (p. 421) – but he still stands, and nothing is meant to mar our sympathies, apparently. But the large disgrace of Maria and the lesser sliding of Julia, the extirpation of the Crawfords and the cauterizing of Norris might seem to lead one to conclude that the reader is being compelled to say something like 'it is so, let it be so, with an *ungenerous* heart'. The famous and dramatic narrative gesture – 'let other pens dwell on guilt and misery' (p. 420) – overwrites or overrides the fact that there is a good deal of dwelling on both. Yet the very sense of strain which attends, in particular, something like the extirpation not only of female sexuality but even of female sprightliness, shades the conclusion with a sense of ambiguity which must include 'ideological' ambiguity.

Even 'Socratic' irony has been associated with sensuality, and irony, whether Socratic or Austenian, returns, licensed only by a wedding licence, in a conclusion which unites Fanny and Edmund with the 'white magic' of an (implausible) reversal of fortunes. Irony itself is 'rehabilitated' as a brotherly–sisterly *rapport* becomes a marital adventure guaranteed as marital by the irony itself: 'She was of course only too good for him. But as nobody minds having what is too good for them, he was very steadily earnest in his pursuit of the blessing' (p. 430).

Pride and Prejudice, with some strong qualifying points, might have been subtitled 'In Defence of Irony'. *Mansfield Park*, on the contrary, looked at first blush like a redoubt against it. Irony is the outward and visible sign of alienation, the 'effect of education' (p. 243) which enables one to see through things. Seeing through things is a dangerous pastime where the implicit commitment is rather to save the sum of things.

Yet, as we see from *Mansfield Park*, saving the sum of things and dispensing with irony exacts a high price, and the irony of ironies here is that irony is rehabilitated after the ironists have been put to flight. Yet it can hardly expunge and raze the euphoric unpleasantness, the glistening malice of Mary and Henry without indulging a slightly distasteful euphoria of its own.

As Mary Poovey remarks of the conclusion, 'our sense of triumph comes not from Fanny, but from the tone and mischievousness of the narrator, whose vitality is far closer to Mary Crawford's energy than to Fanny's passivity' (p. 235). Perhaps we shouldn't bridle at a little magic in the *peripeteia* after which the good brother and the good sister enter into a *ménage* which itself unites the idea of marriage with that of the brotherly–sisterly rapport to achieve a sense of the ultimate intimacy as a kind of incestuous innocence (Mary says of Fanny, 'you *have* a look of his [Edmund's] sometimes.' Shelley's 'Her voice as the voice of my own soul' is something Edmund might well say of Fanny – although Sir Thomas might also want to lay claim to this line. Indeed, conspicuously unlike any of his siblings in this, Edmund has adopted many of his attitudes and might be said to be a 'version' of him, whereas in Fanny herself Sir Thomas had 'found the daughter that he wanted' (p. 431) for reasons which included, as we have seen, erotic feelings.

Clearly Fanny, who began by being taxonomically indeterminate in terms of class and status, not quite a daughter-sibling either of Portsmouth or of Mansfield, now clearly has her hands full as a sister-daughter-wife. If then, we identify with Fanny's triumph then Mansfield is teleologically 'successful' and, in her name, we hail the victory of 'good' over 'evil'.

But it is a victory achieved at considerable cost, and perhaps a final source of discomfort lies in a sense of the relative impotence of 'goodness' itself – so much so, indeed, that it puts the 'goodness' itself into question, awakening a sense that the ethical can hardly be separated from the communal. Fanny and Edmund can minister to each other, yet each has been unable to 'save' either of the Crawfords – Mary, for example, despite strong indications of superior qualities. When Mary draws away indignantly from the fire on hearing Mrs Norris condemn Fanny, growing warm with indignation rather than physical heat, or says of Edmund 'I honour him beyond expression', the reader warms to her. And Fanny herself, we are told, would in time have succumbed to the ardently reformed Henry. Tennyson's Ulysses felt that 'though much is taken, much remains'. In the case of Mansfield, however, it is possible to feel that though something remains, much has been taken.

Thus, in a related way, the famous 'Let other pens dwell on guilt and misery' (p. 420) means 'let other pens dwell on the guilt and misery which I have been at such pains to create.' In a sense, as we have seen, the first half of the book is 'petard-like' preparation for the creation and erasure of guilt and misery. This means, incidentally, that we have to think of guilt and misery as going on elsewhere. 'We' are situated among happiness and conscious rectitude that might look a little like priggery, or remind us of the idea cited by William Empson that one of the pleasures of heaven is contemplating the lot of the damned. And in a sense the 'event' proves Sir Thomas and his regime to have been as morally 'slaughterous' as Odysseus and his 'supporters' were physically so when the time came for him to avenge himself on the suitors.

An interesting essay by D.A. Miller makes explicit the awkwardly antithetical relationship of Jane Austen's attitude to morality and attitude to narrative. This associates 'virtue' with the stasis and closure (consequent on 'openness') – which leaves nothing to be disclosed, nothing to the imagination. 'Virtue' then, is 'stasis' and 'closure', while marriage, as the resolution of imaginary pairings, 'couplings of the imagination', as Emma herself almost calls them, has the connotation of 'eternity'. Marriages are, after all, made in heaven, and Henry himself glances at this in his sly irony about it as 'Heaven's *last* best gift', in Milton's phrasing. (His defiance of Miltonic meaning is significant.)

Miller points out that 'what keeps Henry from reforming is nothing but his unrelenting pursuit of the narrative moment; a moment in which meaning is postponed ... or scattered along the ground of various possibilities'.[49] Thus his flirtation with Fanny is the supreme act of flirting with what might bring it to an end. Movement suggests fluidity of role: making sermons 'would not do for a constancy' and neither would anything nor perhaps anyone else. It is interesting to note further, as Miller does not, that if Henry stands for the postponement of meaning Sir Thomas stands for its absolute imposition, a rock-hard fixity of role, suffocating propriety. (He is Mansfield's 'transcendental signifier' in propria, as it were, persona.)

Such an atmosphere perceptibly descends when the play-acting episode is abruptly terminated by his return from Antigua. When Edmund notes that 'we are sometimes a little in want of animation' (p. 176), and makes further reflections on the theme, Fanny never-theless notes correctly that 'In my opinion, my uncle would not like *any* addition. I think he values the very quietness you speak of' (p. 177). Such inactivity seems to have achieved a death-in-life for *faineant* Lady Bertram. Hence the provocation of early Blake, who cries 'better "devilish" energy than "heavenly" stasis'. What, then, Henry finally embodies for the novelist is an incipiently self-decon-structing distrust about narrative strategies themselves, which are 'doomed to palter with us in a double sense', in Macbeth's phras-ing, as part of their very *raison d'être*.

It is interesting that in Jane Austen's next novel, Knightley, a Sir Thomas purged of imaginative crassness, nevertheless mounts a brisk no-nonsense dismissal of Emma as an 'imaginist', as part of a persistently articulated attack on her pursuit of 'narratable moments' (understandably enough, since Highbury society obvi-ously provides so pitifully few) – i.e. Emma's conjectures as to what will transpire followed by various sleights designed to make them transpire in a particular way. Sir Thomas, himself an ur-Knightley in the patriarchal mode, in his opposition to 'theatrical nonsense' (p. 165) is relatively indiscriminate, and not concerned with the niceties of nastiness – if that is indeed how one would wish to define it – invoked by Inchbald's Kotzebue, a topic which has produced much critical discussion. His opposition, then, we can fairly construe as aimed at *the idea of the theatrical as such*, with its destabilizing potential for 'showing up the subject as an imaginary construct', as Diane McDonell puts it.[50] Sir Thomas, with his evident conservatism and particular interests would claim, after the manner of many inadequate parents, that the subject 'is always given prior to social relations', or, at least, would engage in actions accordant with such beliefs.

In fact it is possible to go a little further and say that the full scope of Sir Thomas's opposition is, strictly speaking, to what Wallace Stevens calls 'the one of fictive music': we might just as well call her the female novelist, who, by means of her own 'theatrical nonsense', projects and sustains the idea of the patriarch, who, if we imagine him imagining what she was up to, would surely repress her. We may take a certain grim satisfaction therefore, in the fact that, although the closure of the novel appears to involve him in a certain 'recuperative' solicitude, this fails altogether to conceal the fact that Sir Thomas's cover has been blown, and the text destroys the patriarchy it appears to sustain and to attempt to 'perpetuate'. Yet it remains ironic for us that here 'Jane Austen' becomes as it were the 'governing presence' of a text whose defining property appears to be 'opposition to spirited critique'. This itself issues from a potentially subversive 'alienation' which has often been pinpointed as, precisely, the spirit of Jane Austen.

Yet the true subject of *Mansfield Park* finally concerns true subjects – that state of subjection for which marginal Antigua provides the central metaphor. Perhaps its presentation of Fanny's ungovernable compliance and submissiveness is its most piquant triumph. Fanny accepts a certain kind of 'subjectivity and subjection' which will lead Sir Thomas to the conclusion that *Fanny* is his daughter, which she indeed is by a kind of spiritual affiliation. Yet it puts a strange 'gloss' on his actual failure as a father. Fanny is indeed his 'true subject', although it has also been shown that this 'subject' is in a double sense an 'imaginary construct', but one which, as the converse of the fatal fluidity associated with the 'Mansfield theatricals', must appear to refuse the very idea of 'impersonation'. It must be refused because the acceptance of 'subjectivity and subjection' must not be relativized.

Perhaps the final dramatic irony of *Mansfield Park*, then, is that it is the despicable Yates, 'bit-player' as he is, 'sawing the air with his hand thus' who contributes most to shattering the bulk of Mansfield. It is, incidentally, surely with 'something like prophetic strain' that he is homophonic with Yeats the poet, since Yeats was at once ideologically 'affiliated' to country house culture, and also drank deep of everything relating to ranting, play-acting, masks and impersonation, as being (as it were) profoundly superficial. Certainly the regret expressed in the famous lines to the effect that

> Players and painted stage took all my love
> And not those things that they were emblems of

is uncharacteristic. In the same way, Yates's 'hardened acting', to use a phrase of Edmund's, is a 'dangerous supplement' to the lifelong 'impersonations' which ensure a sense of stability and – continuity in the family and society, although at a cost which *Mansfield Park* is able not only to imply but actually to articulate so powerfully that its 'reassuring' closure remains somewhat disquieting.

6
Imagining Emma Imagining:
Emma

When I wrote an earlier and very different version of this chapter in the form of an article, I seemed to be bothered by the new, almost paradoxical ways of 'validating' texts, not rejoicing sufficiently in the loss of the new-critical rhetoric of critical inflation which used words like 'great' and 'greatness' as an instant knock-down argument in the High Noon of Leavisite bullying. I was troubled by the idea that 'the text's blindness is the critic's insight and opportunity',[1] and that considerable relish went into demonstrating that at critical points one may say of a text what Coleridge claimed of Hobbes's 'system': 'Its statement is its confutation.'

Combined with such paradoxical valuings was the threat implicit in Terry Eagleton's dramatic image (adduced in an admittedly popularizing work) that 'for Heidegger, our posture before "Art"' must have something of 'the servility which Heidegger advocated for the German people before the Führer'.[2] Or, in other words, not only does 'culture' offer 'documents of past barbarism' (and we are not going to be fooled this time), but, moreover, *we* have ways of making *it* talk.

Perhaps the image seemed particularly resonant for *Emma*. For a start, it seemed to contain its own, Emma-quashing 'Führer', the ultra-patriarchal Mr Knightley, who entered (stage *right*, naturally) as a kind of Village Explainer to explain everything relevant about the village, the text, and specifically the narrative in which he appeared (and seemed also to have attracted a large and uncritical following among 'critics'[3]). Margaret Kirkham gives Knightley too much credit for 'bothering with drains', which indicates only that his feet are firmly planted on his own grounds, but the smell of badly constructed narratives also lingers in his nostrils, which begin to flare slightly when he realises that people have not quite got the (ideological) point.

Emma seemed to lie open to the accusation memorably constructed by Balibar and Macherey that 'the literary text' 'bring[s] about the reproduction, as dominant, of the ideology of the dominant class'[4] (p. 53) with a vengeance. After all, in *Emma* the local landowner enters *in propria persona* to set us all straight, like Mr Dick, or perhaps, more properly, like Theseus in *Midsummer Night's Dream*, the patronizingly elitist (and philistine) explicator. But the very process of sewing things up is enough to sow doubts in the readerly consciousness.

One can see, of course, how it is that 'Jane' became established in the popular imagination as a skilful compiler of legitimating texts for the Tory party at prayer (and when more secularly employed). Yet if we read Jane Austen's *Emma* as an essentially anti-Jacobin 'text' with Marilyn Butler, we are foreclosing on issues and concerns that the text may be opening for us. For her, presumably, the text is still in the prison-house of the 'anti-Jacobinism' ('Jacobinism' entails revolutionary postures) its stable author was saddled with imprinting on the reader, rigidly 'recuperative' (and proud of it). Knightley bestrides the text like a colossus, attacking the wrong kinds of social imaginary (or the imaginative), and his injunction to its imaginists to get real can be read off as an injunction to get realism, as that has been seen as pre-eminently the recuperative form which he as patriarchal supporter of Grand Narratives of his own pre-eminence might be felt to countenance.

Roland Barthes insisted that we are justified in reading (or at least doomed to read) with 'an entirely modern gaze'.[5] This 'modern gaze' (despite the slightly sinister nuances 'gaze' has acquired) is not necessarily a hostile one. And we should realize that it may be unsound to confine oneself critically to 'repeating what is in the script', in Wallace Stevens's phrase, replaying it only on the authentic instruments of its (actually quite hypothetical) contemporary concerns. Charles Altieri's boldly quasi-Hegelian flourish is worth taking into account here. For Hegel, he claims, 'historicism reduces all history to tragedy, by conceiving the monuments of past cultures as empty tombs, irretrievably distant from present needs and concerns'.[6]

Such ideas should prevent *Emma*'s being permanently Bastilled by its cultural matrix. Yet Tony Bennett also seems wrong when he gives the text such a passive role as a mere building (or *Bildung*) site for subsequent *Ideologiekritik*.[7] If the 'work' may be said to prefigure its own deconstructive reading,[8] it has found more work for itself than his critical 'Job Centre' can manage.

Mediating such issues, Catherine Belsey actually invokes *Emma* briefly, but seems disappointingly inhibited by the sense of its 'irretrievability', when she pigeon-holes it as a 'classic realist text' with which, implicitly at least, 'nothing can be done'.[9] There was a moment, apparently, when everyone knew exactly what a 'classic realist text' looked like (whereas for us it's sometimes a little difficult to pick out in the line-up of suspects). There are also some little local difficulties with the terms in question (for Frank Kermode 'classic' meant something like 'alive', but for Roland Barthes it meant something like 'dead'. This at least is the gospel according to Kermode,[10] although he by his own admission has turned out to be something of a recuperative sheep masquerading as a deconstructive wolf [though possibly it is the wolves who are 'recuperative']).

In the circumstances we might pause to defend the classic realist text or pause to defend *Emma* from the imputation of actually being one. But if a classic realist text is, roughly speaking, 'that which resists the kind of "rewriting" that a critical rereading would countenance', then *Emma* is not a classic realist text because it will countenance a good deal of it. Belsey is picking up her argument from Wayne C. Booth, who points out that the reader has nothing to learn except that Emma has had something to learn and learns it. A stable text, apparently: inculcating the need for social stability, it emerges from the (reassuring) Jane Austen stable.

As I suggested, one version of this intellectual 'sealing-off' would be to see in *Emma* merely the anti-Jacobinism of its time – simply a prop to what Jerome J. McGann calls the aftermath of 'the pyrrhic victory of Waterloo. This established the ground for the Holy Alliance and the ghostly return of pre-revolutionary structures throughout Europe'[11] – what we might call the return of the repressive. I am not so much concerned to establish an Althusserian point about not numbering *Emma* among the ideologies as to advocate caution in determining what its ideological 'coefficients' may be.[12] When the Danish critic Georg Brandes delighted Nietzsche by calling him an 'aristocratic radical', he invented a phrase which may seem right for the volatility of *Emma*, as we shall see.

Another problem raised by the critic who gives us a rigidly 'anti-Jacobin' *Emma* is that it cues what may be over-compensating readings, perhaps a little ungenerous, by radical critics. For *Emma*, this means mainly David Aers and Roger Sales. Both are acutely perceptive, certainly. For example, Aers sees that *Emma*, if not Jane Austen, is not necessarily an unequivocal Tory celebrant of the milieu she discloses. Referring in particular to the perilous position of gifted, cultivated, elegant but all-but-fatally penurious *Jane Fairfax*, he points out that 'she shows us central features of the destructive effects such conditions have on the gifted individual'.[13] However, both he and Sales turn in a basically adverse report, to the effect that, in Sales's words, 'she succeeds in uniting the conservatism of the rural gentry with the ethics of capitalist production',[14] very much in line with Ellen Wood's recent claim that 'capitalism in British history was not called into being by the bourgeoisie but by aristocratic agrarian capitalists'.[15]

But that tell-tale 'she' suggests some confusion of the implied author and the actual text, and in both cases 'Jane Austen' is associated with certain imputed anti-radical features of the text, while disclosures which might seem disconcerting or even threatening to such an anti-radical mindset are made to seem somehow inadvertent. (Mrs Elton, for example, satirically embodied as conspicuous consumer, commodity fetishist, seeming at moments to step forth from a 'colour supplement' in her 'apparatus of happiness' is an interesting, if politically ambivalent little vignette.) Yet, if we must invoke the presiding presence of an 'author', it is equally 'Jane Austen's doing that (for example) the degree of *real* adequacy in recognition of talent and cultivation and the *real* extent of the 'care and dear concern' of the (upper) bourgeoisie are disclosed.

There is in fact something involuntarily concessive about Aers's phrasing when he claims that 'Jane Austen' 'covers over the extremely unpleasant features of her class's normal social organization which *her imagination* has momentarily disclosed' (p. 133 – my emphasis). 'Momentarily' is also a prejudicial term. Sales's claim is comparable and equally interesting, but fails to acknowledge the complexity set up by the fact that 'reality' in *Emma* is mediated by Emma's consciousness, and this 'consciousness' is neither disavowed nor accepted as authoritative, so that 'Jane Austen' can actually be demonstrated not to be 'there' in the sense implied or imputed by the critic.

David Aers's weakest moment is also one in which the artistic basis of the text is ignored as he makes his point with a very blunt critical instrument: 'What Austen, Fanny, Edmund and now Duckworth fail to consider is one actually grounded in the coercive 'improvements' and transformation of rural England in the triumph of agrarian capitalism and increased profitability of production for the market ...' (p. 127). In fact the point *is* a jolly good one except for the lumping together of the such different orders of being as Austen, Fanny, Edmund and Duckworth.

It seems to me that much of the 'pleasure' of *Emma* lies in sensing the 'faulting' and 'fissuring' that take place around the central point that Sales imputes to the text as its final didactic posture – the acceptance, against Emma's finally buckling resistance, of Defoe's idea that 'trade in England makes gentlemen' (in *The Complete English Tradesman* [1725]).

But only a partial reading of the book could sustain this idea as its unambiguous outcome. And while it is true that Emma is rampantly contemptuous of Defoe's theory, her contempt is ironically glanced at – although the point is variously figured in relation to the Coles, Robert Martin, Mrs Elton and others. As with much recent critical thought, Sales wishes to make the reader wary of his text, hitching his point to Benjamin's idea that as history is written by the victors, every cultural document is a record of past barbarism. For him, Emma must be taught who the victors are and the nature of the victory.

But if Emma stands corrected, it is hardly to be assumed that all of her hypotheses, postures and assumptions are 'wrong'. In Jane Austen's judgement, that Emma herself will not be liked, the assumption is that Jane as casual peruser of her own cultural productions does, but the reader must also have her/his day, calibrating Emma, *Emma* (and the politics of Emma and *Emma*). 'Floated' as a privileged yet imperilled zone of awareness, the confused murkiness of Emma's perception of who belongs with whom is cognate with her social and political dubieties. Is Elton's outrage at being paired with Harriet outrageous? If clergymen don't know their places, who does? But as Emma herself thinks Harriet is a bit of a goon, or a goose, why shouldn't Elton be allowed to notice the fact? Finally, Harriet is seen to belong to the lower orders, who are naturally thick anyway. In Emma's world, the erotic is subsumed by the marital, which is itself subsumed by the ideological.

Emma is at once 'rescued' and 'quashed' by Knightley. Yet if Knightley appears to furnish an absolute 'rebuke' to the errors of her consciousness ('ideology') it is that consciousness which has installed and enabled the 'repressing' authority. It is of great 'ideological' moment here that 'Emma' is ambiguously 'vectored' in relation to the 'history of the victors'. For example, her own violently discriminatory' consciousness is inflamed by the imbecility which thinks that persons, particularly those of a certain class, are much of a muchness – precisely what she has to contend with in her father, whose 'high claims to forbearance' add further fetters.

Emma is sympathetic because she exemplifies Pascal's point that the more one sees, the more one sees differences. Such 'differencing' unavoidably stratifies, however, and this 'hierarchic' imagination is easily seduced into following the 'ley lines' and conventional demarcations of social class as indices of 'worth'.

The ambiguity of *Emma* itself throws criticism into violently polarized responses. The most spectacular example is perhaps that of Marvin Mudrick, who thinks Mr Knightley must have taken leave of his senses to wish to marry Emma. However, even if critics do not become aggressive towards Emma as Mudrick does, and may even write as professed 'supporters', they may still produce what Jonathan Culler calls 'the literary criticism of a patriarchal culture' (*On Deconstruction*, p. 60). Rachel M. Brownstein, for example, casts her claim in strangely instructive form when she observes that 'both (Elizabeth Bennet and Emma) must *learn* that their fathers are inadequate men ... *learn* from tutelary lovers ... *learn* that, defined only as daughters, they are incomplete' (p. 105). One can also see what is a 'definite false note' in a recent book by Margaret Kirkham when she congratulates 'Jane Austen' on her ability to free herself from 'that extensive class of literature which makes Gods of Baronets or Dukes', en route to the implausible conclusion that *Emma* '*subverts* the stereotype in which the heroine is educated by a hero-guardian'.[16]

One need not concede the point that the text unambiguously installs Knightley as 'Pedagod' in the sense that Emma's response to him might appear to make inevitable. But certainly, as he himself admits, he has a great deal of teaching to do. The culmination of his forceful didacticism, the crushing 'victory at Box Hill', powerfully points up his patriarchal 'care and dear concern' (in Hopkins' idiom), which Emma was never deficient in acknowledging. But his exhortations leave structures in place which leave all too much room for that 'pity' which both Blake and Nietzsche saw as poisonous, with Knightley as a *pharmakon* or poisonous remedy, as a landlord who gives much time to 'settling his accounts', a magistrate administering savage (in)justice.

Noting that Knightley is a landowning JP, licensed to put into force the savage laws of the endlessly 'enclosing' gentry of whom he is one, Sales mischievously but appropriately remarks that 'if the gipsies, who committed the heinous crime of frightening Harriet Smith and Miss Bickerton, had stayed on the outskirts of Highbury, we might have found out what kind of a magistrate he was' (p. 34). His kindness and consideration combine with some acerbity, and his lessons might well make the reader feel the force of the feminist point, not made of Emma, but applicable to her, that 'she is asked to identify with a selfhood that defines itself in opposition to her; she is required to identify against herself'.[17]

In fact, not only is Knightley 'god-like', here, but Emma's 'English Ideology' makes him so. Susan Morgan, in a spirited, absolute contrast of Emma and Clarissa, surely 'overpresses' when she writes that

> marriage is a union with life, and Austen can conclude *Emma* by giving her heroine the 'perfect happiness' of such a union because Emma has opened herself to the world. Clarissa's progress, on the other hand, is necessarily a withdrawal … a child of her Heavenly Father throughout, she has remained essentially unrelated to this life, and ends by entering into his house.[18]

The phrasing of the last sentence actually brushes past a perfectly reasonable account of what happens to Emma herself – except that, at the end of *Emma*, we find her 'Heavenly Father' entering into *her* house. A. Walton Litz throws an interesting sidelight on the matter when he speaks of 'Mr Knightley, who succeeds in the fatherly role where Sir Thomas Bertram failed'.[19] Mr Knightley is obviously so fatherly that it seems unnecessary to mention that he is not, in fact, a father. Sir Thomas Bertram is.

Where Mr Knightley is most palpably presented as a 'Heavenly Father' is in a fascinating passage in volume 3, chapter 9: 'Could Mr Knightley have been privy to all her attempts of assisting Jane Fairfax, could he even have seen into her heart, he would not, on this occasion, have found anything to reprove.'[20] This deliberately 'remembers' the Collect for the Communion Service in the Anglican Communion:

> O God, to whom all hearts be open, all desires known, and from whom no secrets are hid …

The fact that Knightley's very house and grounds are a legacy of what was once part of England's religious endowment makes him eloquent of Emma's English Ideology. 'Our lot is cast in a goodly heritage' is a sentiment quoted by Miss Bates, but one feels that Knightley has considerably stronger reasons to echo the text in an even more heartfelt way. And indeed it may be that Miss Bates has found a way of expressing *ressentiment* in her overdetermined repression of anything like it – her asseverations of gratitude, ecstasy, etc., ironize themselves, as T.S. Eliot would have said, by having no very firm 'objective correlative'.

As it is, everything about Knightley, from his almost absurdly apposite names ('George Knightley') to his Johnsonian traits and almost truculent moralism, make him seem, in part, a fantasy figure supremely apposite to 'rescuing' genteel, talented spinsters. In one of his poems G.M. Hopkins sees Christ as Perseus. Austen-Emma has figured Knightley as 'rescuer' with quasi-theophanic overtones in a 'religion of Englishness' where 'Englishness' is nevertheless an ideologically 'weighted' term (but where the text actually lets us see this). That Jane Austen herself is a 'party' to this arrangement but is also 'troubled' by it is actually reflected in the famous statement about Emma as 'a heroine whom no-one but myself will much like'.

Thus, to accept Knightley as an ultimate authority in a sense which forecloses on the text/reader's arbitrement is a mistake. As we saw earlier, Catherine Belsey seems to be constrained in this way when she mentions the book *en passant*. Yet, curiously, she does give the reader the handle s/he needs when noting, with a perhaps unconscious irony, that '"classic realism" constitutes an ideological practice in addressing itself to readers as "subjects", interpellating them in order that they may freely accept their subjectivity and their subjection' (p. 69). This rather brilliantly (if inadvertently) suggests the idea of a necessary 'subjection' of 'subjectivity', which was Emma's 'problem' as defined by Mr Knightley – a refusal, as he said, to 'subject the fancy to the under-standing', a phrase which seems to augur the eventual 'subjection' of Emma to Mr Knightley. We hear of Emma as an 'imaginist', and of 'that very dear part of Emma, her fancy' (p. 192).

Mr Knightley's imagination being appealed to, he replies cautiously that he 'does not know what he could imagine' (p. 34), a remark elicited by Mrs Weston's asking him whether he could 'imagine anything more beautiful' than Emma. It makes a piquant contrast with Emma's remark, arising out of her critical attitude to

Mr Weston's lack of discrimination (he is the spiritual cousin of Sir John Middleton in *Sense and Sensibility*) to the effect that 'general benevolence, but not general friendship, made a man what he ought to be. She could fancy such a man' (p. 287). In the light of the playing on the word which takes place, the text seems to twit Emma here – she has no need to 'fancy such a man' because she already has an example to hand in the person of Mr Knightley.

But this point turns with even more piquancy towards the fact that Mr Knightley is himself the 'fancy' of an 'imaginist', Jane Austen – an entity at once producing and produced by the text – who, owing to inability or an unwillingness to 'subject the fancy', created a novel whose subject was, in part, that very theme. It is of course somewhat reductive to speak of an ending in which Fancy (Emma) is subjected to Understanding (Knightley). But reductiveness can be instructive. The extent to which Emma is under attack as an 'imaginist' at first suggests a strongly 'rationalist' strain to the text, which, if more obviously 'abstract' after the manner of its author's mentor, Samuel Johnson, might even be imagined as having Spinoza's classic statement as epigraph:

> Men of great imaginative power are less fitted for abstract reasoning, whereas those excelling in intellect and its use keep their imagination more restrained and controlled, holding it in subjection, so to speak, lest it should usurp the place of reason.[21]

Ostensibly, then, *Emma* may be read as a caveat against the contemporary Romantic 'licensing' of the Imagination, against the contemporary enshrinement of which J.S. Mill wrote that 'there never was such an instrument devised for consecrating all deep-seated prejudices'.[22] But Spinoza's statement is also prejudicial. His *aporia* lies in ignoring the perfectly possible conclusion that the excellent intellect may not have much imagination to restrain. Here Knightley himself, despite a 'penetration' (p. 122) conceded by Emma, perhaps shows this in his lack of a sense of what Emma calls 'the difference of situation and habit' (p. 133) in their discussion of Frank Churchill – i.e. he could never be a novelist?

However 'reproved', Emma's habit of mind is the matrix of the text of *Emma*. The reader is asked to consider the claims of a 'sturdy' (cruel?) Johnsonian moralism – Johnson, said Wyndham Lewis, was a god to his biographer, and Knightley looks like an English deity. But something like Shelley's 'sympathetic' imagination is also evoked. However, as I hope to establish clearly, Knightley himself is supremely the beneficiary of Emma's 'imaginism', though he speaks against it. The text does have 'counter-currents' which suggest that Knightley is not simply being investigated with the sovereign authority of anti-radical 'reason' (and indeed that 'Reason' itself is liable to be vectored by various pressures, none of them reasonable).

But the deeper point is the one about the contradictory nature of the enshrinement of Knightley himself as the deity of Emma's English Ideology, which I explain more fully. This leads on to the further point, again developed here, that, stripped of its almost 'fairy-tale' elements – i.e. elements which might virtually be thought to signal themselves as such – the book offers a rather dark vision of the civilization it is often held unsubtly to celebrate. This returns us to our original points about the shrewdly 'counter-textual' thrusts of contemporary critique. Texts are not so irrecoverably the fruit of Benjamin's 'history of the victors' as to offer no resistance to the disabling conditions which precede and surround their genesis. In fact Jerome J. McGann's claim that the texts of the past may show 'grace under pressure' (p. 2) may even seem unnecessarily defensive.

It is in Emma's mediating consciousness that we see George Knightley greet John Knightley in 'true English style' and admire the 'English culture'[23] of Mr Knightley's grounds. 'English' here connotes gentlemanliness, and being cut off with remarkable clarity from its more obvious referential functions, might well be styled both 'aporetic' and ideological in use. The people one might meet on the road could hardly, though inhabitants of the country, be considered 'English' at all. Certainly, destitute and desperate as they might well be, they could hardly be expected to yield much in the line of restraint and understatement. One would probably have to call them 'gypsies', which is what those who assail Harriet in volume 3 chapter 3 of *Emma* are called. Their connection with Egypt, however, is much more conjectural than their connection with England. But, in any case, 'Englishness' in *Emma* is seen with disagreeable clarity to be an exclusive property.

It was, no doubt, such considerations which troubled D.H. Lawrence. After all, he had something like a professional interest in the term, attested to by his 'I am English, and my Englishness is my very vision.'[24] Yet, when he wrote that Jane Austen was English 'in the bad, snobbish sense',[25] he perhaps perpetrates or perpetuates a more dangerous assumption – that the word can easily assume what we might call a disinfected, denotative clarity; while in *Emma* the English Ideology is subtly qualified by the inherently 'dialogic' means of appearing to depict a social dispensation which is not necessarily benign or enabling.

Mrs Elton is an interesting case here. For all her patronizing obnoxiousness as vulgarly *arriviste* intruder on this English rural scene, she actually threatens to take on some of the Blake-like virtues of someone who embarrassingly says, indicates or defines what 'gentility' decrees must be left unsaid. Mrs Elton infuriates Emma because her own sense of 'value' is weak or confused. Although she is (implicitly) scornful of Defoe's claim that 'trade in England makes gentlemen', she herself finds it difficult to retain respect where material means and possessions are not obvious correlatives or signifying agents of gentility. She wishes at once to 'naturalize' and 'spiritualize' gentility.

We have already seen how, piquantly, Mr Knightley's almost 'numinous' quality is correlated with, one might almost say 'extracted from' his house and grounds. (Has the over-determined, almost jokey quality of *George Knightley of Donwell* [=done-well?] been sufficiently remarked?) Emma's famous meditation on his 'goodly heritage' and how it actually signifies the qualities of the owner is a development of the way in which, in *Pride and Prejudice*, the suddenly 'good' or sublimated' image of Mr Darcy rises like an exhalation from Pemberley when Elizabeth visits it:

> She felt all the honest pride and complacency which her alliance with the present and future proprietor could fairly warrant, as she viewed the respectable size and style of the building, its suitable, becoming, characteristic situation, low and sheltered – its ample gardens stretching down to meadows washed by a stream, of which the Abbey, with all the old neglect of prospect, had scarcely a sight – and its abundance of timber in rows and avenues, which neither fashion nor extravagance had rooted up. – The house was larger than Hartfield, and totally unlike it, covering a good deal of ground, rambling and irregular, with many comfortable and one or two handsome rooms. – It was just what it ought to be, and it looked what it was. – And Emma felt an increasing respect for it, as the residence of a family of such true gentility, untainted in blood and understanding. Some faults of temper John Knightley had; but Isabella had connected

herself unexceptionably. She had given them neither men, nor names, nor places that could raise blush. (p. 323)

Emma's meditation on the Knightley 'heritage' is interesting in that it seems to marry an 'aesthetic' with a quite ordinary possessiveness, as her reference to her sister Isabella's marriage to John Knightley makes clear – although she is not of course aware at this point of any desire to be affianced to Mr Knightley himself. But she takes a pride in and relishes the idea of his possession of the estate, and its mute eloquence about its owner's qualities, in a way that makes a fascinating contrast with what might with appropriate paradox be called Emerson's 'unpossessive appropriation' of the landscape:

> The charming landscape which I saw this morning is indubitably made up of some twenty or thirty farms. Miller owns this field, Locke that, and Manning the woodland beyond. But none of them owns the landscape. There is a property in the horizon which no man has but he whose eye can integrate all the parts, that is, the poet. This is the best part of these men's farms, yet to this their warranty-deeds can give no title.[26]

This is a brilliantly explicit resumé of much of what Jerome McGann has called the Romantic Ideology; while Emma's, perhaps more culpably, is that of an English Ideology of ancestral rightness of feeling signified by an appropriated landscape. Yet on the one hand it is Emerson who perhaps comes perilously close to smugness – the reader can certainly see that he is a good deal closer to the poet than Locke or Manning, for example. And Emma, despite her family involvement, speaks from a sense of distance, almost exclusion, partly because her own femininity and/as marginality implant an insecurity which lead the reader to conclude that her emphasis on rank does not proceed from a secure sense of a personal possession of it, as Nietzsche would confirm: 'This need *for* the noble is fundamentally different from the needs *of* the noble soul itself, and is in fact an eloquent and dangerous sign of its lack.'[27]

Without that sense of distance and difference, she would not experience the almost awed ('spilt religion') response to Knightley's grounds, and this makes her musings those of a much more representative English consciousness than her social position and her temporal remoteness would appear to make possible.

It might be helpful, indeed, to develop the idea of these 'Nietzschean' tones of Emma – the Nietzsche, that is, of *The Genealogy of Morals*. In that book, what we normally think of as 'morality' is an 'antithetical' or 'reactive' phenomenon. After the acceptance of 'Christianity', 'morality', at least *selon* Nietzsche, means a spiritual accountancy founded in *ressentiment* – a distillation from the rancour of the repressed or weak. Original 'goodness', on the other hand, was a concept inseparable from the idea of high rank in itself and the qualities which characterized it – a sense of well-being, power and energy and essentially open reactions of whatever variety. The keynote of this morality is shame, not guilt – a distinction largely drawn on in later books, for example E.R. Dodds's *The Greeks and the Irrational*, and by A.D. Nuttall in his recent *A New Mimesis*.

Nietzsche's tenor is in fact well caught in the passage quoted, where her musings come to a very natural conclusion with the reflection that 'she (Isabella) had given them neither men, nor names, nor places that could raise a blush'.

Here moral and social considerations mingle, in a sense blush-makingly. The untrammelled worldliness of the admired attributes ('untainted in blood and understanding' and 'neither men, nor names, nor places that could raise a blush') is breathtaking.

It is important to grasp that these are ideas applicable to Emma's attitude to Knightley rather than ideas with which he would necessarily let himself be associated, though he might act in accordance with them. The idea of having something to 'blush' for here is interestingly picked up in another of the key phrases of the text. Innocuous though it may seem to some, it secretes the idea that one's very being – social, or, as it were, 'ontological' (what's the difference?) – may be something to blush for. Thus, when the secret of Harriet's 'low birth' is out and the idea of her union with Mr Knightley is seen as abhorrent, specifically on account of her low social standing – 'the stain of illegitimacy, unbleached by nobility or wealth, would have been a stain indeed' (p. 438).

As elsewhere, it is not wholly clear from the textual context, complicated as it is by the sense of a fissuring or at least undulating reaction to the presentation of Emma's 'mediating' consciousness, quite what to infer or how to respond. Had the sentence read, for example, 'the stain of stupidity, unbleached by nobility or wealth, would have been a stain indeed', it would, in its suggestion of the slashing, rompish world of the juvenilia, have had a less ambiguous bearing. Here the text disavows at the moment of entertaining the idea that considerations of social rank alone might suspend or over-rule a sentiment about someone's 'character'. But to the extent that it is a joke at Emma's expense, it might be said to have the French Revolution in its bones. The 'text' is, if not 'militantly protean'[28] at least quite 'binary'.

Such comments might also be appropriate on a larger scale. If the reader is 'seeing through' Emma's emphasis on rank, s/he also 'sees through' Mr Knightley's implicit claim to embody Reason and thus act as a kind of rationalist *deus ex machina*, clearing up the 'mess' created by false consciousness and assumptions. One sign that 'Knightley' is not being installed by the text as a 'solving' higher reason, 'untying the text' from within, as it were, is the obvious unawareness of the effect of his 'morally correct' response to Emma's twitting of Miss Bates on Box Hill.

Its crushing impact, in relation to what we have been enabled to discern as his essentially uncomprehending (unimagining) delivery of the magisterial rebuke determines our response to him in a way that he could not conceive – or so we conceive. Another instance of the text's prising apart of Knightley and the notion of an ultimate, authoritative point of view is the context of his rebuttal of what might be called the Versailles pastoralism of Mrs Elton (volume 3, chapter 6), who wishes the strawberry party at Donwell to be 'all out of doors'. In observing that 'the simplicity of gentle-men and ladies, with their servants and furniture, I think is best observed by meals indoor', his phrasing sounds dangerously complacent (quasi-Johnsonian in Johnson's most alienating vein). Unlike the Johnsonian magnanimity which speaks from 'outside' the genteel on its behalf, he speaks as a complacent 'insider' in a tone from which self-congratulation cannot be expunged.

This 'outsider's' rhetoric which, speaking from outside, not only *for* the inside or 'in-side' but as if *from* the in-side are very trouble-some. But the awkwardness also derives from the tension between the complacency of the reference to 'gentlemen and ladies' and the petty pontifications of Mrs Elton. The moralism which is apparently so scrupulous about 'essential human worth' is nevertheless seen to be bound by another set of rules which require the recognition of the absolute cachet of rank, even when 'lady' and 'gentleman' come in the form of a Mr and Mrs Elton.

The towering, authoritative 'Reason' of Knightley is, in the last instance, the function of his class position. 'Everybody has their level', as Mr Elton remarks, but Knightley is too gentlemanly to say so, or to have to. However, even to the extent that Knightley is seen as being invested with the 'sovereign' authority of a (conservative) 'reason', the text has various ways of suggesting that 'reason' is liable to be vectored by various pressures, none of them reasonable.

For example, when Mr Knightley dissuades Emma from contemplating the possibility of a match between Harriet and Mr Elton, he explains that 'Elton may talk sentimentally, but he will act rationally' (p. 59). 'Acting rationally' here turns out to mean 'marrying a harpy for money'. The 'Age of Prose and Reason' might be felt to be showing its hand a bit here ('Romanticism' was in part, at least ostensibly, a revolt against this very 'worldly-minded' rationality).

Again, in a minor but telling way, a similar whiff of 'rationalism' also seems to commit Knightley to a 'definite false note' when he attempts to cheer the 'anti-hymeneal' (or, remembering Derrida, excessively hymeneal!) Mr Woodhouse with the thought that Mrs Weston, formerly Miss Taylor, will have an easier lot by having one '[person] to please instead of two' (p. 9). This catches exactly the kind of fatuous 'polite' reasonableness which found its way even into the talk of a Johnson, and it is significantly trivial in attempting to make plausible essentially irrational, which may mean disabling, social arrangements. (Knightley's fatuity is piquant here as, by virtue of Emma's marriage to him, she will certainly have two to please instead of one, as Mr Woodhouse remains a dead weight to the end.) The 'rational' point of view produces obvious truths, but, as Catherine Belsey puts it, 'if what is "obvious" is also incoherent, non-explanatory or even self-contradictory, it is possible to produce a recognition of the ideological status of what is obvious' (p. 63).

Emma, with its finally quite 'dialogic' role in its exposure of signifying practices is well-placed to produce such recognitions, and indeed to show how 'ideology' as 'false consciousness' is produced. Emma's acutely discriminative awareness is implicitly approved of along the lines of Pascalian praise for awareness of differences, but petrifies into what might be called 'caste-ing', i.e. when it follows the false lures or 'ley lines' of merely class discrimination. (She is a bit of an 'anti-Pygmalion' to Harriet, for example, breathing social life into her but petrifying her again when she requires to be 'trashed for over-topping', as Prospero put it.)

But against her incipient English Ideology and snobbism, the text's sense of the variousness of the relationship of social position to personal attributes constantly breaks through, with its Lady Catherine-de-Bourgh-like Mrs Churchill in the background, its insufferable prosperous Eltons, charitable but penurious Bateses, gifted but apparently doomed Jane Fairfax – her rescue being, as John Bayley has brilliantly demonstrated,[29] of an almost 'fairy-tale' order. Emma's bafflement and significant absurdity are conveyed briefly by her reactions to the Coles, who were 'of low origin, in trade' (p. 186), but who seem, though largely offstage, to behave and express themselves with 'true feeling' and perfect 'propriety'.

Yet the way in which Emma's snobbery strains to mediate class status as spiritual 'essence' is deeply significant. For example, she muses that the Westons had, for a couple of generations, been 'rising into gentility and property' (p. 12). Again, this is a claim unclearly vectored by the text. It is not apparent whether the statement entertains in order to endorse or to disavow the idea that personal qualities, real or attributed, may be a 'function' of material possessions, in which case the 'satirical' point may also be a 'radical' one. On the other hand, the weight of satirical attribution may be presumed to fall on the very idea of 'rising'. The contrast with Mr Knightley here is obvious, as his claims to both property and gentility are ancient, so that no one can 'see the join'. Thus, the irony here might be seen as tilting towards a reindorsement of a rural and quasi-feudal emphasis on the indisputable rights and merits of an ancient landed gentry, but it can also be read as an 'unmasking' device. (On the other hand, it might be seen to be insinuating that Mr Weston's gossipy insouciance may be read off as a sign of his recently acquired gentility.)

In recent criticism a responsiveness that seemed 'natural' for the more obviously 'unanchored' or 'mixed register' texts of modernism has moved towards a more active recognition of the 'variousness' of older texts. Yet, as we have seen, Catherine Belsey, in what has undoubtedly been one of the liveliest and most influential contributions to the 'New Accents' series, was very cautious in her brief references to 'classic realist' texts and *Emma* in particular. Foucault may speak of the author as being merely 'the principle of unity in a group of writings', but it is an unnecessary restraint on a critic to have to posit even this, and this is the area in which recent critique may be said to have 'broken through'.

The form of the breakthrough is seen here in our heightened awareness of the way in which a text like *Emma* represents 'a time ... of deep-seated folding, straining and faulting: old strata and new shifting against each other into fantastic and precarious poises'.[30] The words are G.M. Young's, and indeed 'faulting' does seem a good word to refer to points where a text suddenly appears to be out of alignment with what the reader had previously grasped as its implicit movement of thought. *Emma* may indeed show its 'grace under pressure' in a movement towards the dissolution of the apparent limits of its psycho-social genesis.

At worst it may be seen to *lapse*, as John Bayley has shown, from a bolder conception still present to a critical X-ray, or as a kind of 'watermark'. He points out that in his careless and inconsiderate treatment of Jane Fairfax, Frank Churchill's behaviour is actually very like that of the unfeeling employer she would have ended with as governess, and also that the text is shadowed by a conclusion its ostensible resolution appears to disavow, namely that its true creative logic would see Jane deserted and forced to earn her bread as a governess.

As we saw at the beginning of the chapter, recent heightenings of our awareness of the complications of the act of reading tend to have an apparently 'countertextual' force. They remind the reader that s/he is likely, in terms used by Mrs Weston of Emma's impersonation of Miss Bates, to be 'diverted against her/his conscience'. To say this remains in some degree, for us, true of this very novel. Yet if, in the case of *Emma*, what has been seen as its ostentatious anti-Jacobinism is, on closer inspection, gratifyingly ruptured, there is still no need to conclude that the 'entirely modern gaze' of the reader is, in a famous phrase of Cowper's cited in *Emma*, 'itself creating what it sees'.

In fact, that (amusingly) cowed, Heideggerian deference to what I.A. Richards once called 'Art in Gothic letters' interestingly indicated by Terry Eagleton is not much in evidence in contemporary critiques. There is, rather, a resolute determination not to bow down to what our *parti pris* may tell us is politically incorrect, in the light of which we are likely to end by giving a work like *Emma* much less than anything like full justice. As propaganda, it fails; as art, it succeeds. And to succeed as art, it had to fail as propaganda and become, so to speak, 'impropaganda' (if the reader will forgive me my momentary impersonation of the later James Joyce). Propaganda becoming 'impropaganda' is an informal way of saying what this chapter has hoped to establish about *Emma*, and this book hopes to establish about Jane Austen.

7
'Jane's Fighting Ships': *Persuasion* as Cultural Critique

According to Harold Bloom in his curiously pyrrhic victory of literary elitism, the aesthetic is uncontaminated with the ideological.[1] One gathers that the ideological forms a low diet which can be fed to the troglodytes of cultural studies while the politics-free zone of high culture can be left to the initiated. (Curiously, he has some glowing pages on *Persuasion* which persuade us to share a sense of *Persuasion*'s 'extraordinary aesthetic distinction' (p. 254), a judgement which nothing that follows is intended to diminish or demean.)

Once Bloom embraced Blake and Shelley as avatars of a kinder world than that adumbrated by the fiercely prejudicial ideologies of modernism. But Bloom, if brilliant, is now a cultural conservative. If Eagleton can investigate 'the ideology of the aesthetic', nothing, surely, is plainer than that *Persuasion* offers the aesthetics of ideology, or ideologies.

If we bring to mind the most famous (or hackneyed) points made by Walter Benjamin – to the effect that we must 'brush history against the grain', and that 'every cultural document is a monument to past barbarism'[2] then in many ways it would be as accurate as dramatic to announce that *Persuasion* shows that distinguished inference, 'Jane Austen' brushing her own previous work against the grain, and writing a novel which is prepared in some measure to treat its immediate predecessors as 'past barbarisms'. *Persuasion* is thus, it would appear, something of a recantation, giving its vote to 'the unfeudal tone of the present day'[3] and thoroughly deconstructing phrases and concepts like 'completely the gentleman in manner' (p. 101) to which 'Jane' had seemed, however equivocally on closer inspection, to present as a solid (perhaps even 'transcendental') signified.

'The old order changes, yielding place to new', here as in Tennyson, and, like her other texts, and rather unlike her reputation (or 'image'), 'Jane' does not offer to 'transcend', but boldly grasps the nettle of, ideology. According to Bloom, ideology is an affair of inferior types who inhabit the blue-collar world of a crudely pragmatic lower circle which leaves the world to aesthetes and to him. But on this basis, at any rate, he can hardly expect the 'Jane' of *Persuasion* to join him. Despite what people seem to have been constrained to believe or accept about this author, *Persuasion* is not only what Volosinov said of the Freudian unconscious, 'ideological through and through',[4] it is so in rather startling ways.

Indeed, although *Persuasion* might be said to mobilize its own 'recuperative strategies', to use the kind of phrasing dear to a Fredric Jameson, these may actually be signs of authorial panic in the face of its own success in 'rendering' the crumbling of old certainties and stabilities. (It should be remembered that Jane Austen's novels were perused by all the family members, including Edward Knight, the adopted brother and landowner who granted Jane, Mrs Austen and sister Cassandra the Chawton cottage.)

Although narratology has not often been considered in relation to ideology, the handling of the plot of *Persuasion* is specifically contrived to signify the 'paradigm shift' in the assumptions about society which the novel might be said to 'contain'.[5] This sense of a paradigm shift is in turn embodied in 'structures of feeling' which have political implications. Anne Elliot's world is a very private one. But its very privacy suggests an inner distancing from characteristic attitudes of her social group which in turn suggests 'the political'.

Her tale of marital triumph, her 'rescue', is simultaneously a tale of a certain political liberalizing or even liberation, although emphatically not a liberation from 'the political' in itself, which Jane Austen's novels were once held to assume. This assumption was also a paradigm for what Eliot and Leavis took to be that of 'literary studies' in themselves – freedom from the 'banality' of 'the political'. Indeed, it's surely more than a footnote to Roland Barthes' attack on the idea of the author as a potentially explanatory point of origin to observe that this concept of *Persuasion* destroys the idea, implicit in many critiques, that 'Jane Austen' functions as a kind of *marque*, as a supplier of unfailing, unfading – and virtually identical – commodities, *to the gentry*, of course. 'Jane Austen' is, rather, an image refashioned from moment to moment in the twists and turns of the narrative, an epiphenomenon of the text.

J.-F. Lyotard as an exponent of what he calls 'the breaking of the Grand Narratives'[6] has a conceptual structure like Marxism in mind, but Jane Austen is also thought of as expounding a 'grand narrative' which incorporates an English Ideology[7] of a Burkean kind, transparently Tory, but with 'grace-notes' of qualification, perhaps even momentary revolt. In fact the attributed commitment to a rock-hard conservatism is already seriously disrupted in her earlier novels, often most recalcitrant to such 'incorporation' when apparently most committed to it, despite Alastair M. Duckworth's heroic efforts to turn Jane Austen into a Mr Collins.[8] (It is interesting that from what Lyotard calls a 'scientific' point of view, 'narrative' itself may seem inherently 'Burkean' [see p. 27]). And, with some irony, it might actually be said to be characteristic of 'Jane Austen' in general that she supports (or sports) Burkean notions entailing high regard for tradition, rank, ancestry, gentility, deference and the like, yet consistently putting into question what she might seem to sustain.

But in *Persuasion*, Burkean notions are, on the whole, disavowed. Naturally, there might be qualifications to this because art is defined by being '*among* the ideologies', to adapt Althusser's useful phrase, and without a certain ideological suppleness, or subtlety, the 'polyphonic' effect which accompanies highly creative work like Austen's could hardly be achieved. These conservative notions are most sympathetically embodied in the figure of Lady Russell, but the whole point of this is to show that it is the *inadequacy* in psycho-social diagnosis which springs from Lady Russell's views which precipitates the narrative proceedings. 'The unfeudal tone of the present day' is embraced, indeed like a lover, since Wentworth, who hates snobbery, is the unfeudal tone incarnate (although he surely belongs, if in a new, improved sense, to the 'ordering' classes).

'Feudal' herself, but 'no longer at ease in the old dispensation', Anne, the 'heroine', is yet another version of that watching and waiting femininity, that predatory abnegation, so easily associated with 'Jane' herself. Anne is a kind of Fanny Price *renverse*, a marginal figure as eager *not* to identify with Burke's symbolic patriarchal order as marginal Fanny was, and to be part of and to identify with the 'umbilical' relationships of that specifically naval world to which Fanny had such difficulty in accommodating herself. As with Elizabeth Bennet and the redoubtable Darcy, Anne is proleptically united emotionally and ideologically with

Wentworth, the phallic signifier, who, pen in hand, rewrites the text in that justly celebrated scene of writing which effaces the traces of the narrative's own gloomy Freudian wisdom about the dance of desire.

'Jane Austen' is still, one suspects, a name which stands in most imaginations as the 'author' of 'classics of class', high-class treatments of the upper classes, a kind of novelistic *Debrett's Peerage* (strictly, *Baronetage*). Yet *Persuasion*, in a highly emphatic opening gambit, is specifically a 'new creation' (p. 75), which refuses the *authority* of Debrett's. Debrett's is, for the snobbish Sir Walter Elliot, the 'supreme fiction' precisely because it appears to 'underwrite his existence', and *Persuasion* is also a 'scene of writing' which undermines the underwriter. In fact the quality of the novels is often associated (or confused) with the fact of their dealing ('exclusively') with 'the quality' or 'persons of quality'.

Perhaps one way of inhibiting such premature associations, is to 'defamiliarize' things a little by leaving the prison-house of *genre* and compare Austen's 'new creation' with the mythopoeic narratives of her great contemporaries, the Romantic poets.[9] Byron, the *succès de scandale* of the 'eighteen-teens' is formally present here, but Keats, of the same generation, is much more *à propos*. For example, his 'Ode' 'To Autumn' (1819) correlates very interestingly with *Persuasion* (published 1817), which is also 'Autumnal', but so determined, like the Keats poem, not to succumb to the mode of elegy which the subject might seem to make inevitable ('counteracting the sweets of poetical despondence and meaning to have Spring again' [p. 83]), that in each case this appears to become the subject of the work itself. Indeed the penumbra of pathos which Keats's early death throws over his late work has a counterpart in the effect of our knowledge of Jane's illness and premature death on our contemplation of *Persuasion* (and particularly perhaps in its scorn for exhibitionistic invalidism).

Jane Austen's work in general is 'mythopoeic' in concerning itself with elites and hierarchies, but insofar as it relates the idea of hierarchy to the idea of class it finds the two not to be 'congruent' – an idea which surfaces with greater force here. Contemplating his navel, Sir Walter finds the naval an improper way of bringing persons of obscure birth into undue distinction. Seamen, it seems, finding the hierarchy is rigged, hasten to swarm up the social rigging. In *Persuasion*, notions of necessary and painful change, the quitting of Kellynch Hall being the initial moot point here, make the novel surprisingly comparable to Keats's 'Hyperion' (version 1 drafted 1818, the year after *Persuasion* was published). There is a parallel between the 'ousting of the gentry' theme in one work with the supersession or superannuation of old 'gods' by new in the other.

In a way 'gods', more or less antique creations (Anne's snobbish sister Mary, forever putting her linguistic foot in it, 'never thinks much of your new creations' [p. 75]), are productive of and produced by 'supreme fictions' from Homer to Hammer. As such, they are bound, or doomed, to seem more than a little like high-ranking humans, social 'Titans', while classic godhead, like gentry status, equally unavoidably, brings imputations or overtones of *leisure* and *narcissism*, so that there is something 'Olympian' about Mrs. Clay's characterization of the gentry as 'those who are not obliged to follow any [profession]'(p. 25). This is an apparently favourable, indeed sycophantic pronouncement, appropriate to a cupbearer, which looks, given the ideological swaying and pitching of this narrative, as if perilously easy to transpose or turn seamy side out – and thus to end as critique or righteous *ressentiment.*

Certainly Sir Walter Elliot's sterling incapacity and conceited self-regard seem to be correlated with his absurd over-emphasis on the hereditary principle itself, so that there is a certain rapport with Tom Paine's attack on the repressive and destructive effects of the 'hereditary' view of society. Jane Austen's previous novels were in any case Greek gifts to Toryism, and to her traditional critical reproduction. They seem, in words of Fredric Jameson which are all the more tellingly apposite for *not* being used of 'Jane', to be 'tending to embarrass and compromise even those on whose behalf they seem to testify'.[10]

In *Persuasion*, however, matters are taken a good deal further. There is something quietly frantic about the way in which Sir Walter turns to the hereditary principle in an obsessive 'legitim-ation exercise' which negates the point it might be supposed to establish. Indeed, his abrupt departure from his personal Valhalla, Kellynch Hall, has unavoidable symbolic overtones, rather like an ironic version of Hyperion's supersession in the Keats poem:

So on our heels a fresh perfection treads.[11]

The mode of epic, of heroism which may be literally warlike or involve merely a struggle with 'weak' impulses, resists the mode of elegy here, partly because there is something inherently wrong with 'poetical despondence' (p. 83), but also because it is alleged to be inapposite. But, in *Persuasion*, the sense that the altering social dispensation is *not* one to be regretted is itself painful to Anne, chief 'focalizer' here, and on hand to add the necessary peroration, which concedes that 'they were gone who deserved not to stay, and that Kellynch-hall had passed into better hands than its owners' (p. 119).

Formally the substituted 'Apollo' (for Sir Walter's 'Hyperion'), is Admiral Croft – with faintly comic overtones. Indeed, the 'mythic' resonance here has a positively Joycean ring, since plain-spoken Croft 'wants manner' and outrages the gentry code which emphasizes manner, or manners. But the Admiral is not insensitive; Sir Walter, on the other hand, is. It is a deftly managed ideological 'turn' in itself that, while his manners are not those of a gentleman (not of a *tone* to suit the ultra-Burkist Lady Russell [p. 120]), they in no way diminish our sense of his hale concern for others. As a happy warrior, in Wordsworth's not-so-happy phrase, happily anticipating another war (p. 69), he might be thought to bring his own ideological problems. Strict comparison with Sir Walter's fading feudalism temporarily forestalls the reader's mutiny.

Perhaps a better candidate for Apollo here, though, is Anne's former suitor Wentworth, irresistibly *emergent* where Sir Walter(s) have been *dominant* but threaten to become merely *residual,* to evoke the well-known terms and discussion of these concepts by Raymond Williams.[12] Concepts and ideologies as well as particular characters ensure that the novel resists its own elegiac overtones. Its love theme is interwoven with a sense of its political bearings. It asks to be read in the light of its *resistance* to the regretful plangencies that an (intelligent) commentator like Monaghan sees in it, and very much overemphasizes in it, as it braces itself to be 'ever-changing, living in change',[13] like late Keats.

Emotions, then, are linked to ideologies in *Persuasion* in a peculiarly intimate way. It begins in pain, not only with Anne's painful rejection of Wentworth, but the cleverly compounded awareness that this rejection has been a function of the Burkean attitudes and axioms of Lady Russell, together with the awareness that her gentry family is in fact mean-spirited and in this vital sense actually *socially inadequate.* If, as Burke claimed, 'persons must now support places, and not places persons,' in Anne's family she presents the idea of the *ideologically insupportable* as *socially insufferable* in their 'heartless elegance' (p. 213), a phrase containing its own oxymoronic shock, since elegance has previously had a highly positive inflection for 'Jane Austen'.

There is, equally, an ideological 'turn' here if we consider the Freudian idea, *avant la lettre*, of the 'Family Romance' projected so strongly in Elizabeth's marital elevation in *Pride and Prejudice*. Here it is Anne's gentry family, ignoble in its alleged nobility, which is inadequate for the heroine, while a sense of protection, trust, being valued, comes from the *déclassés*, the penurious Croft and Harville types. These are naval personages defined by Sir Walter as 'persons of obscure birth brought into undue distinction' (p. 24) by events which (presumably) have had a good deal to do with rendering his position untenable and his situation insupportable. People, even textual ones, don't merely represent ideologies, but in *Persuasion* people are close to being ideological vectors or pointers at times. For example, Anne's fancying herself a particular 'favourite' (p. 120) of Mrs Croft has the force of a specifically ideological 'reaffiliation'. In the novel's highly conscious handling of continuity and rupture, adhesion and disconnection, Mrs Croft is in the rough-hewn mode of the protectively maternal, while Lady Russell is a rival mother-substitute or Matron after the manner of the *ancien régime*.

Keats in 'Hyperion' charges the position of the obsolescent deities with a good deal of pathos, and the sense of tension in the artistic position is a key to his relative success. Here too, we can see things partly in a split-level way, and the *ancien régime* cast(e) of thought is seen sympathetically. Wentworth, the 'new man' may be indignant that Benwick, a 'clever man, a reading man' (p. 172), should throw himself away on thoughtless Louisa, and be rather 'pertickular about the schoolmaster' (p. 53) for 'hopeless' Dick Musgrove, but it is Lady Russell who actually gets 'all the new publications' (p. 138). (Might they perhaps include the novels of Miss Austen?) She speaks to a script of education as well as gentility which can hardly be discarded. Also focalized by Anne is that 'pain' which is 'severe in its kind' (p. 119) when Anne is forced to concede that in the heartlessly elegant persons of elder sister Elizabeth and Sir Walter, 'they were gone who deserved not to stay' (p. 119), and this can be seen to correspond with the wound, the trauma which 'Jane Austen' inflicts on her authorial self in 'evicting the gentry'.

Certainly Sir Walter may be seen as nothing more than an *unrepresentative instance* of *genteel incompetence* where matters are unluckily brought to a head by *fiscal incontinence*. Nevertheless, Sir Walter's plight seems to have a symbolically concessive 'inflection'. It concedes, that is, to the 'unfeudal tone of the present day', a tone perhaps personified by Admiral Croft, a 'risen-through-the-ranks' type whose 'manners were not of a *tone* to suit Lady Russell' (p. 120). You could say, possibly with some amusement, that the word *tone* itself has become something of an ideological battleground. Perhaps, indeed, 'tone' has actually been routed (it would only entail 'heartless elegance' again, perhaps), and warm-hearted Crofts and Harvilles shall prevail against it. Any sense of romantic 'affiliation' to the Great House culture of Pemberley, Donwell and Mansfield has gone, although it can hardly be denied that ideological shuffling and 'recuperation' continues, including regret for the loss of 'the duties and dignities of the resident landholder' (p. 130).

Indeed, at the cruellest possible estimate, it might even be argued that 'Jane' stumbles out of the shrubbery of ghastly effete gentry snobbery into a road which leads to the Nazis at the level of their own self-representations. She certainly writes some glorious 'publicity material' for 'happy warriors'. Yet this might be more sympathetically discerned as a Hegelian sense of *morale* which only the proximity or prospect of death will fail to annul. The position, argued in the *Philosophy of Right* (1821), is nicely summarized by Francis Fukuyama:

> Hegel understood that the need to feel pride in one's humaneness would not necessarily be satisfied by the 'peace and prosperity' of the end of history. Men would face constant danger of degeneration from citizens to mere *bourgeois* ... The ultimate crucible of citizenship therefore was and would remain the willingness to die for one's country: the state would have to require military service and continue to fight wars. This aspect of Hegel's thought has led to the charge that he was a militarist. But he never glorified war for its own sake ... war was important for its secondary effects on character and community. Hegel believed that without the possibility of war and the sacrifices demanded by it, men would grow soft and self-absorbed; society would degenerate into a morass of selfish hedonism and community would ultimately dissolve ...[14].

Persuasion, then, is even more 'visibly ideological' than its predecessors. There should be no prizes for noticing this, but the forces of resistance to accepting the implications of this are strong indeed.

Lady Russell, for example, whose large, slow reconnoitring is like that of a worthy institution (or warship) which has failed to move with the times, or tides, is at once laudable *and* culpable. She is a mellow, quite sympathetic embodiment of the impulse to *cleave*, sc. to what Keats called 'faded hierarchies' (sc. *anciens régimes)*, whose hold on the imagination exceeds either their benevolence or their efficacy.[15] What she represents may be fairly rendered, but it is still more significant that the 'object of her "belief"', Sir Walter, is shown to be an unworthy receptacle for her veneration. He is unworthy of the deference with which, in her slowness to imagine or contemplate change, she contemplates him.

In any Battle of the Books, Lady Russell would emerge victorious here. One might even ask if bookishness itself is not being impugned as somehow politically 'blinding', so that 'Jane' may actually be seen to anticipate such expressions of wholesale irritation with prose fiction in such a recent work as Lennard Davis's *Resisting Novels* on the grounds, roughly speaking, that they tend to, or even seek to, prevent change. At any rate, not only for the reader is it plain that Sir Walter 'stands confirmed in full stupidity',[16] as, for pragmatically effective and unadmiring Admiral Croft it was equally obvious that Sir Walter 'would never set the Thames on fire' (p. 35). Yet, for learned Lady Russell he was still, if not an 'aweful object', at least an object of solicitude. Indeed, just as Lady Russell, on the distaff side of the gentry 'party' towers over dull Sir Walter, Mrs Croft is depicted as a keener wit (p. 90) than her bluff, hearty spouse (though neither has the status or the 'occupational outlet for talent' of the men).

Indeed, femininity is here a 'site of ideological tension or contradiction'. It is surely significant that 'Ideal Husband' Wentworth seems to be seriously confused on these matters. One might say that in the presentation of Wentworth, Freud's notorious 'What does a woman want?' is already subject to proto-feminist critique. Even in the apparently enlightened Wentworth such questions are precipitated by *male* confusion and *male* 'aporia' about this. What, it's implied, does a man want a woman to be? is the relevant question here (implying the correct articulation of gender dominance). The answer, even for such an apparent paragon as Wentworth is, it appears, *simultaneous incompatible things.*

It is perhaps a necessary defensiveness which makes Wentworth think that Anne's original refusal of him was from 'weakness', as 'the effect of overpersuasion' (p. 62). Logically, of course, her *acceptance* of him would *also* have been the effect of a persuasion which might itself have been considered 'weakness' by others.[17] He simultaneously considers her as weak for having refused him, continues to cherish an image of her as ideal, while at the same time excluding her from further consideration. This is understandable, yet he still seems confused about the attitudes that he either requires of women or that they require in order to 'be' women – or do we mean *ladies*?

His dislike of having women on board ship seems to say so, is perhaps an indicator of an ambiguous ('sexist') deference. This posture of his, at any rate, draws the fire of his sister, the formidable Mrs Croft, who makes staunchly Wollestonecraftian points to the effect that women should be considered as 'rational creatures' (p. 69). Mrs Croft is given a good deal of moral gunnery here, and we are well within the ambit of Margaret Kirkham's lively attempt to unite Jane Austen with Mary Wollstonecraft against Romantic 'gallantry', and specifically Rousseauvian postures.[18]

Wentworth seems to be paying a naval officer's ambiguous homage to weakness, while his imagination continues to dwell on the biblical motto, 'out of the strong came forth sweetness'. (Convinced that women should be experts in not being persuaded, and inspired by happy memories of male camaraderie, he comes close to the exasperated Professor Higgins asking 'Why can't a woman be more like a man?')

Promoting the headstrong, tomboyish Louisa, Wentworth is Frankenstein-like in 'creating' a monster of self-will as an icon to fill the void left by Anne (until a blow to Louisa's head brings him to his senses). Simultaneously, in a scene of *peripeteia* and comic metamorphosis at Lyme Regis, Anne becomes a kind of captain, ordering demoralized naval officers, now rather 'out of their element', about. It dawns, perhaps, on Wentworth, that she may make an admirable 'first mate', for the second time. Certainly she seems an admirable compromise solution here, able to take charge selflessly where necessary when all else (i.e. masculinity) fails. Anne and Wentworth, experiencing desire as lack, take up with hypothetical partners who supply what they might be supposed to want, the latter with husband-hunting butterfly Louisa, the former with the poetical, self-indulgently sorrowing young widower Benwick. Thanks to a smart, violent bit of plot-wrenching which might incite the envy of a Thomas Hardy, the nervous ('feminine') Benwick and bold Louisa are thrown convalescently together to enjoy 'the sweets of poetical despondence' (p. 83), just what Anne is trying to avoid – after the manner of the Keats of the 'Ode to Autumn' and of 'Hyperion'.

In fact it transpires that Benwick's *claims* to sensibility are themselves a radical *defect* of sensibility. (He tries to get Harville to reinscribe a miniature of himself for Louisa which was originally intended for the delectation of Harville's sister Fanny [pp. 218–19].) 'For the gods approve/The depth, and not the tumult, of the soul' might be Wordsworth's reproof to both of them. Thus, when Benwick sits at the elbow of the now suitably nervous ('feminized') Louisa reading verses, he has obviously got the wrong poet in his hands: Wordsworth would be a 'safer' (to use Anne's emergency services criterion [p. 98]) influence than the 'dangerous' Byron here.

Hazlitt said of Wordsworth that his muse was a 'levelling' one. Abusive reviewing of the deeper poet confines Anne and Benwick to poetry written by Lords, which turns out to be bad poetry written by Lords, as Keats had the 'giant nerve' to point out.[19] But if Anne's worries about the effects of poets on Widower Benwick's shallow melancholia are anything to go by, 'Jane' may be making a not dissimilar point. His self-indulgence led him to Byron or Byron led him to self-indulgence.

We may still feel that Austen's imagination, for what the idea is worth, is 'hierarchical'. Yet, in *Persuasion* at any rate, she provides the materials for a thorough deconstruction of the idea that class levels as such enshrine more than the processes of ideological mystification which perpetrates (but will not necessarily perpetuate) a Sir Walter.

As we have seen, his insecurely narcissistic fascination with Debrett's is brilliantly *à propos*. As a sacred text, it 'underwrites his existence'. *Persuasion*, on the other hand, does not. Indeed, and rather after the manner of recent critique, it 're-writes *English*' so as to destabilize and marginalize his position and his assumptions. The historical irony which underlies *Persuasion* is that mobilizing a military defence of the 'Burkean' society with its emphasis on tradition and stability has itself undermined the very 'stability' it was mobilized to maintain.

The author of *Persuasion*, then, undermines the authority of Debrett's. But it is interesting that, even for dimmish Sir Walter, reality was a 'scene of writing' in which Debrett's, that 'supreme fiction', could appease anxieties of 'person and situation'. It enabled, for example, himself, cold-hearted daughter Elizabeth, or the more insecurely snobbish Mary (the daughter who married Charles Musgrove after Anne turned down his offer to her), to despise *new creations*. Yet as itself a scene of writing, its plot resolved by Wentworth, pen in hand, silently scratching a subtext to Anne's dialogue with Harville about male versus female constancy, *Persuasion* itself is a 'new creation' mischievously bent on ruining the great work of time by casting doubt on 'old creations' and on 'attributing to *place* no sanctity'.[20] It also diagnoses a certain phallocracy at the scene of writing itself: 'the pen has been in [men's] hands,' as Anne observes, just at the culminating moment when, (perhaps by way of comic denouement), 'the pen falls from Wentworth's [hand]' (p. 220), and he is able, having reread the signs, to have Anne's at the second time of asking.

Yet, although *Persuasion* may seem to this extent highly encouraging as a 'scene of writing', it is not entirely clear that in it the pen is indeed mightier then the sword. Itself a war-scarred text, it might be said that it merely reinscribes 'genealogy' in terms of new points of 'origin' by the warrior caste who supplant the effete modern representatives of a formerly dominant warrior caste. There is also, although there may be a certain authorial cunning about this, enough ideological leeway to keep ['(His)Tory'] readers comfortable or at least quiescent. And of course Sir Walter is formally reproved, not for being a country gentleman, but for being a bad one, notably unalert to 'the duties and dignity of the resident landholder' (p. 130).

But such gestures of ideological recuperation or containment are in tension with other points which have put earlier 'keywords' under severe pressure. The emphasis on 'manners' and 'elegance' of an Emma, the mannerly musings of Edmund in *Mansfield Park*, the vigorous, potentially demeaning emphasis on expressions like 'gentleman-like' even of an Elizabeth in *Pride and Prejudice*, are all subject to a flick of 'transposition' corresponding to what Wallace Stevens in his last poem called 'something like / A new knowledge of reality'.[21]

But *Persuasion* may still, in its 'textual politics', be unreassuring. As Mary Poovey reminds us, it celebrates the social group responsible for the defeat of Napoleon,[22] while it simultaneously tilts at the gentry caste which is inclined to look down its collective nose at its benefactors. But 'Jane Austen' may then be said, in Blakean parlance, to admire those who pursue what Blake calls 'corporeal war'[23] for financial inducements. (As we have seen, in general 'Jane' seems, much of the time, to be a bit of a Blakean, perhaps most obviously here in her treatment of Anne's attitude to William Walter Elliot, with his smooth impenetrable mask of gentility.) 'The peace has come too soon for that younker,' observes Admiral Croft, breezily (p. 161). Perhaps a 'younker' is not quite a *Junker*, but either he loves war or he loves gold: 'How fast I made money in her', observes Wentworth of his sloop (p. 66); while the Admiral has sanguinary as well as sanguine hopes that 'we' may 'have the good luck to see another war' (p. 69).

Still, accession to the idea that preoccupation with social forms and rank is 'only a shell, a husk of meaning', is a considerable ideological advance. In particular, William Walter Elliot, 'completely the gentleman in manner' comes off very badly by comparison with plain-spoken Croft (who in earlier novels might have appeared a mannerless monster). And Anne herself is not merely a 'feminine lead' whose fulfilment through her love for Wentworth one can identify with. She 'votes' for the 'new men', identifies with them as a social group against her own caste in an apparent reversal of Freudian 'Family Romance', despite 'shows of deference' to Burkean notions most gracefully purveyed by Lady Russell. Cordelia-like, Anne fails to flatter her father, unlike the tirelessly sycophantic Mrs Clay. Even her opening gambit, to the effect that 'sailors work hard enough for their comforts' (p. 24), may be construed as a genteel kind of mutiny.

This, however, is something of an aporia. When she claims that *sailors* work hard enough for their comforts, she must be understood to mean 'naval officers', but the apparent inclusiveness of the word creates a 'classless society' image which contradicts the 'faineant caste' basis of English domestic society. At the same time, though, it naively overlooks the peremptory élitism which must prevail at sea, the disproportionate awards for the officer class, and the fact that 'sailors' strongly suggests 'other ranks' rather than the officers here. Apposite, perhaps, to the particular narrative voice which picks up on Anne's Wentworth-worshipping partisanship, the final and famous peroration (p. 237) about sailors being 'as distinguished in [their] domestic virtues as in [their] national importance' is troubled by similar considerations. Either you reduce 'other ranks' to 'parergonal' irrelevance, a severely ideological move, or you raise the spectre of the 'girl in every port' stereotype to heckle the carefully wrought rhetorical triumphalism (naval and marital). All this is also quite apart from the fact that 'national importance' is affected by technological advances and developments no less than by the whims of statesmen.

Also (say) John Bayley's reference to the 'proverbial unreliableness of Jack ashore'[24] is a decided euphemism: when a ship docked after a lengthy voyage it was common practice for it to be met by boat-loads of prostitutes, as the 1822 'Statement of Certain immoral Practices in H.M. Ships' reveals:

> Let those who have never seen a ship of war picture to themselves a rather large low room ... with five hundred men and probably three or four hundred women of the vilest description shut up in it, and giving way to every excess of debauchery that the grossest passions of human nature can lead them to.[25]

Wentworth is hardly likely to be 'in there', but then Anne's use of the word 'sailors' can be seen as an aporetic attempt at an imaginary resolution of real class contradictions. However unsnobbish Wentworth is, he is to be sharply distinguished from the brutes in the long low room who have not made twenty thousand pounds out of the war (see p. 74). Thus it is that much of the ideological force of Anne's mutiny against the status quo is lost. I agree that if her/the narrator's[26] remarks comprehend only the officer class, then it is a little unfair to heckle the Austenian peroration with uncomfortable reminders of the 'girl in every port' stereotype; but if 'sailors' means only 'officers', the democratic perspectives the novel opens upon are lost.

But if 'levelling-down', even in *Persuasion*, has its limits, Anne's desire to be 'reborn' into a warm, protective social group is strong enough to cope with penury (at least as an idea). The gratifying re-affiliation brings thoughts of claiming kin with social inferiors – quite a revolutionary move, if itself contradicted by the nature of marriage itself as an exclusionary rather than communal arrangement. No doubt Mrs Bennet would have become almost as ecstatic over Wentworth's 'pin-money' as she was over Darcy's.

There seems to be a deliberate retraction of the priggish, repressed Fanny Price's wincing in the face of the small naval rooms of Portsmouth, where the same mistaken impression that a 'living room' is too small to be anything but a passageway to something decent becomes a tribute to the Harvilles for 'inviting from the heart' (p. 96), i.e. unlike the hosts of the select parties of Bath arranged by Sir Walter and his cronies, they have nothing to be 'vainly ostentatious' about.

But if Anne's 'acceptance' of poverty comprehends her old acquaintance, Mrs Smith, whom she refuses, much to Sir Walter's annoyance (pp. 149–50), to drop, despite her reduced circumstances in Bath, *Persuasion* remains a tale of 'upward mobility' with which the reader can identify. Wentworth is now a war-rich 'catch'. 'This August is like a woman/Who gets men without moving', is a strange moment in Robert Lowell's last collection, *Day by Day*. Anne is understood to have reached October, her tale, in Stevens' idiom, an 'Aurora of Autumn'. Perhaps Lowell is just defining the traditional female role anyway, but Anne in particular is a silent female sufferer in a world made for noisy, bustling men.

She seems, though, to be awarded many 'points' for this very characteristic. As we have seen, unlike many-decibelled Louisa Musgrove, and much like her repressed predecessor, Fanny Price, she feels much in silence, tempted to smile by the absurdities round about, as well she might be – but the trait is not reassuring. It might give some colour to D.H. Lawrence's accusation that 'Jane' is strong in the realm of 'snobbish, knowing apartness',[27] especially where Anne herself has a Blake-like prejudice in favour of 'bursts of feeling' (p. 152) which overcome good manners in the cause of spontaneity.

In almost ludicrous antithesis, the Musgrove girls, softened versions of Julia and Maria Bertram, are as noisy as mariners and headstrong enough to be beyond the persuadability that, for Wentworth, has ruined his suit to Anne – although they are pliable enough to be what he seems to want them to be. And, unlike Anne, they broadcast feeling. When Wentworth claims that he might have been 'lost' in obscure circumstances and 'in a sloop' (p. 66) and thus commemorated only 'in a small paragraph at one corner of the newspapers', 'Anne's shudderings were to herself alone: but the Miss Musgroves could be as open as they liked, in their exclamations of pity and horror' (p. 66).

The problem here is that Anne in her very 'femininity' forgoes the Blake-like warmth and expansive spontaneity she claims to value in others, for example when she notes that the ultra-'correct' William Walter Elliot has no 'bursts of feeling' (p. 152) to testify to a personal warmth.

As we have seen, narrative jocosity as well as the desire to have Wentworth confront Anne again yokes noisy, tomboyish Louisa to the 'too piano' (p. 163), faintly feminine, Benwick – if only after she has shed her noisiness and is returned to what we might fear to be a properly feminine nervousness.

Louisa and Benwick are at once defectives to measure Anne and Wentworth by, and providers of a touch of narrative tension, though not much, about who is going to be together at the end of this particular narrative dance. Irony, again, takes charge. Man of Sensibility and poetry-reader, Widower Benwick forgets his Fanny Harville and 'sits at [Louisa's] elbow, reading verses' (p. 206), no doubt redolent of the 'sweets of poetical despondence' we have seen Anne struggling to refuse. Wentworth, the naval man whose 'nerves [have] never flinched at slaughter', presumably, flees igno-miniously into the country, apparently compromised by Louisa. But he is actually aroused by Anne and specifically by the admiration she has attracted from the fine gentleman at Lyme who turns out to be potentially kissing cousin William Walter Elliot. He is a man to whom Anne should, for all his moral turpitude – so melo-dramatically portrayed by Mrs Smith (p. 187) – be profoundly grateful for kindling Wentworth's 'jealousy' (p. 180).

Wentworth's desire for Anne is desire aroused by the idea of the desire of an 'Other'. The renewal of his addresses might be called 'a repetition which is not one'. In the meantime he has been able to make mental notes, not only comparing Anne with the other ladies who present themselves to him, but of Anne's continuing desir-ability to other men, including Charles Musgrove, who proposed and was rejected, Benwick who recited and was encouraged, and William Walter Elliot, who followed and flattered and met with some temporary success.

All this contrives to refute the final 'scene of writing' in which Wentworth textualizes his love for Anne as a constancy (just as she elaborates the theme to Harville about women being more constant because they have nothing else to think about). He is, of course, writing a necessarily repressive history of his love. In fact J. Hillis Miller's sense of Derrida's telepathy may be excessive,[28] but in his essay on 'Freud and the Scene of Writing', his insight that 'writing is unthinkable without repression' corresponds exactly to the way in which Wentworth's 'sincere' professions of constancy are crossed by the tale told here of the vagaries of his variously vectored desire. As his passionately scratched letter speaks only of a conventional constancy all too palpably ruptured by temporary attachments to others, he writes a version of himself which is created for the occasion. He thus confirms Derrida's idea that 'we are written only by writing' (with its converse 'we are *only* "written" by writing').

Harold Bloom, in his admiring reference to the Derrida text, may be right to point out that Derrida's scene of writing is insufficiently primal. But Derrida also cites Freud's *Problem of Anxiety*. This does sound pretty primal, and in particular sets a very primal scene indeed for the scene of writing in *Persuasion:*

> If writing – which consists in allowing a fluid to flow out from a tube upon a piece of white paper – has acquired the symbolic meaning of coitus ... then writing ... will be abstained from, because it is as though forbidden sexual behaviour were thereby being indulged in.[29]

We have now reached the 'primal scene' of Freudian rhetoric in all its dismaying reductivism. It jars with the genteel trappings of Austen's fiction, although they do disguise their own incisiveness of inquisition into the vagaries of desire and the insidiousnesses of 'gender construction'. But if Anne is indeed a surrogate 'Jane Austen', what could exceed the appositeness of this strong silent type who steps forward to privilege writing over speech?

As for the 'gender construction', the moralistic point that Benwick and Louisa are self-indulgent, one in the *piano* and one in the *forte* mode, comes close to implying that Benwick is a little too like a woman and Louisa a little more like a man than is good for her. (She might be said to have 'fallen' *for* Benwick.) But at least with reference to the navy (which serves as a touchstone, even a kind of 'church' here) it's clear that even a woman may have *anima naturaliter marina* (while some sailors [Dick Musgroves] may be spiritual landlubbers).

Benwick and Louisa, then, have overdetermined functions, and do not merely suggest the possibility of 'queer unions' (in Hardy's idiom), blessedly averted, for Anne and Wentworth, the happy couple. But is the book, for all that, merely a 'thinking woman's' Mills & Boon, where all the nice girls like a sailor in the form of a naval officer who has made twenty thousand pounds?

I have been suggesting that the answer lies in the acutely inflected sense of an ideological drama, a drama which is a function of both theoretical and historical considerations. Even character is a 'function' of this ideological backdrop. The book, I've been suggesting, is a refraction of those 'war-manacled minds' which

Erdman, as cited by Claudia Johnson,[30] speaks of, its achievement inseparable from its provocativeness in this respect. Empson thought Milton great in the sense that a Benin (African) sculpture might be said to be – brilliant but 'savage', alien. (John Carey's claim that *Paradise Lost* is 'great' because 'objectionable' is a weak echo of the idea.) The Austen text also has, at times, a slightly breathtaking barbarity and 'otherness'.

We might, for example, consider the chess-like oppositions and antitheses in the positions the characters occupy in the drama of *ancien régime* and 'new creations': there's 'inaction man' Sir Walter and 'action man' Admiral Croft; well-read, Burkean Lady Russell, and many-voyaged, roughing-it Mrs Croft, with her 'keener powers' (p. 90) than her bluff, man's man spouse; Elizabeth ('heartless elegance' [p. 213]) and the 'inviting from the heart' (p. 96) Harvilles; deep-feeling Wentworth and Benwick's luxuriating emotional shallows; quiet reflective Anne and rompish Louisa; introvert Benwick and hearty Charles; whingeing Mary and sprightly, impoverished Mrs Smith and the like.

But the most offensive of these antitheses is that of Wentworth and Dick Musgrove, yoked by *violence* together, one might say, both in the navy and in Mrs Musgrove's imagination (broaching complacently the idea that Dick would have been such another as Wentworth is [p. 64]). This is reread as an equally raging contrast in Anne's Wentworth-worshipping imagination, more at home with Wordsworth's happy warriors than his idiot boys:

> the real circumstances of this pathetic family history were, that the Musgroves had the misfortune of a very troublesome, hopeless, son; and had the good fortune to lose him before he reached his twentieth year; that he had been sent to sea, because he was stupid and unmanageable on shore; that he had been very little cared for at any time by his family, though quite as much as he deserved; seldom heard of, and scarcely at all regretted, when the intelligence of his death had worked its way to Uppercross, two years before. He had, in fact … been nothing better than a thick-headed, unfeeling, unprofitable Dick Musgrove, who had never done anything to entitle himself to more than the abbreviation of his name, living or dead. (p. 52)

This is the prelude to Mrs Musgrove's 'large, fat sighings' on a sofa – a sight that 'ridicule will seize' – eliciting solicitude for someone whom 'alive, no one had cared for' (p. 68), – precisely why he turned out as he did, and why we sympathize with Dick, especially as his epistolary comments are as pleasant and Wentworth-worshipping as Anne's own – 'A fine dashing fellow, only two pertikular about the schoolmaster' (p. 53), showing a generosity no one will visit on him, apparently. So sending the conjecturally degenerate Dick to Davy Jones's locker creates ambiguity instead of downrightness: we may even associate him with Jane's idiot brother George, rejected by his family and taken care of by the Cullums of Monk Sherborne.[31] (In such a case the aggressive rhetoric is 'inverted' guilt.)

Yet the passage and the incident remain distinctly shocking. If a remark in a famous cognate passage in the letters about casualties of war ('thank heavens one cares for none of them!') contains, as Hugh Kenner has argued, 'more wisdom than callousness',[32] then those about Dick Musgrove seem to contain rather more callousness than wisdom.

This peevish outburst at continuing parental solicitude for the transparently useless is protected from the reader's mutiny as a kind of consideration focalized through Anne, and 'Jane Austen' is 'in the clear', although the narrator's support for Anne is obvious. The unattractive creative logic runs as follows: The overwhelming event of the recent past is the saving of England largely for the benefit of a relatively unappreciative gentry by a band of men, larger than life, or even myth, so that to compare, say, Keats's Apollo to Austen's Wentworth is 'very much to the honour of both', but rather more to the honour of Apollo. Wentworth and his like are sublime creations, much above those of Debrett's.

In a sense the whole game, this game of 'just gaming' in some serious sense, is 'recognizing the god'. This is a tale of how to recognize the uncanniness of Wentworth's canniness: failure, or perhaps refusal, to recognize the 'saviour-figure'; or perhaps *Persuasion* is 'about' *mis*recognition, the following of false gods – in this sense the secular *Persuasion* is a religious text through and through.

Who to bow to around here? Sir Walter and Elizabeth abase themselves before disagreeable, insignificant Lady Dalrymple, Lady Russell defers to the 'full stupidity' of Sir Walter, common Mrs Clay engages in some initially effective grovelling before all of them, while sister Mary, tellingly the most insecure, is perhaps supremely blind to everything but sheer rank.

And Wentworth in particular is given two significant moments of repudiation of this rampantly snobbish ethos. On the walk to humble Winthrop, when Mary boasts that she has scarcely ever entered the home of the poor Hayters, she receives from Wentworth an 'artificial, assenting smile' (p. 84), followed by a look of contempt which only Anne notices. Forced to hide feeling, Anne and Wentworth are already, as it were, secret sharers, their marriage already consummated as part of a war on such 'false consciousness'. The 'libidinal investment' which the reader is 'forced' to make in wishing for Anne and Wentworth to be united, or reunited, is at one with the fact that they are already 'at one' in an 'ideological' rightness which no one else comes near to sharing.

Persuasion's last laugh is that just as the Bristol voice of Mrs Elton deploring the low-key nuptials of Knightley and Emma was its very celebration, the crass socialite vision of Mary adds the final touches, as she uses Wentworth to bait the lowly social niches of Hayters and Musgroves. She winces only at the 'restoration' (ironic word?) of Anne to 'the rights of seniority' and the ownership of 'a very pretty landaulette' (p. 235). A 'hermeneutics of suspicion' might whisper that Mary is indeed there as a sort of 'compensatory' principle, able to orchestrate crasser gratifications than Anne the heroine would be allowed to. In much the same manner, Mrs Bennet's joy over 'pin money' etc. lets the reader wallow a little in Elizabeth's lottery-winning in *Pride and Prejudice* in a way the severe couple in question would hasten to discountenance – despite the fact that Elizabeth herself had once let herself go with a joke about the glories of Pemberley.

For Marx, social being was held to 'determine consciousness'. But it all depends how determined you are. Mary seems determined to determine social being itself. That 'social being' is a fluctuating concept is imperiously determined by *Persuasion* itself, which is apparently determined to play illuminating games with phrases like 'man of consequence', 'nothing but himself to recommend him' (p. 30), 'with that [i.e. property] he will never be a contemptible man,' (p. 75), etc.[33]

'Man of consequence' is a phrase ironically used of Sir Walter's self-assessment as he moves with stultified and stultifying snobbery and heartless elegance from private party to private party in the littleness of an effete and 'superstructural' town. In context he is himself of course of supreme *inconsequence*, a fact writ large from his being surrounded by war heroes who have been about matters of some consequence. The man with 'nothing but himself to recommend him' (p. 30) was Wentworth himself under the shuddering contemplation of the misguided Lady Russell, a phrase which the text once more hastens to surround with happy irony, as, having only himself to recommend him, he promptly becomes a war-rich commander.

Of course once Wentworth, originally despised, has shown his mettle, he is now ironically counterpointed with the high-ranking nonentities of Bath that Sir Walter and Elizabeth delight to follow and flatter. But Wentworth of course, *has* as well as *is*, no matter how Anne might protest the irrelevance of this. Charles Musgrove uncovers the values of the time in saying that, as Charles Hayter has something to inherit, with his land and property 'he will never be a contemptible man' (p. 75), making his acquisitions bespeak personal qualities, and thus exposing, once more, a kind of 'false consciousness'. This must be a phrase for ironic contemplation given that 'Jane' gave us, inter alia, *Mansfield Park,* with its booby Rushworth (who, if not 'rich beyond the dreams of avarice', was at least rich enough to inspire them).

Wentworth has another chance to show his mettle, when his response to an invitation card to a private party (graciously presented to him by Elizabeth) is meant to atone for past patronage. Mary, always at hand to misconstrue, assumes he must be delighted (a fairly crude touch, this, although it also shows how we tend to interpret in a way that confirms our assumptions about the assumptions that underlie the behaviour of others). But Anne, as usual, knows better, and is also on hand to construe correctly his 'contempt' (p. 214). The card and the parties signify an exclusiveness which makes to define an élite. Yet Anne and Wentworth know that the élite is elsewhere, defined, as it were, by kind hearts rather than coronets, by sterling qualities rather than mere money.

This is a bit too cosy, though, to be any kind of peroration here. It is exciting to realize that the supposedly non-political Jane Austen was operating all manner of ideological levers, pulleys and switches, but the results derive from ideological tensions rather than resolutions. Finally they resist any easy imputation of simple political correctness. *Persuasion* seems contaminated by what it seems to oppose. For example Sir Walter, in a sustained and comic tirade, attacks Anne's incomprehensible visits to sick impecunious commoner Mrs Smith ('Mrs Smith, such a name!' [p. 150]). Anne muses, again in that silent privacy of hers (no bursts of feeling from her of the sort she requires from others, apparently) that 'Mrs Smith was not the only widow in Bath between thirty and forty, with little to live on, and no sirname of dignity' (p. 150).

This is a reference to Mrs Clay, in league with William Walter Elliot and in pursuit of Sir Walter. It's a pyrrhic victory, though, as she is now a prisoner of his snobbish terms of reference, not realizing, that 'names are nothing' (Derrida has a powerful passage on the 'violence' of naming). To similar effect is the narrator's attempt to muster a bit more indignation against Sir Walter and Elizabeth's neglect of Lady Russell and Anne, describing them as 'bestowing [their] affection and confidence on one who ought to have been nothing to her but the object of distant civility' (p. 21).

The last phrase is a chilling reminder of the tone of British society with its finely calibrated concern. Ideologically, then, once more, the text is 'vectored' in an ambiguous way. The argument 'against' Mrs Clay sounds a bit like that used by Sir Walter against the navy as bringing 'persons of obscure birth into undue distinction' (p. 24), as well the argument against 'noticing' Mrs Smith.

Yet Sir Walter, in a sense, *justly* fears the new order, the new men that 'history' is bringing to prominence. He might be said in a piquantly emphatic sense *dimly* to apprehend Weber's point that established power is sustained only by subjective belief in its legitimacy. Sir Walter himself can hardly supply such sustenance, and this shows the text's 'deconstructive turn' towards the idea that such sustenance is no longer possible or desirable.

At the same time, though, we remain within the ambit of the satirical portrait of the stupid, snobbish landowner, the unrepresentative instance. If only, this reading says, Sir Walter would be more prudent, more cunning, could feign a little more concern for his tenants, be less showy, less extravagant, less self-indulgent – in a word, more bourgeois – then, perhaps, all would be well for him and his like. Yet, on the whole, and again surprisingly for those who like their Jane Austen Tory, the ideological inflection of the narrative (despite its 'unreassuring' aspects) does seem significantly concessive to Paine's sardonic remarks to the effect that

The aristocracy are not the farmers who work the land, and raise the produce, but are the mere consumers of the rent; and when compared with the active world are the drones, a seraglio of males, who neither collect the honey nor form the hive, but exist only for lazy enjoyment.[34]

It might be said that the novel's conservatism lies in the fact that a certain 'substance' is understood to be necessary for one to gain an entrée, not to Sir Walter's private parties, but *to the novel itself*. An exception here is the Harvilles, there to show naval solidarity and Wentworth's qualities, marginal but there (workmen appear briefly to admire Louisa's fall at the Cobb); but there's an emphasis, also, on a competitive ethos in which the weakest (i.e. Dick Musgrove *et hoc genus omne*) go to the wall.

It also has an undercurrent of deadly female competitiveness *for* men of success or consequence, attending the other competitiveness as a 'secondary' phenomenon. Anne herself is, in fact, 'at war' with the Musgrove girls for Wentworth – a disagreeable business, particularly as the Musgroves themselves are not at all disagreeable, unlike their prototypes, Maria and Julia in *Mansfield Park*. In fact even the narrator has to resort to violence to bring Wentworth to his senses, to make Louisa 'feminine' again, to 'promote' Anne to temporary captaincy (or perhaps 'first mate') and make her a help-meet for Wentworth in the mould of Mrs Croft, his sister. This is significant indeed, as Wentworth is an admirer of her match with the Admiral. Much revolves here upon Wentworth's likes, and what he likes best is the idea of a female so strong-willed that nothing apart from his own persuasion can persuade her to change her mind. The result is a knot of ironies the denouement will unravel.

Louisa's hubristic self-will (firmness) has earlier attracted the attention of Wentworth on the occasion of the walk to Winthrop. Louisa, he thinks, will be an anti-Anne in her utter unpersuadability, and he expatiates on the theme, unwittingly within earshot of Anne, in the course of which he elaborates what might be called the Parable of the Nut, in which a handsome specimen is said to be 'happy' because 'firm' (p. 86). 'Nut' is, interestingly, a colloquialism for 'head'; not a respectable one, of course, though it has been noted that, for example, the French word for head [*tête*] derives from the Latin *testa* (= pot), and must in its origin have been at least as slangy as the English word 'nut' (when used as a synonym for head).

The association of Louisa with the 'nut' having been made as firmly as the association with a certain intellectual vacuity, it is interesting to note that we are finally 'reassured' about Louisa in an unnaturally short paragraph informing us that

Louisa's limbs had escaped. There was no injury except to the head. (p. 109)

Suspiciously unelaborated, this seems positively to encourage the idea that nothing of great moment is involved, as an injury to Louisa's head was less worrying than one to her limbs: a headless Louisa would not be much worse off, but a limbless Louisa would be unthinkable. But Wentworth's unhappy attempt to symbolize Louisa's firmness in the excitingly singled-out nut, which achieves an unhappy and unintended appositeness, is also implicitly corrected by the references to that 'elasticity of mind' which makes passively heroic Mrs Smith 'like' Captain Harville, equally afflicted with poor health and penury from his active service.

Persuasion, then, retains 'objectionable' qualities, whether it may be said to be 'great' because it is 'objectionable' or not. We have come to expect such a work to be encouragingly suggestive in terms of a 'political unconscious', yet its political 'conscious' seems to be doing quite nicely as it is. Its treatment of desire also engenders a much less constricting perspective than its Mills and Boon aspect might have been felt to encourage, though its knowledge of the vagaries of desire might constitute its unconscious in the (Lacanian) sense of 'knowledge that can't tolerate one's knowing that one knows'.[35]

And if the 'classless society' image of the navy turns out to be another form of false consciousness, the image it provides of hearty democratic inclusiveness survives the naivety of commitment. This was inspired, perhaps, by Jane's Admiral brothers, to whom, indeed, the navy-intoxicated peroration may be addressed.

Although its political inflections are not quite those of the earlier 'mature' novels, *Persuasion* also encodes in an even more 'radical' way what may be implied about the other works: that is, however they may seem to be locked into an ever more refined examination of the 'ethical' in a manner seen by the late Raymond Williams as, inevitably, rather limiting,[36] they are so far from being the 'ideological vehicle' for 'concrete structures of power and domination', that we discover a good deal of a directly opposite tendency – discover it, that is, in what would at one time have been considered the most unlikely of places: the work of Jane Austen.

8
Props and Properties: Social Imaginaries in Recent Screen Adaptations

Curiously, although much is said of radical alternatives, not so much is said of doubts that may legitimately arise as to precisely which alternative that *is*. In this case we may suspect academic suspiciousness about the processes which put Austen, or what purports to be Austen, on screen. Are all such fuddy-duddy enemies of progress who rush to quell popular cultural initiatives with post-Leavisist ferocity? Do the forces that put 'Jane Austen' before so many more people than could have thought of her as a possible source of pleasure and 'profit' 'abide our question'?

It goes without saying that a particular kind of Janeite or Austen Industrialist to whom 'everything is grist', and to whom everything that may appear to boost 'Jane' cannot be bad, is also *sous rature*. (There is also a 'sort of "Cultural Studies"' perspective for which the text is a mere pretext, a score awaiting its performance, actually inferior, not merely anterior, to its transposition into screen presentation.) But if sixteen million British people switch on to see Elizabeth slalom round the obstacles which stand in the way of Darcy, or vice versa, can sixteen million Britons be wrong?

Well, they might be if 'Jane Austen' were utterly traduced in the process, or if it were, perhaps somewhat paradoxically, at work to put into circulation 'a crypto-feudal culture imposing idealized, mythologized versions of the national past from above'.[1] Against this, some commentators claim that heritage films may often 'ironize the caste culture of Old England' (Dave, p. 112), and it has also been argued that such representations are politically 'nomadic',[2] so that 'the nightmare of caste culture is dissolved by a playful retro style culture' (Samuel, p. 246).

If this were indeed the case, we might welcome all such efforts with open arms (or eyes). But while hoping it might be so, there are so many contra-indications here that such optimism sounds like *carte blanche* to *kitsch*, not to mention the crypto-feudalist conspiracy theory which makes the process sound a little less 'nomadic' than Raphael Samuel somewhat blithely assumed.

In general, heritage culture theories, which do tend to look like perfectly rational conspiracy theories, often seem to 'bracket' questions of local accomplishment and 'quality'. But, for example, the general release film of *Emma* was much less successful than the televised version of *Emma* for BBC television, and there is little doubt that this had everything to do with the ideological coefficients that the watchdogs of 'Heritage' are anxious to pinpoint. Although the superiority is partly 'technical' (for example, the use of the ironically 'hypothetical' flash-forward to present Emma's ideas of 'happy' marriages was brilliantly carried off in the BBC version and has no equivalent in the large-screen *Emma*), the ideological 'platform' is different.

The BBC version is 'British' in its incarnation of what Tom Nairn defines as a distinctively English Ideology, fruit of the highly mediated and unmodern English 'revolution', which precipitated an archaic caste system, and it was made quite clear that the motor of capitalism in England was not the bourgeoisie but aristocratic agrarians.[3] The general release version of Emma sat comfortably within a modern, quasi-American paradigm of class as 'status conferred by money', which caused it to lose interest in many of *Emma*'s preoccupations, so that it seemed so much more perfunctory and so much more obviously a dumbing-down. But as dumbing-down itself may become, somewhat ironically, a journalistic parrot cry which is part of the disease it claims to 'reprehend', it is necessary to pursue the idea. The film has lost touch with the motivation of its 'original'.

Paul Dave, in his interesting summary of recent responses to 'heritage' productions in general, does not mention any of the recent adaptations of Jane Austen(!), but for that very reason makes fascinatingly relevant points about such productions inadvertently – for example, when he claims that 'the view that heritage cinema is simply the celebration of the spectacular pomp of the *ancien régime* is suspect' (p. 112). Curiously, he himself arms the suspicion by using Tom Nairn's latest book as one of his props here. It claims that the earliness of the English Revolution left structures of 'Old

Corruption' in place, leaving a bias towards aristocratic forms of capitalism and classic paradigms of arrested ideological development projected in just such 'folklore from above'[4] as the film verson of *Pride and Prejudice* may be felt to have (de)posited.

It is possible to share this ideological dyspathy while maintaining a kind of technical sympathy for those who undertake this sort of thing: Jane Austen is to be transposed to the screen, ergo we must change things; Jane Austen is to be transposed to the screen, ergo we must preserve things; 'Jane' is 'added to' by screen productions; 'Jane' is sharply reduced by screen productions.

More, paradoxically, often does seem to mean less here. In Blakean parlance, what was imagined is now real – Elizabeth and Darcy stand before you, Rosings (Baroque) is to the right and Pemberley (Palladian) to the left. Emma's Hartfield was always the monstrously grandiose Trafalgar House, it seems, while Knightley's Donwell rises before you as a hotel-complex-sized horror. Again, in the recent film version of *Sense and Sensibility*, Marianne, Elinor and Mrs Dashwood, types of impoverished and marginalized femininity, gaze, faintly dismayed, at a house, supposedly Barton Cottage, which the chairman of a privatized utility might not have disdained.

What you see and get is in a new (but not improved) sense 'material culture' – 'cultural materialism', even – in which all those props, properties and appurtenances lurch forward into a hugely semiotic prominence, and that 'National Trust Catalogue with Dialogue' effect nicely noted by one reviewer becomes heavily significant. Such productions are enacted in that 'heritage space' pleasantly defined by Andrew Higson as 'a place for the display of heritage properties rather than for the enactment of dramas'.[5] In 'Jane's' texts Great Houses stand at most for 'social security', but, even when textually foregrounded, usually bespeak the qualities of their owners as architectural embodiments of those educated, ethical perspectives which result from good taste. Unfortunately, as seen on TV they tend to evoke *arriviste* acquisitiveness, and the breathless accents with which Joanna David as Mrs Gardiner invited Elizabeth to admire Pemberley was alienating, as was the long build-up of (out-of-shot) 'our Darcy' as 'our perfect man', improving his image for Elizabeth – the actors, as if in involuntary response to all this rather grovelling mawkishness, ironized things disastrously.

Then, *enfin Darcy vint*. He made a Siegfriedean entry (Carl Davis's musical periodicities were, let it be said, immensely affective throughout[6]), dived briefly into a D.H. Lawrence novel as he swam through one of his own ponds, then out and into some Andrew Davies dialogue full of alfresco 'camping' in which he took a shine to the sensible Gardiners. I am not sure that at this point, with a fascinating glance at the idea of 'intention', it doesn't deserve Claire Monk's phrasing, again used of another film, of 'straining towards a post-heritage aesthetic in its melodramatization of the spectacle of property and landscape' but 'laps[ing] into a complacent Tory tract on the pleasures of property'.[7]

Again, though, it must be conceded that in the BBC films the novels were adapted with admirable fanaticism by the purveyors of authenticity, often in the sense of the authentic reproduction of that which never was, a truly post-modernist pursuit (and a lucrative one). Indeed, in the later one-part adaptation of *Emma* by the same 'team', an 'instant-tradition-style' addition to Miss Bates's house, despite its being in Lacock National Trust Village, proved to be necessary, consisting of wood and polystyrene.[8] A 'village' owned by the National Trust and eked out by polystyrene filmed as a version of a Jane Austen novel which contains only what Wallace Stevens called '[wo]men made out of words' (fitting Joel Weinsheimer's argument that 'Emma Woodhouse is not a woman nor need be described as if it were'[9]): forget Baudrillard, this one's a real simulacrum. One needs to be alert to the sheer strangeness of the process of transposing a Jane Austen novel to the screen to 'read' it properly, yet huge modern forms of expertise and technical innovation give that seamless 'realistic' gloss and naturalized inevitability to process and product on which it is difficult to get a proper critical purchase: this is significant, as what emerges may be precisely the opposite of what a genuinely modern reading of Austen would confirm.

You may be getting a Mills & Boon Jane Austen, a Barbara Cartland sort of Jane Austen, perhaps even the National Trust as Jane Austen, while Jane Austen herself fades into impalpability as we witness, simultaneously, 'the commodification of the past and the disappearance of history' (see Dave, p. 113). For example, at the time of showing the six-part BBC *Pride and Prejudice*, someone had discarded part of a *Daily Telegraph* on my commuter train with a front-page article which caught my eye. It was headlined 'A House to Die For', signalling, presumably, the preoccupations of the readers of the *Daily Telegraph*, at least as those are imagined by the editorial staff. The house in question was Luckington Court, that used by the BBC in the filming of the six-part adaptation of *Pride and Prejudice* to represent the house temporarily owned by Mr Bennet which was entailed away to Mr Collins. Although dying for Luckington Court does seem a little excessive, complaints of viewers and reviewers of screen versions of Austen novels might be felt to coalesce in the feeling that they consist almost entirely of houses to die for. In general Austen's quiet, and actually quite ambiguous and shifting *'prédilection d'artiste'* for the genteel considered as an ethical haven (or culture club) tends to be megaphoned into a plutocratic emphasis on Property disconcertingly twinned with 'sterile nostalgia' (Jameson) for a past which never was, leaving us somewhere between *Antiques Roadshow, Dallas* and a 'Royal Wedding' with much the same sense of bogus, 'Ukanian'[10] unity, in a costume ('made out of original Austen material') drama – arranging, in effect, those famous Althusserian imaginary resolutions of real social contradictions.

Would it really matter if it were, say, Galsworthy, who provided the foundation for the remake, given the prominence of clothes, buildings, appurtenances, astonishing meals, all the forms of expertise that give that seamless 'reality-effect' (on which it's difficult to get real critical purchase)? If James Joyce with finely inverted imperiousness declined to allow characters who earned more than a thousand a year an entrée to his works, adaptors of Jane Austen, mindful of the Great Expectations of their audiences as they imagine them, obviously feel that the attitudes to be catered for are those of all of us who, in Yeats's Country House idiom, 'shadow the inherited glory of the rich'.

Unfortunately, as Jane Austen is a text, she is doomed to suffer mutilation, and even her dialogue, not to mention her delicate narratorly focalizations, disappear and resurface as fragments, or are grafted on to the wilder stock of whatever the rewrite men may come up with, and even an Andrew Davies as the author of the quite unAustenian *Getting Hurt* (1989) is not entirely reassuring on this 'score'. Fragments and splinters of 'Jane' are sprayed in a kind of collage against a plutocratic backdrop which relegates the text to a subsidiary role. There is a flattening out into continuously mimetic presentation of those phases in which things go rather quietly diegetic, dulling to distance all that insistent mimesis would and in this case does, problematize.

For example, according to Sue Birtwhistle, the novel is about 'sex and … money' (*Making of Pride and Prejudice*, p. v). (She weighed in again with her 'sex and money' on the BBC Radio World Service [26.12.96], where she was worthily opposed by Valentine Cunningham, who indeed opposed such adaptations outright, earning a sneer from the World Service announcer at the end of the programme advising all Oxford professors to switch off as another classic novel adaptation was already on the broadcasting horizon.) While the novel is, anyway, about 'power, sex and money', with Darcy as a Nietzschean nobleman hereabouts, it is, if inadequately, about the *resistance* to, or female integrity in the face of, 'power, sex and money', which leads Darcy to 'identify against himself' in Judith Fetterly's phrase, used of the predicament of women, and accept the whiplash of Elizabeth's discursive contempt.

Sue Birtwhistle's naive account of the moment of original, (or in this case not very original) conception is alienating and surely more than a little patronizing – 'I know what I'd like to do: *Pride and Prejudice*, and *make it look like* a fresh lively story about real people' (*Making of Pride and Prejudice*, p. v): 'make it look like' is particularly rich, I think, in its conviction that the text can be, and needs to be 'added to' like this (and seems to imply that in its original form *Pride and Prejudice* is stale and dull); 'story' is wrong anyway, as novels come in ideological fancy dress or with class cladding; are not suspended in the neutral conceptual space of 'story'.

In the event, the BBC's *Pride and Prejudice* sucked viewers into a mass hysteria over its matrimonial *terminus ad quem*, perhaps in a transposition of emotions released by Royal Weddings which had failed or staled (more 'thoughtless, thoughtless Lydias' than brilliant feisty young Lizzies in high places, it seems). Identifying upwards with this folklore from above enabled a positively 'anthropological' re-ratification of tribal identity in which 'states of fantasy' produced a 'fantasy state'.[11] Yet Austen's text actually projects beyond the marital moment, significantly elided, to present a sense of what Hardy would call 'aftercourses', and creates a sense of what might be called the nuclear community, curiously intimating a 'Utopian' moment paradoxically conjured with *ancien régime* impedimenta. The BBC *Pride and Prejudice* ended Hollywoodishly with the Kiss which Jane failed to provide. However, the final point of the 'work' is ideological, not carnal: Pemberley itself provides the grounds of enchantment, Elizabeth becomes an emanation of the Gardiners, and the marriage is located 'within the City-Crown matrix' (see Dave, p. 121) in a 'fake model of festive inclusivity' (Dave, p. 119). Capitalism's early rise in Britain meant that traditional principles of stratification were undermined and this potentially dangerous situation was dealt with, paradoxically, by reinforcing old ideologies (see Dave, p. 121). Uniting Darcy and Lizzie in TV's *Pride and Prejudice* transparently enacted an allegory of this baroquely gilded, vampiric hegemony.

Curiously, if as Nairn sketches it, such *tableaux vivants* will include the symbolic spaces (we might call them phallic spectacles) which allude to the Crown, the City and even, that no unreclaimed conceptual space remain, the *Royal* Highlands, all this was mirrored in the oneiric geography of TV's *Pride and Prejudice*, where Darcy's Buckingham House-like residence, and solid Cits and City, each with their apposite musical projection, were eked out by a wild, but recuperable Derbyshire which suggestively affected a breathless Lizzie with sublimatedly erotic transports. This was an ideologizing of the aesthetic with a vengeance, en route to a libidinous notional (or 'national') unity suggested by the matrimonial transports.

EMMA (BBC); EMMA (General Release)

It is precisely the provocative quality of *Emma* which ensures its subversive potential: characters' wincing or mincing preoccupations with moral nuance and scruple may themselves become wince-making. But reviewers who responded with rage to the apparent glorification of the unspeakable in full possession of the eatables were not proving that screen *Emma* or text *Emma*, or indeed screen Emma or text Emma, were 'bad', merely that *Emma* is visibly ideological in a way that was calculated to outrage viewers rather than placate them. Bourgeois-trashing as it is (it was clear in the BBC version that Robert Martin, beneath Emma's notice till Mr Knightley explains, inhabited a 'desirable residence' by ordinary as opposed to heritage-spectacle standards), it seems well-placed to alienate its target audience; and the film version actually ruptured the idea it seems elsewhere to be sustaining, that 'the *ancien régime* is "for" you' in both senses of 'for'.

Interestingly, reviewers charmed into acquiescence by the seductions of *Pride and Prejudice* hastened to make amends with fiercely contemptuous notices of *Emma*. Two particularly unnuanced assaults were those in the *Sunday Times* and the *Observer* (each 1.12.96). A.A. Gill in the former was a little hectic, if not hectoring, including the feeling that Emma was 'horrible' and 'still stalks the earth' and the desire that the equally 'horrible' Georgians might have been swept, however anachronistically, off the board by Mongol hordes, was accompanied by a fervent wish that 'we' had not won the Napoleonic Wars. Unfortunately, a number chose to turn a fundamentally ideological rage on the actors themselves, which was transparently unfair.

Andrew Davies actually turned up the volume of potential offensiveness here by including tableaux designed to conscript the text for a kind of 'angry nostalgia for a time of fairness' (*Making of Emma*, p. 58). This included a Mr Knightley voice-over for strawberry-picking which hailed or haled the audience into the absurd business, with flunkies moving knee-cushions for the Versailles pastoralists and shots of harvesting with grateful peasants hailing the all-appropriating Knightley, while this abject paternalism was undercut by virtually simultaneous hints of omnipresent squalor and penury. It was notable that Robert Martin could not forgive Emma's snobbish attempt to wreck his happiness, despite her gracious walk down the Great Hall to 'make friends' Royalty-style in the unscripted 'harvest home' at which the folk were regaled by folklore from above once more. But if 'in ideology', it was at least, for the most part, within hailing distance of Austen's, and the Frank Churchill/Jane Fairfax imbroglio, and Emma's implication in it was brilliantly handled with reference to its caste-and-cultural-capital tensions.

It is obvious that *Emma* remains at least as provocative as Shakespeare's *Coriolanus*, its triumph largely an ultra-textual feat of delicate narrative focalization, and that would-be Directors and Producers should tread warily. Unfortunately, the general release film of *Emma* trod so warily that it leaped out of the ideological mould provided by Austen altogether into a dreary pyrrhic victory of generic Hollywood characterization and invented incident. We may even feel that Emma is a more congenial person than in the novel, but that much is lost thereby, rather as if Coriolanus's mother were pointing out that he had always been kind to butterflies.

Deserting the fierce antipathies and hateful siege of ideological contraries of the text, this production turns all to favour and to prettiness, or tries to. It strikes a 'modernist-American' note about class as status or simply 'easy money', and masks its insipidity with much bosky, bowery loveliness – this *Emma*'s ethos is often Dickensian warm-heartedness partly signified by those home fires burning to announce the cosiness in the heart of that Olde

Englande which is one of the imagination's dearest possessions. Indeed, a Dickensian twinkle infects the whole, and Jane's wince-making words are subsumed. It is interesting that, escaped from the ideological 'parergon' of the text, the characters fall apart, partly because their interrelationships depend upon nuances of class, old style, which went out the window with the cast(e)-ing couch. Just as, in chess, if knights move anyhow they cease to be knights, the characters fall apart when not strictly defined by ideological *différance*.

Mr Knightley is young and smart in the British rather than the American sense, with an aura of almost preening self-regard which could only be praised as a bold portrayal 'against the Knightley stereotype' (!) Not only is he a boyish show-off, at the ball for example, what he conspicuously lacks is *gravitas*. Jeremy Northam really is a good actor but a most inapposite Knightley. He turns this avatar of almost snarling English downrightness into a rather oleaginous sort of chap, promoting cosiness in coy, self-regarding accents, and dances with an exhibitionistic winsomeness which would have made the 'real' Mr Knightley growl gruff Johnsonian epigrams into Emma's ear.

The whole thing, as it proceeds, is quite vacuous quite often, with much wining and dining, and the ambience is, at all times, of a vague firelit affluence one would expect to accompany the soap-operatic rich. But occupying the fireplace is a quite meta-morphosed Mr Woodhouse, originally, one assumed, a valetudin-arian dormouse, but now a martinet-ish little stickler with clinical fixations alarmingly in excess of those vouchsafed by his original. Miss Bates is a comic turn from many another film, wearing spec-tacles to show she isn't very sexy (although she looks no more than thirty) and is given heaven-sent idioms like 'lovely, lovely, lovely', which could be conscripted for satire (involving, that is, a satirical disrespect for the 'original') – simple pantomime stuff. Old Mrs Bates offers comic deafness and Miss Bates shouts monosyllabic *précis* in a tone of acrimony which might have had some point as a possible parallel to the trials of Emma with her tottering, vale-tudinarian Dad, except that he himself is strangely altered here. The whole thing is in the mode of a sort of postmodernist parody, unsure of its bearings. Afraid to face the ideological abrasivenesses of Emma, it opts for something more familiar, and might well, or might as well, be a costume drama of an early Dickens novel (with Greta Scacchi as an outrageously domineering Mrs Weston, as if to compensate for Knightley's reduced or enfeebled status): in Mr Knightley's idiom, it was badly-done *Emma*, badly done indeed. But such is the nature of *Emma* there will always be those who prefer to seek refuge in Hollywood.

SENSE AND SENSIBILITY (Film on General Release)

In the film version of *Sense and Sensibility*, there is a beguiling sequence involving the arrival of the Dashwoods at Barton, with Robert Hardy as warm-hearted, chuckle-headed Sir John Middleton and Elizabeth Spriggs as Mrs Jennings: a computer-assisted skyline and schmaltzy music lead into their 'heartiest welcomer' roles, which they hammily fill. In this way they compose a neat rural opposite to the 'heartless elegance' of the John and Fanny Dashwood world, and their healthy bantering attitude, focalized by Margaret, a character Austen does nothing with, shows at once the defectiveness of the Dashwoods' repressions and the limitations of Marianne's exquisite sensibility – she walks away from them as they greet the outcast family with overpowering warmth ('Delightful creatures; I feel I know you all already'; 'I will not brook refusal; I'm quite deaf to them you know' ...): it all seems most acceptable, and even, at this point, something of an improvement on Austen, whose touch in *Sense and Sensibility* is far from sure, and who smudges all this by trying for too many effects at once instead of sustaining the clear contrast between healthy rural concern and insidious metropolitan grasping – but nothing verbal, as I recall, was *in* the original text.

And more notable is the ideological closure which the Austen text refuses: Lady Middleton is absent, and Mrs Jennings combines with Sir John here to naturalize the hegemonic, at least with regard to the rural gentry. The gilded ones of the metropolis remain *sous rature*, certainly. For example, Hugh Grant as Edward created a nice sense of rapport with Margaret, with the world of the child, and neatly communicated a sense of good values which brought him and Eleanor together while John and Fanny Dashwood, types of metropolitan gentility, compute the ullages and slaver over the silver. Harriet Walter as the metropolitan, if not queenly, Fanny was formidable indeed, all cut-glass vowels, sartorial sumptuous-ness, heartless elegance, crocodile jaw, and insane acquisitiveness, and thus extraordinarily effective as an embodiment of the kind of 'false consciousness' the novel set itself to assail. By contrast, Grant's Edward speaks nicely and consistently of his hatred of London. There is, though, a subliminal message slightly at odds with this: Grant's actual appearance and manner – as the picture of sartorial elegance even after driving through all those muddy lanes, and the too proud possessor of a certain kind of drawling – suggest a character concerned with the figure he cuts and worldly minded enough to compose only a Tweedledum-and-Tweedledee contrast with his brother, Robert the Fop. Heritage productions, then, find it difficult to escape from deeply conservative ideologies even when they seem to 'bend' themselves (and 'Jane Austen') in order to do so.

Notes

1 INTRODUCTION: THE POLITICS OF 'JANE AUSTEN'

1. Louis Marin, 'On the Interpretation of Ordinary Language: A Parable of Pascal', in *Textual Strategies: Perspectives in Post-Structuralist Criticism*, ed. Josue M. Harari (London: Methuen, 1979), pp. 239–59.
2. Edmund Burke, *Reflections on the Recent Revolution in France* (1790; Harmondsworth: Penguin, 1976), p. 46.
3. See Tom Paine, *The Rights of Man* [1791–2] (Harmondsworth: Penguin, 1969).
4. Alison G. Sulloway, *Jane Austen and the Province of Womanhood* (Philadelphia: University of Pennsylvania Press, 1989), p. 6, citing Shaftesbury [1790] ('"Tis the persecuting spirit has raised the bantering one'), grimly adding that 'there was much to be "revenged" by the bantering spirit'.
5. Eugenio Donato, 'Edging/Closure: On Derrida's Edging of Heidegger', *Yale French Studies*, 67 (1984), 22.
6. Marilyn Butler, 'History, Politics and Religion', in *The Jane Austen Handbook*, ed. J. David Grey (London: Athlone Press, 1986), p. 190.
7. Fredric Jameson, *Marxism and Form* (Princeton: Princeton University Press, 1971), p. 358.
8. Kenneth Clark, *The Romantic Rebellion: Romantic versus Classic Art* (London: John Murray, 1973), p. 26.
9. Marilyn Butler, *Jane Austen and the War of Ideas* (Oxford: Clarendon Press, 1975), p. 3.
10. Terry Eagleton, 'Irony and Commitment', *Stand*, 20, no.3 (1978), p. 25.
11. Terry Eagleton, *Criticism and Ideology: a Study in Marxist Literary Theory* (London: NLB, 1976), p. 70.
12. M. Butler, *Jane Austen and the War of Ideas* [Introduction to 1975 ed.], p. 1.
13. See Roger Gard, *Jane Austen's Novels: the Art of Clarity* (London: Yale University Press, 1992), p. 228.
14. See, for example, M.M. Bakhtin, *The Dialogic Imagination: Four Essays*, tr. Caryl Emerson and Michael Holquist (Austin, Texas: University of Texas Press, 1982); and David Lodge, *After Bakhtin: Essays on Fiction and Criticism* (London: Routledge, 1990). For a lively, if difficult, discussion of critical misuses of Bakhtin, 'theory', etc., see Tom Cohen, 'The Ideology of Dialogue: the Bakhtin/De Man (Dis)Connection', *Cultural Critique* 33 (Spring, 1996), 41–86.
15. As K.M. Newton puts it, for Althusser 'works of art have to be seen as "overdetermined", a term he borrowed from Freud, rather than being the product of socio-economic forces in any simple sense', in *Theory into Practice: A Reader in Modern Literary Criticism* (London: Macmillan, 1992), p. 243.

16. Roland Barthes, in *S/Z* tr. Richard Miller (London: Cape, 1975), p. 15.
17. See Paul Bové, *Mastering Discourse: The Politics of Intellectual Culture* (London: Duke University Press, 1992), p. 66.
18. See Roger Gard, *Jane Austen's Novels: the Art of Clarity*, pp. 7–8; see also his slightly mischievous treatment of the quite 'theoretical' John Dussinger on p. 232.
19. Stephen Cohan and Linda M. Shires, *Telling Stories: a Theoretical Analysis of Narrative Fiction* (London: Routledge, 1988), p. 143.
20. See *The Critical Decade: Culture in Crisis* (Manchester: Carcanet, 1993), p. viii.
21. See Henry James, 'The Lesson of Balzac', *Atlantic Monthly*, 96 (1905), 166–80. One of the most convincing and engaging refutations of this critical patronage in older styles of criticism is in Irving Ehrenpreis's *Acts of Implication: Suggestion and Covert Meaning in the Works of Dryden, Swift, Pope and Austen* (London: University of California Press, 1980), pp. 112–45.
22. See Charles Rosen, *Schoenberg* (London: Fontana, 1976), p. 11.
23. Mark Twain, letter to W.D. Howells (18 January 1909); see *Jane Austen: the Critical Heritage* (II), ed. B.C. Southam (London: Routledge & Kegan Paul, 1987), p. 232.
24. Kate Fullbrook, 'Jane Austen and the Comic Negative', in *Women Reading Women's Writing*, ed. Sue Roe (Brighton: Harvester Press, 1987), p. 42.
25. Fredric Jameson, *The Political Unconscious* (London: Methuen, 1981), p. 114.
26. V. Volosinov (M.M. Bakhtin?), *Marxism and the Philosophy of Language* (Cambridge: Harvard University Press, 1986), p. 22.
27. Marjorie Levinson, 'Romantic Criticism: the State of the Art', in *At the Limits of Romanticism: Essays in Cultural, Feminist and Materialist Criticism*, ed. Mary A. Favret and Nicola J. Watson (Bloomington: Indiana University Press, 1994), p. 280.
28. Catherine Belsey, *Critical Practice* (London: Methuen, 1980), p. 69.
29. A. Walton Litz, '"A Development of Self": Character and Personality in Jane Austen's Fiction', in *Jane Austen's Achievement* (London: Macmillan, 1976), ed. Juliet McMaster, 64–78.
30. John Bayley, 'The Irresponsibility of Jane Austen', in *Critical Essays on Jane Austen*, ed. B.C. Southam (London: Routledge & Kegan Paul, 1968), p. 9.
31. See their 'On Literature as an Ideological Form' (1974), reprinted in (e.g.) *Contemporary Marxist Literary Criticism* (London: Longman, 1992), ed. Francis Mulhern, p. 53.
32. See David Aers, Jonathan Cook and David Punter, *Romanticism and Ideology: Studies in English Writing 1765–1830* (London: Routledge & Kegan Paul, 1981), p. 127.
33. Roger Sales, *English Literature in History 1780–1830: Pastoral and Politics* (London, Hutchinson, 1983), p. 34.
34. Michael Riffaterre, 'Undecidability as Hermeneutic Constraint', in *Literary Theory Today*, ed. Peter Collier and Helga Geyer-Ryan (Oxford: Polity Press, 1992), p. 123.

35. See her *Fictions of Authority: Women Writers and Narrative Voice* (London: Cornell University Press, 1992), p. 75.
36. See her *Jane Austen and Narrative Authority* (London: Macmillan, 1995), p. 1.
37. Susan Sniader Lanser, *The Narrative Act: Point of View in Prose Fiction* (Princeton: Princeton University Press, 1981), p. 175.
38. 'Ideologemes': see Fredric Jameson, *The Political Unconscious*, p. 87. This term seems much too good not to 'use', although Jameson may feel my use gives it a rather 'Pickwickian' sense.
39. See Marilyn Butler, *Jane Austen and the War of Ideas*, pp. 108, 141.
40. David Carroll, *The States of 'Theory': History, Art and Critical Discourse* (Oxford: Columbia University Press, 1990), p. 9.
41. Roland Barthes in (e.g.) *Untying the Text: A Post-Structuralist Reader*, ed. Robert Young (London: Routledge & Kegan Paul, 1981), p. 42.
42. Roland Barthes, 'Theory of the Text', *Untying the Text*, p. 33.
43. See his *Narrative and its Discontents: Problems of Closure in the Traditional Novel* (Princeton: Princeton University Press, 1981), p. x.
44. Edward Said, 'Jane Austen and Empire', (1989), rpt. in *Contemporary Marxist Criticism*, ed. Francis Mulhern (Harlow: Longman, 1992), p. 110.
45. Sir Walter Scott [review of *Emma*] *Quarterly Review*, October 1815; and see Rachel Trickett, 'Jane Austen's Comedy and the Nineteenth Century', in B.C. Southam (ed.) *Critical Essays on Jane Austen* (London: Routledge & Kegan Paul, 1968), pp. 163–5.

2 THE CANNY 'BECOMES' THE UNCANNY: *NORTHANGER ABBEY*

1. Peter Medawar, *Memoir of a Thinking Radish* (Oxford: Oxford University Press 1986), p. 89.
2. Claudia Johnson, *Jane Austen, Politics and the Novel* (London: Chicago University Press, 1988), p. 28: 'Jane Austen's earliest literary productions are the fruit of unparalled self-assurance'; while Raymond Williams ascribes 'a remarkably confident way of seeing and judging' to her in *The Country and the City* (London: Hogarth Press, 1985), p. 115.
3. Samuel Johnson, *The History of Rasselas, the Prince of Abissinia: A Tale* (1759), title of chapter 43.
4. All quotations from text of *Northanger Abbey* (Harmondsworth: Penguin, 1995), ed. Marilyn Butler.
5. Olivia Smith, *The Politics of Language, 1791–1819* (Oxford: Oxford University Press, 1984), p. 15; but Claudia Johnson raises doubts on this score, pointing out that 'many progressive writers perceived in Johnson a potentially, if not actually, sympathetic figure', Johnson, op. cit., p. 79.
6. Claudia Johnson, op. cit., p. 37.
7. The relation between Henry and Catherine in fact perfectly illustrates Hélène Cixous's claim that 'woman has always referred back to the opposite signifier which annihilates its specific energy and

diminishes or stifles its very different sounds', in 'The Laugh of the Medusa', rpt. in *New French Feminisms*, ed. I. de Courtivron and E. Marks (Brighton: Harvester, 1981), p. 257.

8. J.P. Hardy notes a specific unassignability of irony at key points in the text. See his *Jane Austen's Heroines: Intimacy in Human Relationships* (London: Routledge & Kegan Paul, 1984), p. 11. (In general, though, much Austen criticism has roughly the same relation to its original as, say, Lamb's *Tales from Shakespeare* have to Shakespeare, so that as a rule one feels that the reader might well be advised to 'betake himself to the original at once', in the words of *Jane Eyre*.) For a comparable sense that things may tilt against Henry rather than Catherine here, see Karl Kroeber, 'Subverting a Hypocrite Lecteur', in *Jane Austen Today*, ed. Joel Weinsheimer (Athens: Georgia University Press, 1975), p. 38.

9. W.H. Auden, 'Macao', in *Collected Poems*, ed. E. Mendelson (London: Faber, 1976), p. 145.

10. A.W. Litz, *Jane Austen: a Study of Her Artistic Development* (London: Chatto & Windus, 1965), p. 64.

11. This occurred on 16 August 1819; Shelley's *The Mask of Anarchy* was based on this event. See *Complete Poetical Works*, ed. T. Hutchinson (London: Oxford University Press, 1904), p. 341.

12. Reprinted in *Jane Austen: the Critical Heritage*, ed. B.C. Southam (London: Routledge & Kegan Paul, 1968), p. 106.

13. As Nicholas Tredell reports in *Culture in Crisis: the Critical Decade* (Manchester: Carcanet, 1993), p. 140, this word is actually used of British workmen by the historian Corelli Barnett.

14. William Blake, 'To the Christians' ('Jerusalem', plate 77), *Complete Poetry and Prose* (Berkeley and Los Angeles, 1982), p. 231.

15. As Frederick M. Keener agreeingly puts it in *The Chain of Becoming: the Philosophical Tale, the Novel, and a Neglected Realism of the Enlightenment: Swift, Montesquieu, Voltaire, Johnson and Austen* (New York: Columbia University Press, 1983), p. 241, 'not even "narrative voice" is a priori perfectly reliable'. Barbara Benedict argues that 'Austen challenges the authority of narrative control itself' in 'Jane Austen's *Sense and Sensibility*', *Philological Quarterly* 69 (1990), 454.

16. But again, Claudia Johnson feels that 'Johnson's legacy could, and did, go both ways', and that he 'legitimized the energy generated by our desire for happiness' , op. cit., p. 80.

17. Shelley, *The Mask of Anarchy*, referring to paper currency, and (incidentally) anticipating many Marxist themes and ideas; Jane Austen *is* depicting in her own way a similar process of fraud and usurpation, only in an implicit, *sotto voce* fashion.

18. See Susan Buck-Morss, *The Origin of Negative Dialectics: Theodor Adorno, Walter Benjamin and the Frankfurt Institute* (Brighton: Harvester, 1977), p. 167.

19. James Boswell, *A Journal of a Tour to the Hebrides with Samuel Johnson* (1909), p. 53.

20. Luce Irigaray, cited in *French Philosophers in Conversation*, ed. Raoul Mortley, (London: Routledge, 1991), p. 64. It is, therefore, difficult to

agree with lively, opinionated Roger Gard when he claims that 'it is quite possible to find something mitigating, even appealing, in the General's excessive compunction over the health of an heiress' in *Jane Austen's Novels: The Art of Clarity* (London: Yale University Press, 1992), p. 55.

21. Anne Crippen Ruderman also notes her 'artless simplicity that is more like Harriet Smith than like Emma' in *The Pleasures of Virtue: Political Thought in the Novels of Jane Austen* (London: Rowman & Littlefield, 1995), p. 35; but after all, *Northanger Abbey* is in its way a kind of *Bildungsroman*, so perhaps we should expect the heroine to be in a fairly formative, not entirely predictable (or even volatile) condition. Incidentally, by 'political' she seems to mean Aristotelian in the sense of F.H. Bradley's parody of the spiritual guidance of Matthew Arnold: 'Be virtuous, and on the whole you will be happy', which in most eyes would seem to provide a death-warrant rather than a 'warranty' for 'the political'.

22. This instability is partly the result of the process by which '[Jane Austen] asserts the possibility of a woman's morality and a woman's resistance, even as she perpetuates the tradition which has made both so necessary and so difficult to represent'. See Jane Miller, *Seductions: Studies in Reading and Culture* (London: Virago, 1990), p. 37.

23. As René Girard puts it, 'The coquette does not wish to surrender her precious self to the desire which she arouses, but were she not to provoke it, she would not feel so precious.' (In *Deceit, Desire and the Novel: Self and Other in Literary Structure* [tr. Yvonne Freccero], (London: 1965), p. 105).

24. John Dussinger acknowledges the resemblance between Henry and Mr Bennet in his *In the Pride of the Moment: Encounters in Jane Austen's World* (Ohio: Ohio University Press, 1990), p. 123.

25. Quoted by Juliet McMaster, 'Love and Marriage', in *The Jane Austen Handbook*, ed. J. David Grey (London: The Athlone Press, 1986), p. 231.

26. See, e.g., D.A. Miller, *Narrative and its Discontents: Problems of Closure in the Traditional Novel* (Princeton, NJ: Princeton University Press, 1981) who speaks of 'a central tension in the traditional novelistic enterprise: namely, a discomfort within the processes and implications of narration itself'. Curiously, although he devotes a long chapter to Jane Austen, he does not so much as mention *Northanger Abbey*, although its poisedly flustered conclusion about 'the telltale compression of pages' might be thought to exemplify his point perfectly.

27. That sounds a little pugnacious, but (e.g.) Marilyn Butler is quite provocative when she observes that 'Jane Austen believes as Mrs West or Charles Lucas [Tory mediocrities?] believe; her feat is to have found so discreet a way of saying it' – rather a back-handed compliment! See her *Jane Austen and the War of Ideas* (Oxford: Clarendon Press, 1975), p. 29.

28. In fact Austen's Catherine fits the idea rather better here than Joyce's Leopold, as Joyce's notion of 'positively charged ordinariness'

(actually a sort of riposte to Lady Gregory's bloodthirsty embodiments of folkloric Celticity) in the form of the masochistic Bloom, seems, with hindsight, a little weird. These matters are nicely handled by Declan Kiberd's essay on 'The Vulgarity of Heroics: Joyce's *Ulysses*', in *James Joyce: an International Perspective* [Irish Literary Studies 10], ed. Suheil Badi Bushrui and Bernard Benstock (Gerrards Cross: Colin Smythe, 1982), pp. 156–68. Gilbert Ryle, in his 'Jane Austen and the Moralists' (in *Critical Essays on Jane Austen*, ed. B.C. Southam [London: Routledge & Kegan Paul, 1968], p. 118) makes his point piquantly when he observes that 'Catherine, though a gullible ninny about how the actual world runs, is quite ungullible about what is right and wrong, decorous and indecorous'; but perhaps it is part of an (unhappy) 'postmodernist' condition to blur this distinction, or to feel that this distinction is blurred.

29. As reproduced in *William Blake: Selected Poetry*, ed. David V. Erdman (London: New English Library, 1976), p. 107.

30. Howard Babb speaks triumphantly of Catherine's 'finally winning Henry, the champion of reason', Henry being a figure for whom male pedagogues have ready sympathy, in *Jane Austen's Novels: the Fabric of Dialogue* (Columbus: Ohio State University Press, 1962), p. 98; or, as Katrin Ristkok Burlin puts it: 'he is an eager teacher, she, an ardent pupil; she is fond of him, he is fond of admiration', in 'The Four Fictions of *Northanger Abbey*', in *Jane Austen: Bicentenary Essays*, ed. John Halperin (Cambridge: Cambridge University Press, 1975), p. 91.

31. William Blake, 'The Marriage of Heaven and Hell', in *The Complete Poems*, ed. W.H. Stevenson (London: Longman, 1971), p. 115.

32. Keener suggestively refers to *Northanger Abbey* as 'a sister of *Rasselas* and *Candide* in form, meaning and conceptual framework' (op. cit., p. 249). Catherine surely has Candidean traits aplenty.

33. But Patricia Beer, in *Reader, I Married Him: a Study of the Women Characters of Jane Austen, Charlotte Brontë, Elizabeth Gaskell and George Eliot* (London: Macmillan, 1974), has even stronger words for Austen's heroes: 'They have traces of arrogance, conceit and sadism, but these traces are well-concealed. They teach, humiliate, punish, frustrate and tantalise the women they love' (p. 68); and Henry in particular is himself far from being universally loved: B.C. Southam (ed.) *Jane Austen: 'Northanger Abbey' and 'Sense and Sensibility'. A Casebook* (London: Macmillan, 1976), thinks Henry is 'condemned out of his own mouth', and he is also attacked (e.g.) by Sandra M. Gilbert and Susan Gubar in *The Madwoman in the Attic: the Woman Writer and the Nineteenth-Century Literary Imagination* (London: Yale University Press, 1979), pp. 138–40, and Judith Wilt in *Ghosts of the Gothic: Austen, Eliot and Lawrence* (Princeton: Princeton University Press, 1980), pp. 149ff.

34. Shlomith Rimmon-Kenan, 'Deconstructive Reflections on Deconstruction: a Reply to Hillis Miller', *Poetics Today*, 2 (1980–81); reprinted (e.g.) in *Modern Literary Theory: a Reader*, ed. P. Rice and P. Waugh (London: Edward Arnold, 1989), pp. 185–9.

3 A SENSITIVE SUBJECT: *SENSE AND SENSIBILITY*

1. Pascal, *Pensées*; see Louis Marin, 'On the Interpretation of Ordinary Language: a Parable of Pascal', in *Textual Strategies: Perspectives in Post-Structuralist Criticism*, ed. Josue M. Harari (London: Methuen, 1979), pp. 239–59.

2. Edmund Burke, *Reflections on the Recent Revolution in France* (1790; Harmondsworth: Penguin, 1976), p. 46.

3. Janet Todd in *Gender, Art and Death* (Cambridge: Polity, 1993), p. 147 alleges an 'implacable hostility to sensibility' in her work which might constitute its own 'implacable hostility' to what I'm trying to establish, but concedes that in *Sense and Sensibility* 'the conservatively supported nuclear family is the locus of boredom and nastiness'. As Alison Sulloway observes in *Jane Austen and the Province of Womanhood* (Philadelphia: University of Pennsylvania Press, 1989), the effect of Marianne is hardly that of Edgeworth's Julia who prefers 'only to feel', with disastrous results (p. 39). Although the industrious Janet Todd is not wrong to claim in *Sensibility: an Introduction* (London: Methuen, 1986), that 'ultimately' *Sense and Sensibility* 'socializes the scream of Marianne into sensible rational discourse', there is a gap here between the text's structural requirements and its ideological effects which is explored by more probing, though not necessarily more erudite, critics.

4. J. Habermas, 'Technology and Science as "Ideology"', in *Towards a Rational Society* (Boston, 1970); quoted in R. Roderick, *Habermas and the Foundations of Critical Theory* (London: Macmillan, 1986), p. 41; and H. Marcuse, 'Industrialisation and Capitalism in the Work of Max Weber', *Negations: Essays in Critical Theory* (London: Allen Lane, 1968), pp. 223–5.

5. Joe Fisher, *The Hidden Hardy* (London: Macmillan, 1992), pp. 7–19.

6. This and subsequent quotations from the Oxford edition of *Sense and Sensibility*, ed. Claire Lamont (Oxford: Oxford University Press, 1975), p. 91.

7. In *The Dark Side of the Landscape: the Rural Poor in English Painting 1730–1840* (London: Cambridge University Press, 1980), p. 11.

8. See Valentine Cunningham, *In the Reading Jail: Postmodernity, Texts and History* (Oxford: Blackwell, 1993), p. 31.

9. Norman Sherry, *Jane Austen* (London: Evans, 1966), pp. 58–9.

10. William Blake, 'The Marriage of Heaven and Hell', *Complete Poetry and Prose of William Blake*, ed. D.Erdman (Berkeley and Los Angeles: University of California Press, 1982), p. 43.

11. Hermann Melville; quoted by Charles Swann, '"Benito Cereno": Melville's De(con)struction of the Southern Reader', *Literature and History*, 12, no.1 (Spring, 1986), 12.

12. Walter Benjamin, 'Goethe's *Wahlverwandtschaften*'; see Susan Buck-Morss, *The Origin of Negative Dialectics* (Brighton: Harvester Press, 1977), p. 246.

13. J. Derrida, *Marges de la Philosophie* (1972), p. 389; see Jonathan Culler, *On Deconstruction* (London: Routledge, 1983), 127–8.

14. Robert Polhemus, 'Jane Austen's Comedy', in *The Jane Austen Handbook* (London: Athlone Press, 1986), ed. J. David Grey, pp. 60–71.
15. Anne K. Mellor, *English Romantic Irony* (London: Harvard University Press, 1980), p. 3.
16. See, for example, Marilyn Butler's *Romantics, Rebels and Reactionaries* (Oxford: Oxford University Press, 1981).
17. Byron, *Don Juan*, Canto 1, st.194; in (e.g.) *Poetical Works* (Oxford: Oxford University Press, 1904), p. 658.
18. K. Mannheim, 'Structural Analysis in Sociology', in *Essays in Sociology and Social Psychology*, ed. P. Keskemeti (London: 1953, p. 89; quot. in D. Punter, *Blake, Hegel and Dialectic* (Amsterdam: Rhodopi, 1982), p. 13.
19. Fredric Jameson, *The Political Unconscious* (London: Methuen, 1981), p. 114.
20. Judith Fetterly, *The Resisting Reader: a Feminist Approach to American Fiction* (Bloomington: Indiana University Press, 1978), p. xii.
21. Tony Tanner, *Jane Austen* (London: Macmillan, 1986), p. 102.
22. Toril Moi, *Sexual/Textual Politics* (London: Methuen, 1981), p. 114.
23. Goethe, *The Sorrows of Young Werther* ed. and tr. Harry Steinhauer (New York: Bantam Books, 1962), pp. 91–2.
24. William Blake, 'There is no Natural Religion' (in, e.g., *The Selected Poetry of Blake*, ed. D. Erdman (New York: Signet, 1976), p. 45.
25. Byron, 'A Vision of Judgement', st.12 [1822]; in (e.g.) *Poetical Works*, p. 158.
26. My feelings seem to be compatible with J.F. Burrows' findings. In his analysis of Marianne's idiolect, he perceives 'not so much a character as a succession of loosely-fitting roles', in *Computation into Criticism: A Study of Jane Austen's Novels and an Experiment in Method* (Oxford: Oxford University Press, 1987), p. 147.
27. Jean-Jacques Rousseau ['*c'est la chaine des sentiments qui ont marqué la succession de mon être*]; in (e.g.) *Oeuvres Complètes [1]: Les Confessions; autres textes autobiographiques* (Paris: Gallimard, 1959), p. 278.
28. Wallace Stevens, 'Asides on the Oboe', *Collected Poems* (London: Faber, 1955), 250.
29. William Blake, *Complete Poetry and Prose*, p. 40.
30. Kant, *Third Critique*; and see Cynthia Chase, *Decomposing Figures: Rhetorical Readings in the Romantic Tradition* (London: Johns Hopkins University Press, 1986), p. 113.
31. Samuel Johnson, 'Apothegms, Sentiments, Opinions and Occasional Reflections', collected in *Johnsonian Miscellanies, II* ed. G.B. Hill (London: Constable, 1897), p. 1.
32. Bernard J. Paris, *Character and Conflict in Jane Austen's Novels: a Psychological Approach* (Brighton: Harvester, 1978), p. 16.
33. J. Derrida, 'Fors', quot. Cynthia Chase, *Decomposing Figures*, p. 13.
34. T.W. Adorno, *Minima Moralia* (Frankfurt am Main: Suhrkamp-Verlag, 1969), quot. Buck-Morss, *Origins of Negative Dialectic*, p. 168. For the opposition, pursuing an argument one can respect, David Kaufman, in 'Law and Propriety, Sense and Sensibility: Austen on the Cusp of Modernity', *ELH* 59 (1992), concedes that an emphasis on

propriety 'smacks of oppression and ideological obfuscation, of outmoded ideals and outdated restraints' (p. 385), but argues, following Jane Nardin in *Those Elegant Decorums: the Concept of Propriety in Jane Austen's Novels* (New Albany: State University of New York Press, 1973), that 'propriety is needed in a social whirl that is constituted by selfish, stupid or unmannerly people' (pp. 24–5).However, that his argument is not, finally, entirely innocuous is suggested by his observation that 'like Burke, Austen understands that a certain civility is necessary if capitalism is to work' (p. 396).

35. Fredric Jameson, *The Political Unconscious*, op. cit., p. 84.

4   *PRIDE AND PREJUDICE*: OR PROPERTY AND PROPRIETY?

1. Paul de Man, *The Resistance to Theory* (Manchester: Manchester University Press, 1986), p. 11.
2. Tom Paine, *The Rights of Man* [1791–2] (Harmondsworth: Penguin, 1969), p. 81.
3. Compare, for example, the Nietzschean perspective on the concept of 'Enlightenment' provided by them in *Dialectic of Enlightenment*, translated by John Cummings (1944; London, Verso, 1979), p. 44, comparable with Paine's scorn for the 'puppet show' of the 'hereditary principle', but with a greater scepticism, historically justified, that 'Enlightenment' could itself become a 'tool' in the hands of the newly powerful: '"The Enlightenment" should be "taken into the people, so that the priests all become priests with a bad conscience – and the same must be done with regard to the State. That is the task of the Enlightenment: to make princes and statesmen aware that everything they do is sheer falsehood ..."' [from Nietzche's *Nachlass*]. On the other hand, Enlightenment has always been a tool for the 'great manipulators of government ... The way in which the masses are fooled in this respect, for instance in all democracies, is very useful: the reduction and malleability of men are worked for as "progress"!'
4. See, for example, Anne K. Mellor, *English Romantic Irony* (London, Harvard University Press, 1980), p. 21.
5. All bracketed page references in the text are to the edition of *Pride and Prejudice* by James Kinsley and Frank W. Bradbrook (Oxford, Oxford University Press, 1980).
6. See, for a reminder that 'terrorism' may be *de haut en bas*, Peter Widdowson, 'Terrorism and Literary Studies', *Textual practice* 2,1 (Spring, 1988), pp. 1–21.
7. Leo Bersani, *Baudelaire and Freud* (London, University of California Press, 1977), p. 146.
8. 'Volosinov' (M.M. Bakhtin), *Marxism and the Philosophy of Language* (Cambridge, Harvard University Press, 1986), p. 22.
9. 'At about the period I have mentioned, then, the child's imagination becomes engaged in the task of getting free from the parents, of whom he now has a low opinion [Now, as a result of what?, a social

critique would no doubt wish to ask sharply here], and of replacing them by others, who, as a rule, are of a higher social standing. He will make use in this connexion of any opportune coincidences from his actual experiences, such as his becoming acquainted with the Lord of the Manor or some landed proprietor if he lives in the country or with some member of the aristocracy if he lives in town.' (In Freud, 'The Family Romance', in the *Standard Edition of the Complete Works*, vol. 9 [1909; London, Hogarth Press, 1959], tr. James Strachey p. 239.)

10. All the same, one bridles when Donald Greene, in 'Jane Austen's Monsters', *Jane Austen: Bicentenary Essays*, ed. John Halperin (London: Cambridge University Press, 1975) claims that 'the most egregious example of this combined intellectual and emotional obtuseness – perhaps the most thoroughgoing "monster" of the six published novels of Jane Austen's maturity – is Mary Bennet' (p. 266). Mary, after all, is only following the line of requirements for females to make themselves attractive and acceptable, which would include playing and singing all day, like Mr Darcy's sister, or following the path of 'extensive reading' as also marked out by Darcy, yet also seemingly enjoined by Mr Bennet. Clearly, in fact, Jane and Elizabeth 'affiliate' with their father, while Kitty and Lydia 'affiliate' with Mrs Bennet. Mary is left out – father-oriented, but he refuses to 'notice' her – except, of course, as an embarrassment. Surely, then, either Mary is potentially a figure of pathos, or, as in the case of Lydia, one could imagine the construction of narratives formally more sympathetic to either.

11. As Ross Chambers. *Room for Manoeuvres: Reading Oppositional Narrative* (Chicago: Chicago University Press, 1991), suggestively (for the effect of Elizabeth on Darcy) puts it, 'the discursive practice of irony works seductively to shift desire' (p. xvi).

12. The letter may be read as a kind of repository of all Elizabeth's fears about what Darcy might have been thinking about her family, an imagined or hypothetical construction composed of Mr Darcy's frightening silences and Elizabeth's actual feelings about them and their inadequacies, now assuming formal textual form.

13. A phrase used by Anthony Burgess to refer to the way in which the Russian argot was acquired in *A Clockwork Orange*; cit. Patrick Parrinder, *The Failure of Theory: Essays on Criticism and Contemporary Fiction* (Brighton, Harvester Press, 1987), p. 181.

14. Ivor Morris, *Mr. Collins Considered: Approaches to Jane Austen* (London, Routledge & Kegan Paul, 1987). Mr Darcy and Mr Collins, for example, both feel that their worldly position entitles them to the hand of Elizabeth, and both suffer from angry pride when rejected; their respect for the hereditary principle also makes Darcy vaguely congruent with Sir William Lucas, exquisitely sensitive to matters of rank and unaware that, to Darcy, his implicit principle of exclusivity should exclude himself. Also watermarking the text is a suggestion of Darcy's account of his and Wickham's upbringing as a fantasy of rivals in love (the rival is feared; he is 'artful' and 'more charming', etc.), an area of ethical neutrality, but invaded by compensatory,

insecure fantasies of one's superior moral/financial qualities – superior 'property' and 'properties', as it were.

15. Tennyson, 'Maud: A Monodrama', 11. 464–5 (*The Poems of Tennyson*, ed. by Christopher Ricks [London, Longman, 1969], p. 1063).

16. Terence Hawkes, *That Shakespeherian Rag*: *Essays on a Critical Process* (London, Methuen, 1986), p. 15.

17. D.W. Harding, 'Regulated Hatred: an Aspect of the Work of Jane Austen', *Scrutiny*, 8 (1939–40), pp. 346–62.

18. It is interesting, though, that Luce Irigaray claims that 'property and propriety are undoubtedly rather foreign to all that is female' in *New French Feminisms* (Brighton: Harvester, 1980), ed. Elaine Marks and Isabelle de Courtivron, p. 104); a narrative point of view friendly to Lydia could be constructed. And it seems a little much to expect Lydia to get the point made by Julia Prewitt Brown in *Jane Austen's Novels: Social change and Literary Form* (London: Harvard University Press, 1979), p. 12: 'ironically, Jane Austen's novels show that the period of courtship was the least frivolous period of a woman's life', showing what an insidious trap has been laid for her by 'patriarchal' social arrangements. For a sympathetic account of 'giving oneself' as Lydia does with alacrity, see Raphael Samuel's (unsympathetic) citing of Fred Inglis's criticism of Raymond Williams (in 'Making it Up', *LRB* 18 [no. 13] 4 July 1996) p. 8: '... he hadn't that "mind's recoil upon itself" which makes possible passionate uncertainty, the loss of all gravity which goes with falling in love, the giving-of-oneself, the abandon'.

19. Shakespeare, *The Tempest*, 2. 1. 218.

20. Claudia Brodsky Lacour bridlingly notes, in 'Austen's *Pride and Prejudice* and Hegel's "Truth in Art"': Concept, Reference and History', *ELH*, 59, No. 3 (1992) 'the insufferable Mr Collins, the best argument made anywhere in fiction against the so-called natural right to property of the male' (p. 612).

21. Robert Lowell, 'Caligula', *For the Union Dead* (London, Faber, 1965), p. 49.

22. See, for example, 'Preface' to *On the Genealogy of Morals*, ed. W. Kaufmann (New York, Random House, 1967), p. 17.

23. Wordsworth, 'Tintern Abbey', in *William Wordsworth: Selected Poetry and Prose*, ed. Philip Hobsbawm (London, Routledge, 1989), p. 45.

24. See Susan Buck-Morss, *The Origin of Negative Dialectics*: *Theodor Adorno, Walther Benjamin and the Frankfurt Institute* (Brighton, Harvester Press, 1977), p. 167: 'Now with Brecht in California, Eisler suggested after one lunch with Horkheimer that the Tui novel be based on the story of the Frankfurt Institute: "A wealthy old man (Felix Weil) dies, disturbed by the suffering in the world. He leaves in his will a large sum of money establishing an institute to search for the source of misery – which is of course he himself."'

25. J.M. Bernstein, *The Philosophy of the Novel: Lukacs, Marxism and the Dialectics of Form* (Brighton, Harvester Press, 1984), p. 189.

26. See David Lodge, 'Analysis and Interpretation of the Realist Text: Ernest Hemingway's "Cat in the Rain"', reprinted in K.M. Newton,

Theory into Practice: a Reader in Modern Literary Criticism (London: Macmillan, 1992), p. 69.

27. Roy Pascal, *The Dual Voice: Free Indirect Speech and Its Functioning in the Nineteenth Century European Novel* (Manchester: Manchester University Press, 1977).

28. Bernstein, p. xxii.

29. W.H. Auden, 'Letter to Lord Byron', in *The English Auden: Poems, Essays and Dramatic Writings, 1927-1939*, ed. Edward Mendelson (London, Faber, 1977), p. 171.

30. See Lennard J. Davis, *Resisting Novels: Ideology and Fiction* (London, Methuen, 1987), p. 33.

31. See Paine, *Rights of Man*, esp. pp. 72–3.

32. See, for example, the traditionally-inflected *Jane Austen: Intimacy in Human Relationships* by J.P. Hardy (London, Routledge, 1987).

33. Shakespeare, *The Winter's Tale* 1. 1. 118.

34. See A.D. Nuttall, *A New Mimesis: Shakespeare and the Representation of Reality* (London, Methuen, 1983), pp. 119, 164–6. And cf. Emma's musings on Mr Knightley's house and grounds: 'She [her sister Isabella, married to a Knightley] had given them neither men, nor names, nor places that could raise a blush' (p. 323).

35. And note even Claudia Johnson's Lady Catherine-like reference to Wickham as a 'propertyless upstart' in *Jane Austen: Women, Politics and the Novel*, p. 56.

36. In *Women, Power and Subversion: Social Strategies in British Fiction 1778–1860* (Athens: University of Georgia Press, 1981), p. 54. Yet in 'Can this Marriage be Saved: Jane Austen Makes Sense of an Ending', *ELH* 50 (1983), Karen Newman rightly points out that 'Austen exposes the fundamental discrepancy in her society between its avowed ideology of love and its implicit economic motivation' (p. 695).

37. For Jane Austen as something of a dab hand at 'binary oppositions' (part of the description of Mr Darcy's estate is examined), see Steven Cohan and Linda M. Shires, *Telling Stories: a Theoretical Analysis of Narrative Fiction* (London: Routledge, 1988), p. 43.

38. Wallace Stevens, 'Of Modern Poetry', *Collected Poems* (London: Faber, 1955), p. 239.

39. Walter Benjamin, 'Goethes *Wahlverwandtschaften*', (1924); see Susan Buck-Morss, *The Origin of Negative Dialectics*, p. 246: 'Wanting to make the *Wahlverwandtschaften* accessible to understanding by means of the author's words is a misplaced effort. They are precisely suited for [*sic*] barring criticism from access …'

40. 'SLOW RISES WORTH, BY POVERTY DEPRESSED', 'London: a Poem in Imitation of the Third Satire of Juvenal', in *Poems* (London, Yale University Press, 1964), p. 56 (vol. 6 of the *Yale Edition of the Works of Samuel Johnson*).

41. Shakespeare, *The Tempest*, 1. 2. 98.

42. J.P. Hardy notes the connection in *Jane Austen's Heroines*, p. 129.

43. Charlotte Brontë made several pejorative references to Jane Austen in letters from 1848–1850, documented in (e.g.) Graham Handley,

Jane Austen ('Criticism in Focus' series) (London: Duckworth, 1992), pp. 15–16.

44. As Kathryn Sutherland puts it, in 'Jane Eyre's Literary History: the Case for *Mansfield Park*', *ELH* 59 (1992), 'Austen never forgets that love, too, is among society's commercial arrangements and is therefore historically specific. Consequently, her social criticism, however compromised, is more effective [than Brontë's]' (p. 434).

45. Byron, 'Cain', as quoted in Matthew Arnold, 'Byron', in *The Portable Matthew Arnold*, ed. Lionel Trilling (1949; Harmondsworth, Penguin, 1980), p. 381.

46. Nietzsche, *Genealogy of Morals*, pp. 36–43; 'a man pleased with his own passions and volitions', Wordsworth, 'Preface' to *Lyrical Ballads* edited by W.J.B. Owen, *Wordsworth's Literary Criticism* (London, Routledge & Kegan Paul, 1974), pp. 69–90.

47. Wallace Stevens, 'Imago', *Collected Poems*, p. 439.

48. Her enthusiasm is expressed in suspiciously Johnsonian terms – 'What are men to rocks and mountains!' etc. (p. 138). Compare T.S. Eliot's critique of Johnson's lines in 'London': 'For who would leave, unbribed, Hibernia's land./Or change the rocks of Scotland for the Strand?' as a singularly imperilled rhetorical question: 'The answer is, Samuel Johnson, if anybody', *On Poetry and Poets* (London, Faber, 1957), p. 179.

49. *Paradise Lost*, bk 5, line 297.

50. 'Metonymic analogues' is Meir Sternberg's phrase for the concurrence of qualities between Darcy and his estate, in *Expositional Modes and Temporal Ordering in Fiction* (London: Johns Hopkins University Press, 1978), p. 131.

51. Margaret Kirkham, *Jane Austen: Feminism and Fiction* (Brighton, Harvester, 1983), p. 138, in fact denying that Jane Austen does this.

52. Milton, *Samson Agonistes*, ll. 1479–50.

53. Ann Banfield, in *Jane Austen's Achievement*, ed. Juliet McMaster (London: Macmillan, 1976), speaks of Jane Austen's 'rejection of an aesthetic which effaces the real, which arises from a class's inability to confront the facts of work and the social world' (p. 32).

54. Christopher Gillie, *A Preface to Jane Austen* (London, Longman, 1974), p. 170. An imposing, indeed an intimidating personage, whose silent ponderings are also judgemental, and who fails to suffer fools (sc. 'Mr Woodhouse') gladly; he notices, for example, that Mr Elton is courting Emma and tries to warn her.

55. Robert Burns, 'Is there for honest Poverty?' *Burns Poems and Songs*, ed. James Barke (London: Collins, 1955), p. 642.

56. P.N. Furbank, *Unholy Pleasure: or the Idea of Social Class* (Oxford, Oxford University Press, 1985), p. 97.

57. For Gerald R. Bruns, in *Inventions: Writing, Textuality and Understanding in Literary History* (New Haven: Yale, 1982), who makes of *Pride and Prejudice* a world of hermeneutic coding, 'Elizabeth, indeed, is the most subtle of interpreters … She discovers what … Schleiermacher had formally proposed, namely that interpretation is routinely confounded by prejudice, and that the act of

interpretation is essentially an act of self-correction ... [while] the Gardiners are *reading* the situation, together with the people in it, some of whom ... are more readable or legible than others' (pp. 113–15). Darcy, in particular, it would seem, is a text of jouissance – often rendered as 'bliss' but also referring to 'troubled pleasure', a Wordsworth phrase, corresponding to the 'sexual turbulence' which George Steiner in 'Eros and Idiom', in *On Difficulty and Other Essays* (New York: Oxford University Press, 1978), pp. 95–136, intuits that Austen conveys below the surface of polite conversation.

Confirming this is Ross Chambers's reporting that 'for Freud and Klein as for Bataille, the desire to know – the epistemophilic urge – is ultimately linked to sexuality' (op. cit. p. 9).

58. When, in 'Chance and the Hierarchy of Marriage in *Pride and Prejudice*', *ELH* 39 (1972), 419, Joel Weinsheimer claims that 'the driving force of *Pride and Prejudice* cannot be explained with reference to the pocket book', he is once more reaching to repress, armed, perhaps, with what Terry Eagleton has claimed as the persistent 'idealism of American criticism', that linkage of the ethical and the economic which haunts the text and which nothing can 'exorcise'.

59. Some such awareness, it seems to me, continues to embarrass the 'Utopian' gestures of the novel's marital 'resolution'. Unlike the Hollywood emphasis of the recent TV adaptation – not only is its cut-off point the moment when Darcy kisses Elizabeth (carnal consummation *vincit omnia*), quite a lot of narrative after-imaging in the text (which, incidentally, elides the marriage itself) goes into showing how the various characters slot into or are the beneficiaries of the final (marital) 'move' of the book, and this suggests a (limited) 'communal' sense which Franco Moretti expounds so well: 'If Lukacs had known [it] ... *Pride and Prejudice* would have [been] an unparalleled example of the *Bildungsroman*. In reading it we witness the complete success of a "compromise" as Lukacs understood it in the *Theory of the Novel*: the founding of a relationship, a community, which neither exhausts nor radically modifies reality, and yet is invested with an intersubjective sense: the family, formed on the respect for and command of the *social mediation par excellence*, a perfect sense of the community and its multiple nuances'. See *Signs Taken for Wonders: Essays on the Sociology of Literary Forms*. [rev. ed.] (London: Verso, 1988), pp. 171–2. This being so, it is a bit much to claim, as Leo Bersani does, that 'Elizabeth's marriage to Darcy will presumably provide an ideal social context for her personal worth' in *A Future for Astyanax* (Boston: Little, Brown, 1969), p. 55.

5 'CAPITAL GRATIFICATIONS' AND THE SPIRIT OF MANSFIELD

1. Lionel Trilling, 'Mansfield Park' *The Opposing Self* (1955; Oxford: Oxford University Press, 1980), p. 198. References to Oxford University Press edition of *Mansfield Park*, ed. James Kinsley and John Lucas, 1970.

2. See Geoffrey Hartman, *Saving the Text: Literature/Derrida/Philosophy* (London: Johns Hopkins University Press, 1981), pp. 129–30.
3. Edward Said, 'Jane Austen and Empire', (1989), rpt. in *Contemporary Marxist Literary Criticism* (Harlow: Longman, 1992), pp. 97–113.
4. Alison G. Sulloway, *Jane Austen and the Province of Womanhood* (Philadelphia: University of Pennsylvania Press, 1989), p. 6.
5. Nina Auerbach, 'Jane Austen's Dangerous Charm: Feeling as one ought about Fanny Price,' in *Jane Austen: New Perspectives [Women and Literature]* N.S. 3 (New York: Holmes & Meier, 1983), ed. Janet Todd, p. 210. Hence it seems a little unfair for Janis P. Stout to claim that 'Fanny's silences are rarely significant of anything except her timid self-effacement' in *Strategies of Reticence: Silence and Meaning in the Works of Jane Austen, Willa Cather, Katherine Anne Porter, and Joan Didion* (Charlottesville: University Press of Virginia, 1990), p. 38.
6. Judith Lowder Newton, *Women, Power and Subversion: Social Strategies in British Fiction 1778–1860* (Athens: University of Georgia Press, 1981), p. 73.
7. Paul Ricoeur, 'The Conflict of Interpretations', in *Twentieth Century Literary Theory: a Reader*, ed. K.M. Newton (London: Macmillan, 1988), pp. 193–6.
8. Charlotte Brontë, *Jane Eyre* (1847), ch.15 (Harmondsworth: Penguin, 1953), p. 146.
9. Claudia Johnson, *Jane Austen: Women, Politics and the Novel* (Chicago: Chicago University Press, 1988), p. 96.
10. Tara Ghoshal Wallace, *Jane Austen and Narrative Authority* (London: Macmillan, 1995), p. 59.
11. Arnold Kettle, *An Introduction to the English Novel* (New York: Harper & Row), 1951, pp. 93–4.
12. See, for example, James Boswell, *The Life of Samuel Johnson*, ed. John Canning (London: Methuen, 1991), p. 119; and Patrick Cruttwell, in his 'Introduction' to *Samuel Johnson: Selected Writings* (Harmondsworth: Penguin, 1986), p. 25.
13. David Lodge, 'Mansfield Park', in *The Modes of Modern Fiction* (London: Edward Arnold, 1977).
14. Avrom Fleishman, *A Reading of Mansfield Park* (London: Johns Hopkins University Press, 1967), p. 45.
15. Clive Bloom, *The Occult Experience and the New Criticism* (Brighton: Harvester Press, 1986), p. 18.
16. Mary Poovey, *The Proper Lady and the Woman Writer* (London: University of Chicago Press, 1984), p. 216.
17. Tom Paine, *The Rights of Man* (1791–92; Harmondsworth: Penguin, 1969), p. 73: to him, Mr Burke was 'accustomed to "kiss the aristo-cratic hand that hath purloined him from himself!"'.
18. W.H. Auden, 'Dover', (August 1937), *Collected Poems* (London: Faber, 1976), p. 124. (ed. Edward Mendelson).
19. Clive Bloom, *The Occult Experience*, op. cit., pp. 25–6. Together with Mary's point about '*Rears* and *Vices*' in the context of a work like *Mansfield Park*, I find helpful Lacan's reference to the unconscious in an unpublished remark cited by Shoshana Felman as 'knowledge

that can't tolerate one's knowing that one knows' in *Jacques Lacan and the Adventure of Insight* (London: Harvard University Press), p. 77.

20. Fredric Jameson, *The Political Unconscious: Narrative as a Socially Symbolic Act* (London: Methuen, 1981), p. 117.

21. Karl Marx's analysis, although coming much too late to refer directly to the world of Jane Austen is still highly *à propos* here. In particular, it pursues the connection between 'rents' and 'rants' which is Mary Crawford's at once indispensable and inadmissibly offensive characterization of the relation between economic base and linguistic superstructure: 'Up to 1846, the Tories passed as the guardians of the traditions of old England. They were suspected of admiring in the British Constitution the eighth wonder of the world; to be *laudatores temporis acti* ... enthusiasts for the throne, the High Church, the privileges and liberties of the British subject. The fatal year, 1846, with its repeal of the Corn Laws ... proved they were enthusiasts for nothing but the rent of land, and at the same time disclosed the secret of their attachment to the political and religious institutions of Old England. The year 1846 transformed the Tories into protectionists. Tory was the sacred name, Protectionist is the profane one; Tory was the political battle-cry, Protectionist is the economical shout of distress; Tory seemed an idea, a principle, Protectionist is an interest. Protectionists of what? Of their own revenue, of the rent of their own land.' (Karl Marx, 'British Political Parties', *New York Daily Tribune* (1852); rpt. in *Karl Marx: Selected Writings*, ed. D. McLellan (Oxford: Oxford University Press, 1967), p. 326.

22. Samuel Johnson, *Lives of the English Poets*: 'He thought women made only for obedience' (1779–81; London: J.M. Dent, 1925), p. 93.

23. Quoted in John Peter, *Vladimir's Carrot* (London: André Deutsch, 1987), p. 104.

24. From a toast proposed by Samuel Johnson which Edward Said might like to consider when writing about Johnson's most distinguished 'student', Jane Austen. See James Boswell, *The Life of Samuel Johnson*, vol. II (London: Everyman, 1992), p. 141.

25. Edward Said, 'Jane Austen and Empire', op. cit., pp. 107–10.

26. Yeats, 'Meditations in time of Civil War', *The Poems* (London: Dent, 1990), ed. Daniel Albright, p. 246.

27. Yeats, 'Meditations', op. cit., p. 251.

28. Claudia Johnson, *Jane Austen: Women, Politics and the Novel* (London: University of Chicago Press, 1988), p. 120.

29. Marilyn Butler, *Jane Austen and the War of Ideas* (Oxford: Clarendon Press, 1975), p. 219.

30. *Measure for Measure*, 1. 4. 34.

31. See the argument of Margaret Kirkham's *Jane Austen: Feminism and Fiction*, most succinctly put in the observation that 'Rousseau excluded *women* from liberation through enlightenment' (p. 45).

32. See *Mansfield Park*, pp. 76–7, passim.

33. Moliere, *Dom Juan*, 1.2.: in (e.g.) *Tartuffe. Dom Juan. Le Misanthrope* (Paris: Gallimard, 1973), p. 161.

34. William Blake, 'The Clod and the Pebble', *Complete Poetry and Prose of*

William Blake, ed. D.V. Erdman (Berkeley: University of California Press, 1982), p. 19.

35. Byron, letter to Douglas Kinnaird, 26 October, 1819, in (e.g.) *Romantic Criticism*, ed. W.R. Owens (Milton Keynes: Open University Press, 1984) p. 56.

36. Quot. Jenni Calder, *Women and Marriage in Victorian Fiction* (London: Thames & Hudson, 1976), pp. 20–1.

37. D.A. Miller, *Narrative and its Discontents: Problems of Closure in the Traditional Novel* (Princeton: Princeton University Press, 1981), p. 22.

38. From 'The Dawn' (1881), in (e.g.) *The Portable Nietzsche*, tr. and ed. Walter Kaufmann (London: Chatto & Windus, 1971), p. 78.

39. Nietzsche, op. cit., p. 79.

40. Dr Fordyce, *Sermons to Young Women* (1766) : quot. Kirkham, op. cit., pp. 43–4.

41. Mary Wollstonecraft, *A Vindication of the Rights of Woman* (1792), p. 179; quot. Kirkham, p. 42.

42. D. Devlin, *Jane Austen and Education* (London: Macmillan, 1977), p. 126.

43. A.S. Neill, *A Dominie's Log* (1915; 2nd edn, London: Hogarth Press, 1986), pp. 151–2.

44. As Daniel Cottom puts it, in *The Civilised Imagination: a Study of Ann Radcliffe, Jane Austen and Sir Walter Scott* (Cambridge: Cambridge University Press, 1985), p. 105, 'the portrait that emerges [from *Mansfield Park*] completely transfers desire from the realm of individual expression and spontaneous affinity ... to a realm where it is little more than the intersection at a particular place and time of a great host of vagrant attachments and supplantations'.

45. For a more 'orthodox' discussion of the whole subject, see Warren Roberts, *Jane Austen and the French Revolution* (London: Macmillan, 1979), pp. 133–7.

46. See, for example, D. Devlin, *Jane Austen and Education*, p. 11: 'For Locke the four great aims of education are "virtue, wisdom, breeding and learning". "You will wonder perhaps that I put learning last, especially if I tell you I think it the least part"' – John Locke, *Some Thoughts Concerning Education* (5th edn, 1705), section 134.

47. John Donne, 'Of the Progress of the Soul: the Second Anniversary,' *Selected Poetry*, ed. John Carey (Oxford: Oxford University Press, 1996), p. 177.

48. For an account of Gramsci's Sardinia, see A. Davidson, *Antonio Gramsci: Towards an Intellectual Biography* (London: Merlin Press, 1977), pp. 1–47. In particular, a traveller (1843) relates: 'The father of a nobleman now holding one of the highest appointments under the Piedmontese government was ... walking with his friend in one of his feudal estates on the island, and feeling tired, called to one of his vassals then working in the field, to come to him. The poor peasant obeyed, and was immediately ordered to place himself "on all fours" ... upon the ground, which having done, the feudal baron leisurely sat upon his back till he was rested' (pp. 7–8). Pozzo and Lucky indeed, and no doubt Antigua was more enlightened. The

underlying psychic pattern was perhaps not so different, however, and, by transposition, was actually very much in evidence at Mansfield itself, where Sir Thomas spends so much of his time 'sitting on' people.

49. D.A. Miller, *Narrative and its Discontents: Problems of Closure in the Traditional Novel*, op. cit., p. 22.

50. Diane McDonell, *Theories of Discourse* (Oxford: Blackwell, 1986), p. 61.

6   IMAGINING EMMA IMAGINING: *EMMA*

1. See Edward Neill, 'Between Deference and Destruction: "situations" of recent critical theory and Jane Austen's *Emma*', *Critical Quarterly* 29 (1987) 39–54 (39). Edition referred to here: *Emma*, ed. David Lodge and James Kinsley (London: Oxford University Press, 1971).

2. In *Literary Theory: An Introduction* (Oxford, Basil Blackwell, 1983), p. 65.

3. See, for example, Rachel M. Brownstein, *Becoming a Heroine: Reading about Women in Novels* (Harmondsworth, Penguin, 1981), p. 105. Indeed, there is a general desire to be reassured about *Emma* in the old criticism which finds Knightley reassuring which modern readers will find it difficult to share, from Julia Prewitt Brown's ringing declaration that 'Mr Knightley is Jane Austen's most attractive character … he is a conservative because he is a realist …' (Julia Prewitt Brown, *Jane Austen's Novels: Social Change and Literary Form* (London: Harvard University Press, 1979), p. 21), which chimes with Mark Schorer's deferential presentation of him as 'the humanely civilised man' in 'The Humiliation of Emma Woodhouse' (see Ian Watt, ed. *Jane Austen: A Collection of Critical Essays* [Englewood Cliffs, NJ: Prentice-Hall, 1963], p. 110), while for ultra-conservative Anne Crippen Ruderman in *The Pleasures of Virtue: Political Thought in the Novels of Jane Austen* (London: Rowan & Littlefield, 1995) p. 50, Mr Knightley is 'the standard of perfection' and for Janet Todd in *Women's Friendship in Literature* (New York: Columbia, 1980), 'the voice of truth and conscience in the novel' (p. 277). Note also the sheer complacency and critical strangeness of Julia Prewitt Brown's idea that Miss Bates 'represents Highbury's fluidity and mobility, its tolerance of past and future classes, or part of the sensibility that helped England avoid a French Revolution'. More rational worries about Knightley's actual role in society are expressed in the Aers, Cook and Punter collection and the discussion by Roger Sales mentioned above. As Frederick Keener puts it in *The Chain of Becoming: the Philosophical Tale, the Novel, and a Neglected Realism of the Enlightenment: Swift, Montesquieu, Voltaire, Johnson and Austen* (New York: Columbia University Press, 1983), p. 274: 'to the extent that Emma and *Emma* idealise Mr. Knightley, the novel may ironically subvert Emma and her readers'.

4. See 'On Literature as an Ideological Form' (1974), rpt. in *Contemporary Marxist Literary Criticism*, ed. Francis Mulhern (London: Longman, 1992), p. 53.

Notes

165

5. See *Untying the Text: a Post-Structuralist Reader*, ed. Robert Young (London, Routledge & Kegan Paul, 1981), p. 42.
6. Charles Altieri, *Act and Quality: a Theory of Literary Meaning and Humanistic Understanding* (Brighton: Harvester Press, 1981), p. 327.
7. See *Formalism and Marxism* (London: Methuen, 1983), p. 174.
8. In *Blindness and Insight* (quoted in Culler, *On Deconstruction: Theory and Criticism after Structuralism* [London, Routledge & Kegan Paul, 1983], pp. 126–7).
9. See *Critical Practice* (London: Methuen, 1980), p. 79. She buttresses her position here with Wayne Booth, *The Rhetoric of Fiction* (Chicago, University of Chicago Press, 1961), p. 265. Booth has interestingly shifted ground in favour of a rather more 'open' response in 'Emma, *Emma* and the question of feminism', in *Persuasions: the Journal of the Jane Austen Society of North America* (16 December 1983), no. 5.
10. Frank Kermode, *The Classic* (London: Faber, 1975), p. 136.
11. Jerome J. McGann, *The Romantic Ideology: a Critical Investigation* (London, University of Chicago Press, 1983), p. 110.
12. Attitudes to *Emma* are so involved with attitudes to Emma that it is possible to be interested by and to feel the critical appropriateness of the following comment without feeling that the 'reconciling' they speak of is a permanently achieved linguistic 'fact': [in *Emma*] the focus is on the way in which two competing perspectives on the central character, Emma, are developed and finally reconciled to each other through modulation' (in David Lee, *Competing Discourses: Perspective and Ideology in Language* [London: Longman, 1992], p. 137).
13. See David Aers, Jonathan Cook and David Punter, *Romanticism and Ideology: Studies in English Writing, 1765–1830* (London: Routledge & Kegan Paul, 1981).
14. Roger Sales, *English Literature in History 1780–1830: Pastoral and Politics* (London, Hutchinson, 1983), p. 34.
15. Ellen Meiskins Wood, *The Pristine Culture of Capitalism: a Historical Essay on Old Regimes and Modern States* (London: Verso, 1991), p. 2.
16. Margaret Kirkham, *Jane Austen: Feminism and Fiction* (Brighton: Harvester Press, 1983), p. 138.
17. Judith Fetterly, *The Resisting Reader* (quoted in Culler, *On Deconstruction*, p. 52); the point is not, of course, that Emma is right to make fun of Miss Bates, but in the nature of the relationship which has developed between Emma and Knightley.
18. Susan Morgan, *In the Meantime: Character and Perception in Jane Austen's Fiction* (London, University of Chicago Press, 1980), p. 47.
19. In *Jane Austen: a Study of Her Artistic Development* (London, Chatto & Windus, 1965), p. 134.
20. See Jane Austen, *Emma* (London: Oxford University Press, 1971), ed. David Lodge, p. 355. All page numbers in subsequent quotations refer to this edition.
21. Quoted in W.R. Valentiner, *Rembrandt and Spinoza: A Study of Spiritual Conflicts in Seventeenth Century Holland* (London, Phaidon Press, 1957), p. 153; but see also Paul Wienpahl, 'On Translating

166   *Notes*

Spinoza', *Speculum Spinozum 1677–1977* (London, Routledge & Kegan Paul, 1977), pp. 403–4.

22. J.S. Mill, *Autobiography*, ed. Jack Stillinger (London, Oxford University Press, 1971), p. 134.

23. This primarily 'agricultural' reference is, nevertheless, organically connected with Mr Knightley's own attributes and attitudes.

24. Letter to Lady Cynthia Asquith, 21 October 1914 (*Letters*, vol. 2, ed. B. Zytaruk and J. Bolton [Cambridge, Cambridge University Press, 1981], p. 414).

25. Quoted in Laurence Lerner's *The Truthtellers: Jane Austen, George Eliot, D. H. Lawrence* (London, Chatto & Windus, 1967), p. 23.

26. R.W. Emerson, *Nature* (1836); quoted in F. Lentricchia, *After the New Criticism* (London, Athlone Press, 1980), pp. 82–3.

27. Nietzsche, *Beyond Good and Evil*, trans. R.J. Hollingdale (Harmondsworth, Penguin, 1973), p. 296; quoted in Gilles Deleuze, *Nietzsche and Philosophy*, trans. Hugh Tomlinson (London, Athlone Press, 1983), p. 81.

28. Bakhtin's phrase, quoted in Allon White, 'Bakhtin, Sociolinguistics and Deconstruction', in *The Theory of Reading*, ed. Frank Gloversmith (Brighton, Harvester Press, 1984), p. 141.

29. John Bayley, 'The Irresponsibility of Jane Austen', in *Critical Essays on Jane Austen*, ed. B.C. Southam (London, Routledge & Kegan Paul, 1968), pp. 18–19.

30. G.M. Young, *Portrait of an Age*; quoted in Noel Annan's *Leslie Stephen: the Godless Victorian* (London, Weidenfield & Nicolson, 1984), p. 43.

7 'JANE'S FIGHTING SHIPS': *PERSUASION* AS CULTURAL CRITIQUE

1. Harold Bloom, *The Western Canon: the Books and School of the Ages* (New York: Harcourt, Brace &, 1994), pp. 18, 253–63.

2. Walter Benjamin, 'Theses on the Philosophy of History': 'There is no document of civilisation which is not at the same time a document of barbarism. And just as such a document is not free of barbarism, barbarism taints also the manner in which it was transmitted from one owner to another. A historical materialist therefore dissociates himself from it as far as possible. He regards it as his task to brush history against the grain'. (See, for example, Susan Buck-Morss, *The Origin of Negative Dialectics: Theodor Adorno, Walter Benjamin and the Frankfurt School* [Brighton: The Harvester Press, 1977], p. 48.)

3. This and all subsequent quotations from *Persuasion*, ed. John Davie (Oxford: Oxford University Press, 1970), p.131. Quite against some of the arguments made here is Claudia Johnson, whose chapter on '*Persuasion*: "The Unfeudal Tone of the Present Day"' is reproduced in *Mansfield Park and Persuasion: Contemporary Critical Essays*, ed. Judy Simons (London: Macmillan ['New Casebooks'], 1997). To buttress her case, Claudia Johnson cites the historian David Spring's 'Interpreters of Jane Austen's Social World', in Janet Todd's *Jane Austen: New Perspectives*, p. 65.

4. Volosinov, *Marxism and the Philosophy of Language* (1922; Cambridge: Harvard University Press, 1986), p. 22.
5. As Tara Ghoshal Wallace puts it, 'In *Persuasion* ... Austen takes away the code book that had allowed readers to interpret, in familiar ways, the subtleties of her text ...' in *Jane Austen and Narrative Authority* (London: Macmillan, 1995), p. 99.
6. Jean-François Lyotard, *The Postmodern Condition: a Report on Knowledge* (Manchester: Manchester University Press, 1984), p.15.
7. As an analogy, see J. McGann, *The Romantic Ideology: a Critical Investigation* (London: Chicago University Press, 1983).
8. See Alastair M. Duckworth, *The Improvement of the Estate: a Study of Jane Austen's Novels* (London: Johns Hopkins UniversityPress, 1971).
9. For Nina Auerbach, in '"O Brave New World": Evolution and Revolution in *Persuasion*', *ELH*, 39 (1972), 'she felt and recorded the vibrations of her age as the Romantic poets and prophets did ... emotional extremes meet and marry in an intensity of feeling' (p. 128).
10. Fredric Jameson, *The Political Unconscious: Narrative as a Socially Symbolic Act* (London: Methuen, 1981), p. 203.
11. Keats, *Hyperion*, bk 2, l.212, in (e.g.) *The Poems of John Keats*, ed. Jack Stillinger (London: Heinemann, 1978), p. 347.
12. Raymond Williams, 'Marxism and Culture', in *Culture and Society* [1958]; rpt. in Rick Rylance (ed.) *Debating Texts* (Milton Keynes: Open University Press, 1987), p. 210.
13. Wallace Stevens, 'A Primitive like an Orb', *Collected Poems* (London: Faber, 1955), p.443; for David Monaghan, see *Jane Austen: Structure and Social Vision* (London: Macmillan, 1980), p.145, e.g. the society into which Anne is entering ... remains too chaotic and disorganised to be considered an adequate substitute for such beautifully ordered worlds as Pemberley and Highbury', a conservative and, in terms of textuality, naive observation, which even on its own terms is inaccurate, as Pemberley can only be compared with Donwell, Knightley's oversized home in *Emma*. Highbury, a populous village, is mainly offstage, and might not be quite as productive of these 'ideas of order' as the critic appears to assume here.
14. Francis Fukuyama, *The End of History and the Last Man* (London: Hamish Hamilton, 1992), p. 329. Roger Gard, situating himself as a universal observer, notes the apparent paradoxicality of the fact that 'it is almost universally observable that professional military men tend to be the most humane and affable of persons in civil life', in *Jane Austen's Novels: the Art of Clarity* (London: Yale University Press, 1992), p. 192.
15. For Marvin Mudrick 'she is a good woman whose judgement is almost fatally incapacitated by the proper assumptions that she accepts without question from her class and time'. *Books Are Not Life But Then What Is?* (New York: Oxford University Press, 1979), p. 335.
16. John Dryden, 'MacFlecknoe' (1682), *Poems*, ed. J. Kinsley (Oxford: Clarendon Press, 1958), p. 265.
17. Interestingly, according to Peter Smith in 'Jane Austen and the Secret Conspiracy', *Cambridge Quarterly* 24 (1995), 283, the novel's title refers

not merely to the explicit counsel that the older woman bestows on the heroine ... persuasion is rather to be taken as a permanent state of mind, perhaps specifically one whose implications involve a degree of error', following the line of Janice Bowman Swanson's more formal academic procedure in 'Toward a Rhetoric of the Self: The Art of *Persuasion*', *NCF* 36 (1981), pp. 1–21, which investigates 'a history of ethical uneasiness regarding the power of persuasion', finding a sort of seduction *renversé* in this case, emphasizing 'the suggestion [Aristotle's, mainly] that rhetoric can exploit or usurp the passions and impair the free use of judgement', which uncovers 'the morally contrary possibilities inherent in persuasion'. This idea that the 'persuasion' trope in Jane Austen's novel is 'all throughther', in Hopkins' Joycean idiom, or as the words 'Brighton Rock' are all the way through Brighton Rock, finds even more formal academic definition by Lloyd W. Brown's observation that 'whenever conceptual terms dominate Jane Austen titles they are pointers to the divergent moral nuances on which she bases her ironic structures'. See his *Bits of Ivory: Narrative Techniques in Jane Austen's Fiction* (Baton Rouge: Louisiana State University Press, 1973), p. 15; while Stanley Fish, investigating the rhetorical bullying involved in psychoanalysis, suggestively concludes that 'the primal scene is the scene of persuasion', in 'Withholding the Missing Portion: power, meaning and persuasion in Freud's *The Wolf Man*', in *The Linguistics of Writing: Arguments Between Language and Literature*, eds Nigel Fabb, Derek Attridge, Alan Durant and Colin McCabe (Manchester: Manchester University Press, 1987), p. 170.

18. See Margaret Kirkham, *Jane Austen: Feminism and Fiction* (Brighton: Harvester Press, 1983).
19. 'Giant nerve', *Hyperion*, bk I, l.175; *Stillinger*, p. 334; 'bad poetry by Lords': see Keats, 'The Fall of Hyperion', (1819), ll.207–8; *Stillinger*, p. 483.
20. Milton, *Paradise Lost* bk XI, ll.836–7, in (e.g.) *Paradise Lost*, ed. A. Fowler (Harlow: Longman, 1971), p. 605.
21. Wallace Stevens, 'Not Ideas about the Thing but the Thing Itself', *Collected Poems*, p. 534.
22. Mary Poovey, *The Proper Lady and the Woman Writer: Ideology and Style in the Works of Mary Wollstonecraft, Mary Shelley and Jane Austen* (Chicago: Chicago University Press, 1984), p. 224.
23. William Blake, 'Preface' to 'Milton: A Poem in Two Books', in *Complete Poetry and Prose*, ed. David Erdman (London: University of California Press, 1983), p. 95.
24. John Bayley, *An Essay on Hardy* (Cambridge: Cambridge University Press, 1979), p. 147, as depicted in *The Trumpet-Major*, though hardly with the full-blown squalor of the report cited below!
25. Cited in C. Lloyd, *The British Seamen* (London: Paladin, 1970), p. 225.
26. David Lodge, *After Bakhtin: Essays on Fiction and Criticism* (London: Routledge, 1990), shows, with the help of Bakhtin and others, including Genette, how the Platonic distinction between *diegesis* and *mimesis* is subverted in modern prose fiction, to produce that sense

of a cross-over between the narrator's and the focalizing character's voice which is so crucial in the appreciation of 'the achievement of Jane Austen'.

27. D.H. Lawrence, 'A Propos *Lady Chatterley's Lover*' [1929]; discussed with reference to its prejudiced and prejudicial context in Christopher Gillie's *A Preface to Jane Austen* (London: Longman, 1974), p. 141.

28. See his discussion of Derrida's anticipation of Hardy's 'The Torn Letter', in *Taking Chances: Derrida, Psychoanalysis and Literature*, eds J.H. Smith and W. Kerrigan (Baltimore: Johns Hopkins University Press, 1984), pp. 135–45.

29. See Harold Bloom, *A Map of Misreading* (New York: Oxford University Press, 1975), pp. 48–9.

30. In Claudia L. Johnson, *Jane Austen: Women, Politics and the Novel* (London: University of Chicago Press, 1988), p. 166.

31. See David Nokes, *Jane Austen: A Life* (London: Fourth Estate, 1997), p. 43 [etc.].

32. From a letter embodying her reactions to newspaper reports of the Battle of Albuera, in the Peninsular War, on 31 May 1811: 'How horrible it is to have so many people killed! – and what a blessing that one cares for none of them!' (*Collected Letters*, ed. R.W. Chapman [Oxford: Oxford University Press, 1952]); for his comment, see Hugh Kenner, *The Invisible Poet: T.S. Eliot* (London: Methuen, 1959), p. 24.

33. As Jocelyn Harris points out in 'Anne Elliot, the Wife of Bath, and Other Friends', in *Jane Austen: New Perspectives* [Women and Literature, New Series, vol. 3] (London: Holmes & Meier, 1983) '"possessioun" is to Sir Walter the second sign of a gentleman. Wentworth's brother had no property and so is nobody' (p. 279).

34. Tom Paine, *The Rights of Man* (1791–2; Harmondsworth: Penguin, 1969), p. 115.

35. In Shoshana Felman, *Jacques Lacan and the Adventure of Insight* (London: Harvard University Press), p. 77.

36. Raymond Williams, *The Country and the City* (London: Hogarth Press, 1985), p. 108–19.

8 PROPS AND PROPERTIES: SCREEN ADAPTATIONS

1. See Paul Dave, 'The Bourgeois Paradigm and Heritage Cinema', *New Left Review* 224 (1997), pp. 111–26.

2. Raphael Samuel, *Theatres of Memory* (London: Verso, 1994), p. 205. The 'nomadic' metaphor is borrowed from Kant's description of the sceptical intelligence.

3. Ellen Meiksins Wood, *The Pristine Culture of Capitalism: a Historical Essay on Old Regimes and Modern States* (London: Verso, 1991), p. 18.

4 Tom Nairn, *The Enchanted Glass: Britain and its Monarchy* (London: Verso: 1988), pp. 174–89.

5. See Andrew Higson, 'Representing the National Past: Nostalgia and

Pastiche in the Heritage Film', in Lester Friedman, ed., *British Cinema and Thatcherism* (London: Verso, 1993), p. 117.

6. Consider the brisk (actually quite Haydnish) tones of early Beethoven summoned by Melvyn Tan's forte piano conscripted for Elizabeth's proto-Romantic 'free spirit' and the healthy stability of the Gardiners, with apposite entrées for the stilted baroque grandiosity of Lady Catherine's Rosings and the wholly bassoonish Mr Collins, to the Siegfriedian overtones of Darcy in temporary defeat and as eventual rescuer; and the splendid dance scene at Netherfield.

7. See Claire Monk, 'Sexuality and the Heritage Film', *Sight and Sound* 5, no. 10 (1995), pp. 33–4.

8. Much information about the whole process (maimed a little by its understandable tone of self-congratulation) is provided by books compiled by Sue Birtwhistle and Susie Conklin, *The Making of 'Pride and Prejudice'* (London: BBC and Penguin, 1995) and *The Making of Jane Austen's 'Emma'* (London: Penguin, 1996).

9. In *Poetics Today* (1979, p. 187).

10. For this neologistic sense of Britain as a forged site of identity and identification, see Tom Nairn, *The Enchanted Glass: Britain and its Monarchy* (London: Verso, 1988), p. 17.

11. See Jacqueline Rose, *States of Fantasy* (Oxford: Clarendon Press, 1995).

Index

Adorno, Theodor W., x, 8, 39, 41, 48, 51
Aers, David, 10, 97–8
'Alice in Wonderland', 27
Althusser, Louis, 97, 114
Altieri, Charles, 96
Amis, Kingsley, 72
Antigua, 77
'Apollo' (Keats), 130
Arnold, Matthew (*Culture and Anarchy*), 87
Auden, W. H., 17
Auerbach, Nina, 71
Austen, Cassandra, xi, 113
Austen, George (brother), 130
Austen, Jane
NOVELS
Northanger Abbey, x, 6, 15–30; *Sense and Sensibility*, x, 6–7, 31–50; *Pride and Prejudice*, x, 7–8, 51–69; *Mansfield Park*, x, 8, 70–94; *Emma*, x–xi, 8–9, 11, 95–111; *Persuasion*, xi, 9, 18, 112–35; 'Lady Susan', 22
CHARACTERS
Allen, Mr, 20; Allen, Mrs, 23, 26, Bates, Miss, 29, 102, 110; Bennet, Elizabeth, 7, 51–69 *passim*, 71, 85, 114, 136; Bennet, Jane, 53, 59, 69; Bennet, Kitty, 53, 59; Bennet, Lydia, 22, 53, 55, 56, 57, 59, 63, 73; Bennet, Mary, 53, 59; Bennet, Mr and Mrs, 7, 59; Bennet, Mr, 24, 55, 56, 59, 60, 63, 73, 87; Bennet, Mrs, 28, 59, 60, 68, 125; Benwick, Captain, 118, 121, 122, 127, 128; Bertram, Edmund, 8, 23, 73, 75, 80, 84, 85, 88, 90, 94, 123; Bertram, Julia, 77, 78, 79, 83, 84, 89, 134; Bertram, Maria, 73, 78, 79, 81, 82, 83, 84, 86, 87, 89, 134; Bertram, Sir Thomas, 71, 72, 74, 76, 77, 78, 79, 80, 84, 85, 88, 89, 90, 91, 92, 93, 101; Bertram, Tom, 25, 78, 88; Bickerton, Miss, 101; Bingley, Charles, 65; Bingley, Caroline, 61; Brandon, Colonel, 31, 43, 47, 49; Clay, Mrs Penelope, 116, 124, 133; Collins, Mr, 51, 52, 54, 57, 60, 63, 64, 73; Crawford, Henry and Mary, 8, 79, 81, 87, 89, 90, 91; Crawford, Henry, 73, 76, 79, 80, 81, 82, 83, 86, 91, 92; Crawford, Mary, 70, 75, 77, 82, 83, 88, 91; Morland,

Catherine, 15–30 *passim*; Churchill, Frank, 29, 103; Churchill, Mrs, 110; Cole, Mr and Mrs, 99; Croft, Admiral, 117, 119, 124, 129; Croft, Mrs, 118, 120; Dalrymple, Lady, 130; Darcy, Georgiana, 55, 64; Darcy, Mr, 7, 9, 51–69 *passim*, 114, 125, 136; Dashwood, Elinor, 31–50 *passim*; Dashwood, Fanny, 6, 32, 38, 50; Dashwood, John, 6, 32, 38, 41, 46, 50, 63; Dashwood, Marianne, 31–50 *passim*; Dashwood, Mrs, 36; de Bourgh, Lady C., 7, 25, 51, 52, 58, 60, 61; Elliot, Anne, 113–35 *passim*; Elliot, Elizabeth, 123, 129, 133; Elliot, Mary, 123, 129, 130, 131, 132; Elliot, Sir Walter, 9, 18, 115, 116, 118, 122, 123, 131, 132, 133; Elliot, William Walter, 124, 126, 127; Elton, Mr, 87, 108, 109, 110; Elton, Mrs, 22, 98, 99, 105, 108, 110, 131; Fairfax, Jane, 98, 110, 111; Ferrars, Edward, 31, 35, 40, 47, 48; Ferrars, Mrs, 38, 50; Ferrars, Robert, 36, 50; Gardiner, Mr and Mrs, 7, 53, 54, 62, 64, 67; Harville family, 118, 122, 125, 127, 134, 135; Hayters, 131; Hayter, Charles, 132; Knightley, Mr, 8, 29, 33, 43, 54, 64, 66, 84, 106, 95–111 *passim*; Knightley, John, 54, 64, 104; Jenkinson, Mrs, 60; Jennings, Mrs, 49, 50; Lucas, Charlotte, 57, 63; Lucas, Maria, 51; Lucas, Sir William, 51, 54, 57, 64; Martin, Robert, 99; Middleton, Sir John, 44, 103; Middleton, Lady, 35, 37, 38, 44, 50; Morton, Miss, 38; Musgrove, Charles, 127, 129; Musgrove, Dick, 118, 128, 130; Musgrove, Louisa, 118, 121, 126, 128, 134, 135; Musgrove, Mrs, 129; Norris, Mrs, 74, 76, 79, 89, 91; Price, Fanny, 38, 70–94 *passim*, 114, 125, 126; Price, Mr, 73; Price, William, 75, 76, 84; Rushworth, Mr, 71, 73, 75, 81, 86, 87, 88; Russell, Lady, 114, 117, 118, 119, 120, 129, 133; Smith, Harriet, 21, 24, 86, 99, 101, 104, 109; Smith, Mrs, 126, 127, 129, 132, 133, 135; Steele, Lucy, 33, 34, 35, 50; Steele, Nancy, 34; Tilney, Eleanor, 16; Tilney, Frederick, 17, 21, 25; Tilney, General, 17, 19, 20,